Star Rising

A Coastal Hearts Novel

Janet W. Ferguson

Southern Sun Press, LLC

Southern
Sun Press

ISBN-10: 0-9992485-2-9
ISBN-13: 978-0-9992485-2-2

Acknowledgments

My thanks go out to:

The Lord. He deserves all the praise for any good I do.

My husband, Bruce, for supporting me and for taking me on a dream trip to Ireland.

Lorna Palmer, my Irish beta reader.

Michèle Phoenix, Alicia Sellers Braswell, Lisa Cantrell, Shirley Gould, Shelia Stovall, Carol Dyer, and others for answering questions about international mission work.

Eric Middleton, Cheyenne Causey, and Vance Purtell for answering questions about piloting or working on a flight crew.

Patricia Bradley for the information on working with clay, making pottery, and the lesson that went along with it.

For those of you who shared with me privately how domestic abuse has affected you or your family.

For those who shared about how rheumatoid arthritis has affected their lives.

To my friend Marilyn Poole for recommending Buntratty Castle. We so enjoyed that tour, and I highly recommend it!

My fabulous ACFW critique partners and my street team.

My readers and friends who told me about their funny-not-so-funny vacation stories.

My amazing ACFW critique partners, volunteer proofreaders (you know who you are!), and my book launch team.

Editor Robin Patchen, mentor author Misty Beller, and cover artist Carpe Librum Book Design.

"You are my witnesses," declared the Lord, *"and my servant whom I have chosen...."*

Dear Reader

I hope you enjoy Star and Paul's story. I was blessed that my husband took our family to Ireland for a vacation, and it was so much fun to revisit those places while writing this novel.

As an author, I did a few mean things to my character Paul in this story, but sometimes life is not fair, right? Sometimes we are attacked by the enemy of our souls. Other times, our own actions land us in sorrowful places. Every now and then, the Lord has to give us a hard lesson to wake us up to our own selfishness. When God disciplines, though, it's in His perfect love and always for our own good. I know miracles don't always happen, like in this story. However, in my own life, my father was given six months to live due to a cancer diagnosis. He ended up living thirty more years, to a ripe old age of ninety-four, proving God is in control. Not us or any doctor.

Star was a character who came out of a horrible home life. Her past was not a happy one—domestic abuse rarely is, and it leaves scars inside and out. Love isn't supposed to be violent and controlling. The apostle Paul writes in the book of 1 Corinthians that love is patient, love is kind... It always protects, always trusts, always hopes, always perseveres. While none of us humans are perfect, if you find yourself in danger, please get help. Don't let shame or fear hold you captive. If you or someone you love is being personally affected by domestic violence, please reach out to your local shelter, domestic violence organization, or someone you trust.

God healed Star from the wounds of her past, and He wants to do the same for all his children. The good news is that you can trust Him. You are not alone.

In Him,

Janet W. Ferguson

Chapter 1

One year of sobriety, already.

Star Youngblood fished the chip that marked the milestone from her jacket pocket. Her steps slowed on the sidewalk leading to the art studio attached to the back of the gallery. In the late afternoon light filtering through the ancient moss-covered trees, she stared at the coin. The piece of bronze she'd received the night before in the AA meeting wasn't much to look at, but the small token represented twelve months of surviving an emotional roller coaster in St. Simons, Georgia. Twelve months of craving. Twelve months of meetings. Twelve months of resurrected memories.

Having a clear head unleashed her anxiety, reawakened her nightmares. A year of sobriety had given free rein to hideous memories that tore loose like floodwaters breaking through a dam. Buried pieces of her childhood resurfaced. Fragments of horror she'd just as soon have kept locked up.

How did she forgive a mother who failed to protect her children? Much less the man who'd terrorized them.

Still, the counselors kept advising her to wrestle with her past so she could move forward.

The door to the art gallery studio flung open, and her friend Davis stomped through, wearing his usual black athletic pants and a Re-Claimed T-shirt. His dark blond hair ruffled in the cool Atlantic breeze. Lately, he'd grown a short beard. It spread with his larger-than-life grin when he spotted her.

"Hey, hey, Star." He squinted to study her face in the low

light, and his wide grin faltered. "You look like the wheel is turning, but the hamster's dead."

"Thanks." Always the blunt truth with Davis. Yes, she was a little frazzled.

"Remember, you can't. God can. How about you let Him?"

She couldn't help but smile. "Trying."

Somehow Davis always seemed to know exactly what to say to lift her spirits. He held the door for her, and she stepped into the large room connected to the back of the gallery. Canvases covered the wall, some waiting to go up front to sell, others drying from art therapy classes the night before. A faint smell of paint still lingered.

Davis had been sober a year longer than she had, and now he was taking online classes to become a minister while serving at the sober living houses. Everyone at the Re-Claimed ministry looked to Davis for spiritual encouragement and truth.

And humor.

Okay, he was really goofy, but something about him was cute too.

The thought smacked her like a fist to the stomach. She'd been wrong about men before. She knew all too well how people could pretend to be normal—nice even. But when they got you behind closed doors, the real monster inside would surface.

Like her ex-fiancé, Vince.

And her stepfather.

"I cleared the room of the easels and set up the pottery wheel for you and Mrs. Kelly over by the back wall for after exercise class." Davis's voice broke into her dark thoughts. "I left two chairs beside it and brought in the clay plus the other supplies." He flexed his bicep and waggled his brows. "That

2

stuff's heavy. Lucky, I've been going to your workouts."

The bulge of bicep did look nice and firm. Not that she wanted to notice. "Coming tonight?" Star slipped off her windbreaker and threw it on the counter.

"I don't know." He clicked his tongue. "Got a lot on my plate—besides food."

"If you're scared, say you're scared." She shot him a challenging look.

"Hey, Miss I'll-kill-you-with-a-hundred-squats, I have a paper to write."

"Oh, right." She lost the teasing tone in her voice and patted his shoulder. Which happened to be rock-solid as well. "Your homework is important."

"Hmm." His gaze held hers for a long moment, sending a bit of heat to her cheeks. "I heard the brain works better after exercise, so watch me bust a move." He broke into a hip-hop two-step and smiled, his teeth white and straight. "Plus, I wouldn't want to hurt Mrs. Kelly's feelings if I didn't stay for her presentation."

"Oh, *now* I see the real reason you'll put off your homework. You can't say no to the well-off older ladies." Star teased, but tension squirmed inside her. She had to admit she liked Davis—a lot—but she didn't want him to think she was flirting.

Unless that would be okay with him…

Shoot, what a head-case she was. One minute anxious, the next indulging in a silly attraction. When would she ever learn? The men in her life had always been bad news, and that would probably never change.

"We're here," a low female voice sang, and Gabby marched through the door. "Primed up for exercise and Mrs. Kelly's devotional." The stately sober living director stood at least six feet tall. Her light brown eyes shone below short black hair and above a sunny smile. The two-dozen or so Re-Claimed residents followed behind her.

"I'm ready," Star chimed back. Perfect timing. Now she could forget everything—including men, past and present—and let strength training and cardio claim her focus.

The residents had been willing to let her practice on them. Once she got back in the groove of leading classes, she hoped to teach at a local fitness club. Her certification didn't run out for a few more months.

One girl in her late twenties caught Star's attention. Thin and pale, she took a spot near the back of the group. Just standing there seemed to require colossal effort. She was newly sober, and Star remembered that feeling. If only she could encourage the girl with hope that things would get better.

She'd love to have a job serving God, giving back to the One who'd given her so much. A job like Davis was doing, becoming an outreach minister. But she didn't have any real skills to offer. She'd never even finished high school.

Of course, she wanted to keep her job as an aide for Mrs. Kelly. She loved serving God by serving the sweet lady. They'd talked, and Mrs. Kelly felt like they'd manage with a flexible schedule. Working for her had been such a blessing this past year. For the first time in…well, for the first time ever, Star had found a place to belong. Sort of like having a friend and a mother for a boss.

Star tsked. Not that she knew much about having a normal mother. She walked to the counter and turned on the stereo. The music started, and she blocked out the negativity begging to blast to the surface.

"Okay, people." She focused on the music's beat. "Let's move those feet. March."

One of the ladies groaned. "I'm still sore from the planks yesterday."

"Don't worry." Davis smirked and flopped down into a pushup stance. "She'll probably have us do burpees or downward dog, and then something else will ache worse tomorrow."

Star tried to keep a straight face. "It's okay to be a little sore, but don't hurt yourself. And we're marching now. Not doing burpees, Davis." She gave him a stern look.

"Yes, ma'am." He stood and saluted.

She kept them busy for a good forty minutes, then sent them to get a sip of water and retrieve the yoga mats from the corner of the room. Her body felt great, her muscles alive. This had to be what she was made for. She'd set up interviews. One of the gyms in town should hire her. The extra money would cover rent and utilities when she moved out of Re-Claimed. She'd always paid her own way, and she didn't want to leech off the ministry or Mrs. Kelly.

The cool-down song began, and she led the group in balance and stretching positions. "Okay, lie on your mat and let your eyes close." She lowered her voice and talked them through relaxation exercises.

"Oooh." Davis's voice broke into her meditation. "Can I get a massage now?"

"Shut up," Gabby squawked. "This is my favorite part."

Star couldn't stop a laugh. These goofballs had become good friends. One part of her couldn't imagine leaving the Re-Claimed house, but another part of her wanted a steady place to call her own. A home. Something she'd never known in her twenty-plus years. If only she could afford a decent rental.

As the class came to a close, she savored the stretch and meditation. The quiet had become her favorite part, too, now that she'd come to know God. When her mind calmed, she tried to connect with Him. She focused on Bible verses she'd learned and prayed.

I praise you because I am fearfully and wonderfully made.

But when you are tempted, He will also provide a way out so that you can endure it.

Do not fear, for I have redeemed you.

Then the music ended. Time to move, even if she'd rather stay put. She pushed herself to a sitting position and clapped. "Great job! You did it. Drink plenty of water to stay hydrated."

The studio door swung open, and Mrs. Kelly hobbled in, using her cane. A sweet smile lit up her pretty face, as usual. Even though rheumatoid arthritis had twisted her body much too early, the sixty-five-year-old never let her pain steal her joy. "Looks like y'all had a wonderful workout."

"She's brutal." Davis gave an exaggerated groan.

Laughing, Mrs. Kelly shook her head. "Poor baby. You can recover while we demonstrate the pottery wheel."

"No rest for the weary." He hopped to his feet, proving she'd hardly worked him enough. "Gotta set up chairs."

Star glanced around the room. "What if y'all just keep the mats out to watch? No sense doing all that work."

"I like how you think, lady." Davis made a megaphone with his hands to his mouth. "People, slide your mats toward that contraption over there and get comfortable."

While everyone complied, butterflies banged around Star's stomach. She'd agreed to help Mrs. Kelly with the clay, but now anxiety flared up. Leading exercise was something she knew. This special devotional of Mrs. Kelly's zoomed out of her comfort zone. The talk might come off as preachy, and the topic couldn't be more awkward. How did Davis lead talks like this all the time?

Unfazed, Mrs. Kelly took a seat beside the wheel and waited. Her eyes locked on Star. *You can do this*, she mouthed.

Reluctantly, Star took her place. Arthritis had robbed Mrs. Kelly of her ability to create, so she'd been teaching Star. The idea was sweet, and Star wanted to share her faith, but this lesson...

"Start the wheel, and let's begin." Mrs. Kelly gave the instructions, then turned toward their little audience. "In order to make something, the clay must be centered."

That was Star's cue to throw the clay on the wheel and get it smooth under her hands. Some days the process came easier than others. Today was one of the easy days—the wobbly clay smoothed under her guidance. But that wasn't what Mrs. Kelly wanted, so Star pushed the mound a little off-center.

"Life doesn't go as well as it could if we just do what we have to do to get by. If we aren't centered." Mrs. Kelly pointed at the swirling mass. "Open the clay with your thumbs and then press the bottom."

Star did as she was told, and knowing the next step, she applied pressure and pulled the clay up. Being off-center, the mass folded under her hands.

"See what happens when pressures come from inside and pressures push from the outside. The walls build—at first. But this piece wasn't centered from the beginning, so the clay collapses. Makes a mess." Mrs. Kelly looked at the group. "What do I do? Throw it away?"

No one answered. They all stared at Star, upping her anxiety.

"No." Mrs. Kelly shook her head. "We reclaim the clay. Just like we don't throw away our lives when we mess up. We start over. We center it right this time."

Star centered the wet clay as she'd been taught while Mrs.

Kelly continued. The woman reached into a box of supplies and held up two vases. "One of these pieces is made from reclaimed clay, and one is from new clay. Can you tell which?"

"Nope." Davis shook his head.

"Good answer." Mrs. Kelly smiled his way. "If a vase is made from reclaimed clay, you can't tell it from the good clay once we centered it correctly. And that's what I want y'all to learn. We need to center our lives and relationships on God. When you leave this ministry, you'll face temptations. You'll meet someone you find attractive, and you may want to become involved with that person."

Star kept her focus on the clay as her stomach tightened. She hoped the others would show Mrs. Kelly respect like they did for Rivers, their regular art therapist.

"I may be old as the sand on the beach," Mrs. Kelly said, "but as far as men and women and sex are concerned, the same temptations have been around since creation. If you've made a mistake in the past and you gave yourself to someone—the wrong someone—the good thing is you can start over now. Reclaim your life." She held up the vases again. "When you meet a man or woman you are drawn to, stay centered on God. Not the urges of your flesh. Try to figure out what or who that man or woman is centered around. If they aren't centered on God, if their focus is only on what they can see or touch, then your relationship will probably end up in a big sloppy mess. Guard your reclaimed purity. Save your affections for a godly man or woman."

She set the vases on the floor and clasped her hands. "Does that make sense to y'all?"

"It sure does." Davis was the first to speak. "I don't need any more disasters. Thank you very much for the great reminder."

Renee, another resident, nodded. "Been there, done that, and bought the T-shirt. Not looking for more man-drama."

"Yeah." Davis scrunched his nose. "We canceled our subscription to your drama a few months ago."

The group laughed, and a few others made positive comments and thanked Mrs. Kelly for speaking.

Star stopped the wheel and wiped her hands on a damp towel, then began cleaning up some of the mess.

"I hope you have a good evening." Mrs. Kelly stood and angled toward Star. "I'm glad to still be useful."

"You're always useful to me." Warmth for the sweet woman filled Star's heart. "I'm glad we're friends." And she was. They'd spent days talking and fixing up Mrs. Kelly's house. Star had worked in the garden, straightened the attic, painted, and cleaned out the garage, but all the tasks had been enjoyable because somehow Mrs. Kelly made them that way. She told stories of the past, sharing her heart while Star became the hands and feet that disease had twisted so.

The group shuffled out the door, and Davis sauntered toward Mrs. Kelly. "What'cha wanna do with that thing?" He pointed at the wheel.

"I talked to Rivers about leaving it here and donating it to the gallery." Mrs. Kelly glanced Star's way. "Maybe someday you'll have a resident potter and sell pieces up front in the gallery."

"You don't mean me, do you?" Star let her mouth hang open a second. She'd been having fun learning from Mrs. Kelly, but... "I'm not artistic."

"Creating takes practice, but you're a..." Mrs. Kelly swayed, then took a step and wobbled. Her hand lifted to her chest.

Star shot to her side and put a steadying arm around her friend's waist. "Are you okay?"

Blinking, Mrs. Kelly shook her head. "I don't know. I'm dizzy like when I had my sinking spell."

"Oh no." Icy fingers clutched Star's throat, squeezing out the air. "It might be her heart again. My cell's in the car." Her gaze searched the room. "Where's a flipping phone around here? We need to call 911!" Panic laced her words. She surveyed the room for Mrs. Kelly's purse.

"It's gonna be all right." His voice calm, Davis moved to the other side of Mrs. Kelly. "Let's set her back in the chair." Once they had her steady, Davis jogged to the counter and retrieved his cell, then punched in the emergency call. His words jumbled in Star's mind as he gave the address. "Possible heart attack."

Please, God, not her too. Star sent up the desperate prayer. It seemed she never got to keep anyone she loved for long.

Chapter 2

Only a couple of glasses of wine the night before and his head still throbbed. Paul Kelly rolled over and massaged his temples. He knew better. Even in Italy where they made the best Chianti in the world, he should have stuck to beer. Or sparkling water, since he'd probably end up flying today. His boss expected the company pilots to be available for his whims.

"*Buongiorno*, sleepyhead." Francesca sat at the small desk in the Rome hotel room, brushing her hair. The deep espresso color shone in the light streaming through the small window. She'd already dressed and looked as if she'd just stepped off the cover of a magazine. As usual. "Shall I bring you a *caffè americano?*"

"No." The muscles in Paul's stomach tightened at the sweetness in her voice. Another mistake he'd made last night. "But, thanks."

Though he no longer believed all the hypocritical rules drilled into him from birth to seminary school, he still didn't feel right about last night. Francesca was a friend going through a hard time. Her marriage to the Italian soccer player might be on the rocks, but it wasn't over. He shouldn't have hooked up with her. If discovered, their intimacy could cause her more problems, and he didn't want to be in the middle of marital drama.

"It's none of my business, but…" Paul rolled his legs off the bed, grabbed the button-down he'd worn the night before, and slipped it on. Where was he going with this, anyway?

Francesca's marriage was none of his business. Period.

"I know you care." She raised her sculpted brows. "I will give myself time. Last night, I just didn't want to be alone."

"Okay." He managed a smile. "I'm not complaining or anything."

She stood and faced him, her chestnut eyes luminous. "You." She kissed her fingertips then blew him a kiss. "I am late. Call me next time you are in the city."

Not happening, but he kept his mouth shut until she'd flitted out the door. Since he'd met the model at an airport bar a year ago, they'd flirted. A lot. That had been fun. When he'd texted her last night, he'd expected dinner and dancing. He hadn't predicted the rest. Not that there was anything wrong with two people enjoying each other—he'd been down that road a time or two—but his goals didn't include being sidelined by relationship entanglements, especially romantic ones. He was only in Europe until he earned enough money to be free to spend his life how he wanted. And free to take care of his mother as she aged.

The phone on the nightstand began its infernal chirping. His boss's ring. They weren't scheduled to fly today. The man was a self-centered tyrant—constant unscheduled changes that could have been planned for, but his boss didn't bother to share those details.

Paul took a deep breath before answering. "Hello."

"How soon can we be in London?"

Never a *Good morning,* or *How are you?* from Kenneth Martin. The CEO of one of Europe's largest insurance conglomerates hadn't risen to the top because of his congenial personality.

"I can be at the airport in forty-five minutes, but I haven't spoken to Charlie yet today." It was Sunday, so his copilot

12

might have gone to church.

"Find him, and call me when you're ready. Marie is on standby as our flight attendant. Don't make me wait." The connection ended.

Nice. Maybe Charlie had gone to an early service. They both knew Kenneth's whims. The new mistress they'd flown over this weekend was younger and more demanding than those in the previous parade of women Kenneth had dabbled with. She'd give the man a run for his money. And Kenneth controlled an enormous chunk of change.

Paul whipped off a text to Charlie and headed to the lobby for breakfast. He'd fill up while it was free. Only six to twelve more months of putting up with this jerk, and he'd be free too. He'd be able to move home and take care of Mom.

When Kenneth started all his ranting and bullying, Paul always reminded himself he was putting up with it all for her. In a year tops, he'd have enough in savings for his own plane. Nothing big, maybe a Cessna 421. He could take up a friend's offer to buy a flight school near Hilton Head. Maybe run sightseeing flights for extra income. His mother would be close, then, especially if he could get her to move into the retirement center he'd researched. She'd have help there, even while he worked. She didn't need to be in her house alone with rheumatoid arthritis crippling her.

Paul held in a groan. Guilt niggled at his chest. He should have gone to see Mom when she'd had the stents put in last year, but, as always, his boss's demands held him hostage. And he was so close to reaching his goal. Mom claimed she had help now, but how could he be sure without going to see for himself? He'd call her tomorrow from London. Maybe he would even broach the subject of taking a few days off with Kenneth, so he could make a quick trip to the States.

Downstairs, the smell of coffee and chocolate croissants lured him. He needed to stay away from those carbs and stick to the yogurt with fruit, but, man, the pastries at this hotel bordered on sinful. He filled his plate with all of the above, tossing on buffalo mozzarella cheese and prosciutto to at least round out the food groups. Italy produced the best cuisine in Europe, hands down.

He found an empty chair beside an older man reading a newspaper, hopeful for a quick and quiet breakfast. His first bite of the croissant melted in his mouth. Delicious and worth an extra hour in the gym.

"Morning." Charlie pulled a chair to the table. "Guess I need to gobble down this food."

"Yep." Paul's shoulders relaxed. They'd be on time. His copilot was a reliable guy.

"Mass at San Clemente was beautiful."

"You don't speak Italian, and you're not Catholic."

"Still beautiful. I figured this would happen, and the protestant service didn't start early enough." Charlie scooped a spoonful of porridge topped with dried fruit and nuts. He was a reliable husband, too, sticking to the heart-healthy diet his wife had wanted him to follow when his cholesterol had hit the roof. "The Catholics don't mind me attending, and they print the Scriptures on the worship guide."

Paul downed his juice. Another half cup of coffee might help knock out the headache.

"Did you sleep well?" Charlie spoke between bites. The seemingly innocuous question hung between them like dense fog on a Seattle runway. His copilot lived his life steeped in Christian faith, and though subtle in his testimonies at work, the guilt-churning undercurrent still there grated.

Paul took another bite before answering. He'd seen the

hypocrisy in "people of faith"—the vast expanse between their talk and their walk. He'd left religion on a rundown airstrip in Africa, and he was never picking it back up.

"I slept well enough to fly." Paul stood, coffee cup in hand. "You?"

"Great, as usual." Charlie offered a clear-eyed smile. "How's your friend holding up?"

And there it was. The guilt trip. "She'll be fine."

"She's blessed to have a friend like you."

Was he being sarcastic or just naive? Paul set aside his cup. He could get more at the airport. "I'll grab my bag and meet you in the lobby."

He took the narrow winding staircase to the third floor, almost at a run. *Blessed to have a friend like me.* Who said stuff like that? His gut clenched. Even if he didn't believe all that religious nonsense anymore, had he been a good friend to Francesca?

His phone chirped again. This ringtone signaled a call from his mother. What time was it at home? Did she know it was Sunday morning here? He hated when she called on Sundays. She didn't ask if he'd gone to church, but somehow the unspoken subject hovered, despite the fact he hadn't been in seven years. It was bad enough with Charlie's *blessed-talk* and invitations to attend church, no matter where they flew. Couldn't a man just live his life without all the guilting?

Paul pressed the silence button. This wasn't a good time. The extra paperwork and logs they'd have to fill out for the boss's schedule changes were adding to his already dull headache.

Mom would have to wait until he arrived in London. Then they'd have time to really talk.

Chapter 3

"This guy's such a...such a...jerk." Star ended the call when it went to voicemail again and flopped into a hospital waiting room chair beside Davis. She managed to keep from spouting all the obscene names that still popped in her mind even after a year of working to tame her tongue and take every thought captive. Both spiritual disciplines proved difficult, but the thought-capturing seemed to be one that did her in.

"Maybe it's because of the time difference in Europe, or he's busy flying a plane?" Davis raised his brows above grayish-blue eyes and ran his fingers over his bearded chin.

How did he always keep a positive outlook? "I don't care what Paul Kelly's excuses are for not answering the *three times* I've called from his mother's phone. I've helped Mrs. Kelly a year now, and I can count on one hand the times he's been the one to call her." Heat rushed to Star's face, the anger bubbling just beneath her skin. "He should be thankful he has such a good mother. I know I would be. She's in the ICU, maybe dying."

"Don't think the worst." Davis clasped Star's hand, his grip warm and strong. His gaze met hers. "Want to pray?"

"I've *been* praying for hours." Tears pricked her eyes, making her vision fuzzy. She curled over, planting her face against her palm. She wouldn't cry. Crying never changed a thing. Not her mother's depression, not her stepfather's rage, not the aching emptiness after her sister quit answering her phone calls.

Releasing her hand, Davis wrapped Star in his arms and pulled her to his chest. "It's going to be okay. I've got a good feeling. Since she's been here so long now, that probably means they're doing something to make her better and maybe running tests."

Something about his embrace soothed her whipping emotions. He quieted the voices in her head that told her Mrs. Kelly would be yet another person she would lose. If only she could stay here like this, strong arms holding her up, the way Mrs. Kelly had said Jesus held her up after the loss of her husband. Star took a shaky breath. She longed to have a strong faith like that, but this embrace felt nice too.

"God's got this, Star." Davis pressed the words against her hair.

She pulled back to search his face for any sign of his feelings toward her. Most men hit on her in one way or another. Some used fists, others made advances. Except for Blake. Before he'd died last year, he'd acted as a protector, never pressing for anything in return. Of course, he'd been totally messed up with heroin.

She swallowed the lump forming in her throat. "Why are you so nice?"

He blinked at her question and loosened his hold. "God's been good to me."

"Why are you so nice to *me*?" She swallowed hard. "I like you. You're cute. I don't know what it means for you to put your arms around me this way." Her gaze dropped to study the white tile floor. "The guys I've known usually had intentions."

"Star." He breathed her name, shaking his head. "I didn't mean to… I can't—"

Mrs. Kelly's phone rang, and Star retrieved it from her purse, relieved she wouldn't have to hear the rest of what Davis was about to say. Paul Kelly's name registered on the ID, so she took the call. "It's about time."

"Who is this?"

"Your mom's assistant. Didn't you get my message?"

"I saw a message, but I... I called when I landed in London."

"Your mother is in the hospital." Finally, she could give this guy a piece of her mind. She stood and paced in front of the row of chairs. "You need to get over here to see her. She's a good person, and you're lucky to have such a wonderful mother."

"Who are you?"

"My name is Star Youngblood. I've been helping your mother for a year now, which you would know if you ever came to check on her."

The line fell silent for a moment. "What's wrong with her?"

"Something with her heart. I don't know yet."

"Is there a medical professional I can speak to?"

"Yeah. There are a lot of them here at the hospital. Why don't you jump in your jet and come talk to them?"

"I don't know who you think you are—"

"Someone who cares about your mother."

The call ended, and Star tossed the phone back in her purse. "Maybe Paul Kelly got the message."

Davis snorted. "Ya think?"

"He was mad, but so what? Maybe he'll get his selfish behind home."

"If that didn't shame him into it, I don't know what else would." He rubbed the back of his neck. "About what you asked before the phone call... It's hard navigating friendships when you've been in a lot of messed up relationships. I get it."

Friendship. "It's cool." Star shrugged and collapsed back

into the chair. "I was just checking." She should have known better. A nice guy would never be interested in her if he truly was nice. She had way too much baggage.

"It's not that you aren't the whole package or anything. I've just—"

"Don't." She held up her palm. "That makes the discussion more awkward."

"Do *not* let us be awkward." He bumped her with his elbow.

"Ow." She rubbed the spot. "Elbow me again, and I'll smack you."

"See, back to normal. Awkward over."

Yeah, for him. He wasn't the one who'd made a fool of himself.

~ ~ ~

He couldn't wait to tell that woman what she could do with her opinions. The wind whipped as Paul stepped out of the rental car onto the hospital parking lot. With eyelids heavy from lack of sleep and a headache throbbing against his skull, he'd done what he had to do and paid what he had to pay to get home within twenty-four hours. Once he gave this Star person a piece of his mind, he'd fire her and arrange for Mom's move to the retirement community in Hilton Head as soon as possible. She'd be safer there until he could move back.

The salty humid air filled his lungs and smelled like home. But this was not how he'd mapped out his return or his future. Next summer, when he had enough cash saved, he could have come back to the States for good, barring any unexpected monetary outflows. That had been the plan to take care of Mom.

He'd always wanted to be there for her after they'd lost Dad. But being jobless and heartbroken had made that

19

impossible at the time. Then, when he'd received the offer from Kenneth, for great money, he'd come up with a plan. He'd work in London until he had enough to start his own business along the Georgia or Carolina coastline somewhere. He had no idea Mom's decline would come this soon. She wasn't even that old, but arthritis had twisted her body and aged her before her time. Now, he might not have to worry about waiting to quit his job because his boss had been irate at the short notice for this trip. Paul massaged the constricted muscles on the back of his neck.

Really, when wasn't his boss irate? Paul couldn't wait to be free of him.

Anxiety churned as he made his way to the entrance. He'd texted his mom's phone before the flight from London to Atlanta. Maybe she received the message instead of that busybody. Someone had texted back the room number. He checked it again before going inside. Man, he hated these places.

But he had no choice. He flung the door open and entered. Inside the hospital, he made his way down the halls, the bright lights and smells of antiseptic agitating his senses. Sad-looking families milled around with weary expressions. His chest ached for what they might be going through. He'd been there.

Memories crashed into him of when he'd arrived home to find his father deathly ill. Even a year spent on the mission field in Africa hadn't prepared Paul for that image. That shock.

Dad had been the picture of health until the flu struck. The resulting pneumonia and strep infection turned into sepsis. Doctors amputated Dad's hands and feet in an effort to save him.

In the end, nothing worked.

Paul shook the horrific images from his mind and checked

his phone again to make sure he was at the correct room number. Lifting his fist to knock, he took in a large gulp of air and held it. What sorrow would he find here?

The old impulse surfaced. The one he'd been brainwashed with his entire life.

But he wouldn't pray. He wouldn't waste his breath.

Because prayer hadn't changed what happened in Africa, nor had it saved his father from an excruciating and untimely death. Nothing would change by whispering words toward the ceiling.

The door swung open. "I'll be back with your tea, and I'll get the mix of sweet and unsweet right this time." A young woman giggled as she walked, her head turned to look back over her shoulder. Caramel-colored hair fell in silky strands from a messy bun and lay against her cheeks.

"You better." His mom's voice sounded weak, but her tone still held that same Southern belle tease.

Relief swarmed Paul, loosening the knots winding across his shoulders. "Is she giving you trouble already?"

"Huh?" The woman pivoted his way, her full lips parted. Her brown eyes widened before drilling into him.

"You must be a friend of my mother's. I'm Paul Kelly." He held out his hand and offered a smile despite his exhaustion.

"I know." She brushed past him without a backward glance.

Confused, Paul continued through the door. How did she know him? High school? She looked too young to be in his graduating class, plus he'd remember a girl that pretty.

"Honey!" His mother waved him closer. "I can't believe it."

He stepped into a small private room, sterile except for a vase of bright flowers and Mom's favorite afghan spread across her thin form.

"You shouldn't have come all this way, but I'm so happy to see you in person instead of that computer screen." She lifted her gnarled hands. "Give your mama a hug."

Paul pressed a kiss on her forehead, and she pulled him closer into an embrace. The fragrance of his childhood enveloped him, something like citrus, sunshine, and a touch of liniment. His eyes slid shut. He'd missed the sweetness from the woman who'd always been there for him—soothed nightmares, bandaged scraped knees and elbows, encouraged him at every turn.

"I love you, baby boy." She patted his cheek.

His chest squeezed as he took in the tubes connected to her chest and her hand. He should have come back sooner.

"I love you, too, Mom. What's going on?"

She waved him off. "Just another stent and a few tests. I should be out soon."

Just another stent? He cleared his throat to keep his voice from cracking. "But why did you need another stent? Is the problem fixed now?"

"I think so, but the doctor should be here at any moment with the test results."

If the doctor gave them good news, the retirement community would be perfect for her. She'd have people nearby day and night who could help her. "We can pick out one of the floorplans I told you about in Hilton Head."

"Paul, no." Her voice cracked. "My life is in St. Simons, and those places won't let me bring Phoenix. "

"You can make new friends. They'll be right outside your door. They have a ton of activities, Mom, and you can't risk your health for that animal—that possum!" His frustration raised his volume louder than he'd intended.

"I have help at the house. You don't have to worry."

"Where is your help? I have a few things to say to that—"

"Excuse me." The cute young woman busted back into the room with the cup, set it aside on the nightstand, and reached for his arm, digging her fingers into his bicep. "I'm right here, and you need to come into the hall."

Now he recognized that snarky voice.

She pulled him out of the room and shut the door. "Cut it out." Her finger wagged at him, but his attention caught on the jut of her angled chin below those full lips. "Your mother's having heart problems, and I didn't call you here to cause her more stress."

"More stress? I'm here to help her."

"By upsetting her while she's still healing? You think badgering her in the hospital is okay?"

A missile launched in his chest and exploded behind his eyes, flaring his headache into a full-blown migraine. "And what gives you the right to tell me what I can and can't say to my mother?"

"I care about her." Her fists planted on her hips, and she squared off with him. "Do you?"

Chapter 4

What was wrong with Paul Kelly?

In the glaring lights of the hospital's hall, Star waited for him to lay into her, but the man pressed his hands over his eyes. Deep hazel eyes that had appeared friendly at first, especially when paired with his nice smile.

The pictures of him at Mrs. Kelly's house didn't do him justice. He stood well over six feet, obviously worked out. Not a strand of his light brown hair lay out of place, though he'd traveled halfway around the world. But no matter how hot the guy was, he'd been a crummy son. And Mrs. Kelly deserved better.

Star grimaced. She'd made a terrible mistake convincing him to come here.

His hands still covered his eyes. Was he crying? Maybe he'd finally realized how awful he'd been and felt guilty.

"Are you okay?" Star ventured to touch his shoulder. "I know I've been a little tough on you, but your mom means so—"

"Migraine." He dropped his hands but pressed his eyes shut another long second before opening them. "Haven't had one this bad in a while, but you've managed to conjure up a humdinger." Sarcasm dripped from his words as those hazel eyes opened and shot her an icy look.

Oh, yeah, blame her for his problems. "I guess you'll be leaving then." And that'd be fine with her. Mrs. Kelly was better off without him.

"I'm not—"

"Excuse me, Star." Mrs. Kelly's doctor approached. She hadn't noticed him coming with all the Paul drama. "Is that you, Paul?"

"Steve Johnson?" Paul's face transformed from the scowl to a smile. "Man, it's been a long time." The two men hugged, patting each other hard on the back before releasing.

"Your mom tells me you're a corporate pilot in Europe now? Where are you based?" The lanky doctor seemed to be in no hurry to visit his patient.

"London, but we travel all over."

"Ever go back to Africa?"

Paul's smile dissolved. He shook his head, a hard line forming between his brows.

Maybe his head did hurt badly. Star held in a sigh. Her sister had suffered from migraines, and they'd seemed awful.

The doctor didn't appear to notice Paul's discomfort. "The month I served with your mission changed my life. I'll never forget those good people. My time there impacted my faith and how I treat my patients, my family… everything."

Paul's lips pinched before he spoke. "The people will do that."

Mrs. Kelly had mentioned Paul living in Africa a while, but she never went into a lot of detail. This clean-shaven, starched-button-down guy didn't look like a missionary. He looked like he'd freak out if his expensive dress shoes got a scratch. She'd seen the type when she waitressed on Sea Island. A tiny chip on the edge of a salad bowl, a fingerprint on a knife, a slightly overcooked steak, and they'd throw a fit, demand a free meal. No tip, either, as if she'd manned the grill herself.

"About Mom. Can you tell me what's going on with her?" Paul nodded toward the hospital room.

"Come in, and we'll talk." The doctor held out one hand directing them forward, his eyes kind behind a trendy pair of glasses.

Finally, some news. Star scuttled in front of them, opened the door, and stepped back in the room.

"Where are you going?" Paul caught her elbow, his voice low. "This is my mother's private health issue."

Ripping her arm from his grasp, Star spun to face him. "Your mother has me go to all her appointments with her." Defenses rising, she took him in, sizing him up. She'd find a way to hold her own if this got ugly. She always did and with a lot worse than preppy-mc-scowl-pants. "And keep your paws off me if you know what's good for you."

"Be nice, children." Mrs. Kelly sighed and smoothed her short salt-and-pepper hair. "Star, he's not like that." She raised one brow as she glanced at her son. "At least he wasn't. And Paul, Star's right. She's my caregiver, so it's best she has information on my health."

"But Mom—"

"What have you learned from my tests?" Mrs. Kelly shifted her focus to the doctor.

"The good news is that the stents will keep you going for a little while longer. The bad news is that your rheumatoid arthritis is causing or worsening your cardiovascular disease. Inflammatory conditions can do that. We need to get you scheduled for coronary bypass surgery."

"Surgery?" Mrs. Kelly's mouth fell open. "Like, open my chest surgery?"

"I'm afraid so."

"Can't we treat it some other way?" Mrs. Kelly's pleading tone had acid filling Star's stomach. She'd do anything to shield her friend from this.

"You're on the best medications," the doctor said. "You claim to eat a healthy diet."

"Maybe I could try water aerobics?" Tears shone in Mrs. Kelly's eyes. "I know I need exercise, but my joints hurt so."

Star neared the bed and took Mrs. Kelly's hand. "They're opening a therapy pool at the gym where I applied." Seeing this sweet lady upset hurt worse than a boot in the chest.

The doctor shook his head. "Water aerobics is a great idea, but I don't think it'll be enough. I know this is a lot to take in, but I'd like to schedule you for the surgery before the end of the year."

Only three months from now? Star's stomach knotted.

"What are the risks?" Paul's voice sounded somber and flat, despite his straight posture.

"The usual risks like bleeding, blood clots, infection, and reaction to anesthesia. Kidney failure can be an issue in some rheumatoid patients if there's already damage there." The doctor removed his glasses and rubbed one eye for a second. "The thing is, Mrs. Kelly, you need to have a healthy heart because you've told me you may be a candidate for knee replacement, even your hips and other joints in the future."

"It's gotten that bad, Mom?" Paul sat on the other side of the bed, hazel eyes becoming glassy. "Why didn't you tell me?"

"I feel okay most of the time, other than my achiness and fatigue." Mrs. Kelly smiled, no doubt trying to make things sound much better than they truly were. "I'll be fine, but I'd like to ask you a big favor."

"Anything." Paul sounded as if he actually meant it.

"Your father and I would've been married forty years this month, and he'd always promised to take me to Ireland for our anniversary someday." She swallowed hard, emotion obvious in her wobbly voice. "Would you take me before this surgery?

I might never get the chance to go."

"Mom, no." Paul stood and crossed his arms. "You can't risk it."

"If it's that important to you..." The doctor tapped his chin. "If you took baby aspirin and promised to move around during the flights."

Paul's forehead squeezed into a knot. "Anyone who's been to Europe knows the old streets and stairways can be treacherous even to a healthy person."

"That's why I want you to go with me." Mrs. Kelly gave him a pleading look. "You can let me hold your elbow and keep me balanced. And I have my cane. I'll even go in a wheelchair if you want."

Paul massaged his temples. "I can't take off right now."

Mrs. Kelly's face dissolved into sad resignation, pinching Star's heart.

"I'll take you. It sounds exciting." Okay, exciting and terrifying, but she could get past that.

"Mom's not going, and that's final." The expression on Paul's face looked as hard as a sculpture carved into the side of a stone mountain.

Oh, this guy would get an earful once they left this hospital.

~~~

Dr. Johnson excused himself, and Paul ran his fingers through his hair. He hadn't meant to sound off the way he had, but he could imagine Mom falling and breaking a hip on the village streets of Ireland or tumbling down a castle stairwell and breaking her neck. A shiver scampered across his shoulders. He refused to lose her so soon. She was all he had left, and this wasn't how he had their lives planned. He hadn't even known arthritis affected the heart.

"Paul, darling." His mother's voice was soft. "Why don't

you take a nap at the house? You have to be jetlagged. And Star made a nice pot of turkey and vegetable soup yesterday. There are leftovers in the refrigerator."

"I'm fine." He glanced at Star. Her stare pinned him. If looks could shoot warheads, he'd be a nuclear wasteland by now. The girl was ferocious, and she seemed to be fiercely attached to his mother. Too much so. It bordered on obsessive. But he dealt in ferocious on a daily basis with his boss, so this girl wasn't going to intimidate him. Especially when it came to Mom.

"You said you had a migraine." Warrior woman just had to interject that little piece of information.

"Paul, really." Mom's head cocked as she studied him. "Rest a few hours. They might even be ready to release me by the time you get back, and you can take me home."

"I can nap here." He pointed to the chair by the bed. "I came to be with you. Your…*help* can leave."

"Listen." The warrior woman kept her tone syrupy sweet, but Paul pictured a cartoon character with steam spewing from its ears. "You need to rest to drive your mom home. Driving without sleep is as dangerous as driving under the influence. We'll call you when they release her, and until then, *the help* will take good care of your mother."

Both women stared at him, neither budging from their blasted stubbornness. "Fine. I'll go eat, shower, and rest. Then I'll be back."

"Give me a kiss before you go." Mom held out her arms. "I'm so happy to see my baby."

"Of course." He hugged her, careful not to dislodge her monitors or IV. "Love you. I'll see you soon." Really soon.

A smug smile lifted Star's full lips as he turned. Man, she got under his skin worse than stepping on a nail. A long rusty nail.

He had to get rid of her to protect Mom. Fast.

The drive to the house passed quickly as he tried to devise a strategy. Before he knew it, he'd pulled into the familiar driveway in front of the gray stucco ranch surrounded by ancient moss-covered oaks. Something about being in St. Simons soaked into his bones, though. Made him feel more relaxed than he had in a long time. He grabbed his duffle bag, stepped out, and took in his childhood home. The yard looked manicured, the front porch freshly painted a vibrant white. Mom hadn't mentioned hiring a contractor.

Inside, the place smelled clean and lemony. The walls sported a fresh coat of pale blue paint. Where had all the clutter gone that Mom usually had lying about? She must have hired a cleaning service.

He dropped his keys and his bag. A clatter pulled his attention to the kennel. He'd forgotten the pet possum.

"Oh, Phoenix." Paul squatted by the cage and unlatched it. "I guess I'll have to show you some attention." Growing up with his father running a veterinary clinic, they'd had their share of wildlife rescues. Warmth seeped through him at the memories of his father teaching him to bottle-feed baby animals, from puppies and kittens to squirrels and raccoons. Even a skunk. They'd seen it all, but this possum was still a trip.

The animal brushed against Paul's leg like a cat. "Okay. You don't have to beg." Paul rubbed the soft hair. "I know you miss Mom. I've missed her too."

His stomach rumbled. Maybe he'd find that soup Star had made, after all. She couldn't poison him when she hadn't known he was coming.

Star. What kind of name was that?

He pictured her honey-colored eyes glaring at him, those loose strands of hair framing her face. She'd looked so young and sweet when he'd first spotted her. Then, like a dark fairytale, she'd transformed into an ogre. What an enigma.

While he ate the stew, he'd figure out how to get his mother away from her. He could call now and see if there was an opening at the retirement village. Maybe he could move Mom before he flew back to London. He could rent a truck tomorrow, hire movers or something.

His mother meant the whole world to him, and he wouldn't let some nut put her in danger here. And certainly not on some harebrained trip to Ireland.

Chapter 5

"Would you really go with this cripple to Ireland?"

Star resisted the urge to help Mrs. Kelly as she lowered on arthritic knees to the side of the hospital bed, dressed and ready to go home.

"We could sneak off," Mrs. Kelly said. "Maybe even this week if our passports are up to date, and Paul wouldn't have to know. I've been researching the trip all year."

"I can go if you're up to it. I wouldn't want you to push yourself too hard." Star sat in the chair beside the bed, holding her knees to her chest. They kept these rooms so cold. She wanted to please Mrs. Kelly, but what if something happened to her overseas? Taking her friend to a foreign country would be a major responsibility. They'd spent hours discussing Ireland, her late husband, and Mrs. Kelly's top-destination bucket list. The discussion was fun, but this trip? Now?

"You heard the doctor say it was okay. Paul's just overprotective."

If the guy was truly protective, he could get his behind back on this side of the globe. And take his mother on the trip she'd dreamed of. Star would love to go, but she could hardly scrape together enough for a deposit on an apartment. "Could I pay in installments? I don't have all the cash right now."

"I'd pay for you to be a traveling companion. You wouldn't need a penny." Mrs. Kelly's face looked so hopeful.

"I'd want to pay something, but I'm saving to find a place to live that fits my budget."

"Have you had any luck?"

Luck was one thing she'd never had much of. "The only thing in my price range, so far, is a room I could rent from a lady in a trailer on the edge of town."

"A room in a trailer?"

"I've lived in worse." Star shrugged. A lot worse, actually. "St. Simons is expensive."

"What if you moved in with me?" Mrs. Kelly lifted her brows above bright hazel eyes, the deep color much like Paul's. "It would help both of us."

Star scoffed. "Your son would be the one having a coronary."

"Absolutely not." Paul strode through the door, his palms facing upward. "She can't live with you. We're moving to Hilton Head."

Had the door been ajar? How long had the guy been standing there, eavesdropping? Star's heart rate accelerated, and adrenaline rushed down her arms. Paul was obviously some kind of control freak. Vince and her stepfather had been controlling too. And she'd been at the wrong end of their fists when things didn't go their way. She wouldn't let anything happen to Mrs. Kelly.

"Then, I can find a place there too." She stood and squared off with Paul.

"She won't need you there. The community takes care of things." His brows scrunched into a deep furrow. "Can't you move in with your own mother and stop obsessing over mine?"

Star's breath caught. He might as well have kicked her in the throat. A wave of grief tore through her and ripped open her memories—her sister, face ashen, screaming that she'd found their mother's body.

"Paul, that's enough." Mrs. Kelly's voice took a firm tone. She scooted from the bed to stand with them and then held up one hand. "You will not talk to her like that. And I'm not moving anywhere right now."

Paul's gaze bounced between them, Adam's apple bobbing as he swallowed, his face and hazel eyes softening as they fixed on Star. "I'm sorry. I'm just worried."

What did he just say? Star cocked her head. Was he for real? Or just sorry like her stepfather always acted after they'd landed a visit from child protective services?

Mrs. Kelly wrapped an arm around Star's shoulders and squeezed. "He didn't know about your mother, sweetie. You have to be exhausted, too, after staying with me up here. Why don't you go home and rest while Paul takes me to the house?"

Go home. If only she had a real home. "Whatever you think is best." Star hugged Mrs. Kelly. The sweet woman meant the world to her, but she wouldn't give Paul a second glance nor his apology—no doubt an attempt to manipulate—a second thought.

~~~

The look on Star's face branded onto Paul's mind, staying with him during the drive to his mother's house. His stomach had roiled once he'd realized she must have lost her mom. What had happened to bring that horror to Star's features?

He'd been downright rude. He was turning into his boss. The girl didn't deserve that. No one did. He was just trying to do what was best for his mother.

Once he had Mom settled on her recliner with Phoenix, he brought her a glass of ice water. He didn't know much about heart conditions, but most ailments required staying hydrated. He sat on the gray leather couch across from her. "What is Star's background?"

His mother stared at the glass, sadness lining her face. "She's had a rough life, but that's her story to tell."

"Can you at least tell me why she got upset when I mentioned her mother?"

Mom chewed her lip before answering. "Both her biological parents died by the time she was sixteen."

His stomach sank. He was a jerk and an idiot.

He'd seen trauma in Africa when children lost their parents to AIDS or typhoid or cholera. So often, they were left alone to fend for themselves—homeless children eating garbage and rotten fruit, begging, stealing, sleeping in caves or trash dumps.

"I'm sorry. I didn't realize."

"Honey." Mom's voice was both stern and tender. "You know from working in ministry that everyone has baggage they carry. She needs me as much as I need her."

"But I'll be moving back here, then you won't need her. Don't you think she should begin to accept that now?" No matter the sad story, Star should move on. His plate would be full enough, starting a new business and looking after Mom. He wasn't going to be someone's counselor. He'd left that job behind too.

Mom's face lit up. "You're moving back already?"

"Not yet. In nine months to a year."

"Oh." Mom sighed, her disappointment obvious. "I'll have to pray about the situation with Star."

Mom and praying. He held in a scoff. What difference would that make? And why did she always have to bring up his past life? He'd made it clear he'd left religion. He changed the subject before she could start bombarding him.

"I like what you've done with the place." He swept an arm around the room. "What company did you hire to do all this work?"

"No company." Mom grinned. "Star did it all. She's as strong as they come and likes to stay busy. She dug up the old bushes and planted new ones, painted the house from floor to ceiling, and helped me clean out. She even fixed the guest bedroom toilet."

A little impressive.

He'd meant to replace the guts of that toilet last time he was home. Over a year ago.

He should have demanded Kenneth give him time off. Only, there were plenty of other pilots waiting in the wings for a high-paying job like his. Biding his time and saving money to come home, permanently, had been his whole focus.

"I'm glad she helped you. I've been trying to get you to declutter this place for years. Where'd she take all the junk you'd hoarded?"

"The ladies from the sober living house have a consignment store, so she took it over there."

A niggle of worry kicked up in Paul's chest. "What sober living house?"

Mom's jaw snapped shut like a wild animal clinging to a scrap of food.

And then he knew.

"Star is from the sober living house, and that's why she needs a place to live, isn't it?"

"I know what you're thinking." Mom's gaze pleaded. "She's been sober a year, Paul. She's not a criminal. Star tried to deal with her difficult past in the wrong way."

"With drugs or alcohol." What if Star hadn't just cleaned out the clutter at Mom's house? What if Star was here to clean Mom out of everything she owned?

This situation was worse than he'd realized. His mom had taken in another stray. Except this time, the abandoned creature was an addict. And she could be much more dangerous than any of Mom's four-legged projects.

Chapter 6

Star's interview had gone even better than she'd expected, and the gym owner was a woman. She'd much rather work with a female. Less chance of being hit on. After working for Vince, she didn't want to go through that again.

Teaching exercise wouldn't be a ministry like Davis's, but she could do her best to watch for people that seemed down at the gym. Maybe try to share her faith with them.

Once she'd parked the VW in front of Mrs. Kelly's house, she gathered the bags from the back seat. Her steps felt light on the walk up the driveway, despite the additional weight of the six full reusable grocery bags cutting into her arms.

The position at the new gym meant she'd be teaching the early morning and evening group classes, plus staying at the front desk at night until closing. It'd be perfect. She'd teach a five a.m. cycle class, then an eight a.m. body sculpting class. After that, she could go home and help Mrs. Kelly until the evening classes started at five-thirty, then she'd stay and work the front desk until nine.

Not a bad gig.

Between the two jobs, she might be able to pay for her car insurance, even save for a better vehicle. Growing up, she'd learned to get by with very little.

But would she *have* two jobs?

She eyed Paul's rental car parked next to the side door of the house. If only he'd never come back, maybe she could have taken Mrs. Kelly up on the offer to move in. She'd be here if

Mrs. Kelly needed her during the night.

No way Mr. Control Freak would allow that now. He was going to get rid of her.

Star pressed her lips together. She never should have called him to come home. She should have kept her big mouth shut. But she'd never been good at that. An unwanted picture of her stepfather blasted through her mind. Angry and fist raised, he'd railed on her mother and anyone else in his wake after he came home from work.

The first few times, Star had hidden under the bed with her sister, Skye, shock making their young bodies quiver.

Until a raging storm built inside her. Until she'd decided she wouldn't hide anymore. Until she'd fought to help her mother, despite the pain it caused.

She had the scars to show for it.

Then she'd gotten smart. She'd planned—armed herself.

No matter how many times her stepfather had gotten rid of baseball bats, golf clubs, or knives, Star had found something to use as a weapon to defend her mother. While he was gone to work on construction jobs, she gathered large sticks and rocks or discarded metal from neighbors' trash. Anything could be used as a weapon if someone were desperate enough.

At only nine years old, she'd threatened to kill the man. He'd smirked and laughed at her until she'd given him a cold stare. *You have to sleep sometime,* she'd said. *And you have to eat.*

Every night after that, he'd locked her in a closet or laundry room at bedtime. Over the years, she'd gotten accustomed to sleeping in small spaces. Well, mostly. Now and then, claustrophobia still hit her.

The storm door swung open, and Paul stepped out, giving Star a needed reprieve from those jagged memories. He wore a starched blue shirt tucked into starched khakis. His clothes were likely as inflexible as he was. But they did fit nicely.

"Can I take something?" His lips lifted in a forced smile.

"I don't need help. It's just groceries for tonight's supper."

"You don't have to cook. In fact,"—he held out his hands to grab the shopping bags—"you can leave these and take the day off."

She pulled the sacks back toward her. "I don't want the day off."

Paul held on, and their seesaw continued. "We're not going to be here, so you're not needed."

The muscles in Star's jaw tightened, and so did her grip. He was the one who wasn't needed. "I can cook and clean while you're gone."

"I'll take Mom to dinner *and* clean the house this evening." His hazel eyes sparked. "We'll still pay you if that's what you're worried about."

Steam rose from her core, and Star fought the urge to scream at him. *Tame the tongue. Tame the tongue.* "I *do not* care about the money." Except that she did have to pay her car insurance.

His eyes rounded. "Sorry. That came out wrong."

Sorry? He'd apologized again?

A bit of the steam receded. Now, she couldn't help but notice that Paul stood so close that she could reach out and trace the nice angle of his smoothly-shaven jaw.

Or slap it for being so irritatingly attractive. Or just plain irritating.

Star cleared her throat, which had suddenly thickened. "Where are y'all going?"

His gaze dropped, and he let go of the grocery bags. "We have an appointment."

40

"With the doctor?" Her heart thudded. "I didn't know about it. What's wrong?"

He shook his head and shifted his feet on the concrete sidewalk. "It's not medical."

Realization dawned, resurrecting her anger. "You're taking her to look at that nursing home, aren't you?"

He held up one hand. "It is not a nursing home. Sparkling Pines is a retirement community, and it's—"

"You disgust me."

Star set the groceries on the ground in front of him and scowled. She'd leave, but she'd investigate this place on her own. And she'd be back, armed with knowledge.

~ ~ ~

He disgusted her?

The comment seemed extreme. Over the top. He shouldn't care what the woman thought, but oddly, the words stung. That and the look of revulsion on her pretty face—the disappointment in her brown eyes.

"Is Star here?" his mother's voice snapped Paul from his stupor. He hadn't heard her open the door.

"She left." Guilt pricked him. Mom wouldn't be happy with his sending Star away, but he didn't need the woman stirring up more trouble today. He glanced over his shoulder at his mother.

"Why did she leave? Is she sick?" Mom arched a brow. "Did you hurt her feelings again?"

Maybe he'd hurt Star's feelings, but he hadn't intended to. "I gave her the day off." Paul grabbed the grocery bags and made his way toward the house.

"Oh, Paul." A second look of disappointment from a woman in one day. And it was still early. "I wanted to hear about her interview with the gym. And if we have to go, I

41

wanted to take her with us to Hilton Head. I value her opinion."

"Her opinion is biased."

His mother chewed her lip, worry creasing her brow.

"Don't you have another friend you could take?" He tried to keep his tone gentle. He knew thinking about relocating was hard on her.

"They'll be busy with such short notice."

Moving closer, he gave her an apologetic look. "I was looking forward to catching up with you on the drive. I can't stay in the States much longer, and we can have lunch at your favorite French restaurant over there. Just the two of us."

His mother's expression softened, and her normally affectionate disposition returned. "That does sound nice. I guess I'm ready to go then."

Two hours later, Paul ushered his mother into the spacious lobby of the Sparkling Pines Retirement Community. She had a tight grip on his arm as they crossed the hardwood floors, passing men and women sitting at game tables or quietly talking on couches. She held on as if he'd leave her any second, and she'd be locked up against her will. He hated for her to feel scared like that. This was supposed to be a really nice place.

At least she'd commented on how beautiful the grounds had been along the driveway. And she was right. Trees lined the road, and a large lagoon with lush landscaping boasted a sparkling fountain. They even had biking and walking trails, not that mom could bike, but still.

"Welcome." A middle-aged woman in a gray suit greeted them. "I'm Miranda Luckett."

"Paul Kelly. We spoke on the phone." He nodded toward his mother. "And this is my mother, Priscilla Kelly."

"Of course. Nice to meet you." She offered a polite,

professional smile to Mom. The kind of greeting that reminded him of a flight attendant's welcome. Friendly, but all business. "Would you like something to drink? We have freshly squeezed lemonade or cucumber water on the bar." She gestured to a low table near the receiving desk.

His mother eyed the carafes that held beverages as if they contained arsenic. "No. Thank you."

"Would you like to take a tour?" Lines crinkled Miranda's temples. She'd obviously seen the look on Mom's face before.

Probably an everyday occurrence in her job, and she recognized the anxiety. Like a pilot could spot someone who had a fear of flying.

"Okay." His mother's voice was barely audible.

"Let's take the golf cart and look at the cottages. After that, I can show you the apartments in this building."

"Cottages?" Mom perked up. "Like my own cottage? By myself?"

"Yes." Miranda gave a vigorous nod. "Just like home, except we keep the lawn and do the maintenance, even offer housekeeping and meals if needed or desired. Of course, you can always eat in the dining room here. Some residents buy their own golf carts and ride up for meals and parties. We have entertainers, movies, and singing groups once or twice a week."

His mother's eyes narrowed. "What about pets?"

"You can have a pet, but it has to be on a leash if it comes out of your dwelling." Miranda crinkled her nose. "And use a pooper-scooper."

"Oh, he uses a box, so that wouldn't be a problem."

Not until they realized the animal using the box wasn't a cat but a possum. Paul nearly chuckled at the reaction the animal would likely get.

They exited the building, and Paul helped his mother

43

aboard the golf cart. The skies were clear, and the temperatures hovered in the upper seventies. Gentle winds blew from the east. They couldn't have scheduled a better day to be outside.

The stucco cottages were small but new, and they had plenty of room for one person. Some even had a guest bedroom. Not much of a yard to speak of, but a golf course backed up to the property, offering an attractive view.

Mom seemed fairly impressed, and they finished their tour in the main building. Relief wrestled with guilt in Paul's chest. Mom even appeared to be considering the move.

It had to be the best thing for her. Right? This place came highly recommended. He'd done his research.

But the scowl on Star's face had carved into his mind.

You disgust me.

If only he could erase the woman's image for good.

No such luck.

Chapter 7

With her adrenaline pulsing since she'd left Mrs. Kelly's driveway, Star had gone for a jog around the neighborhood where the Re-Claimed house stood in an attempt to shake off the fury swirling in her chest. When running had done little to calm her, she'd worked on her Bible study, caught up on some reading, taken a shower, and eaten lunch.

Nothing helped. She set out down the street again on the short walk to the gallery. She had to talk to someone. It seemed Paul Kelly brought out the worst in her. Like *Beyond Thunderdome* worst.

Much of her life, she'd used alcohol or drugs to numb the storm of emotions that blasted through her. But her problems still waited to be dealt with when she sobered up. Over the past year, she'd learned to take her pain and anger to God. And then turn to a Christian friend or counselor if she still needed to vent.

So here she was at the art gallery owned by her friends, Rivers and Cooper Knight. They operated the business with the assistance of Re-Claimed residents. And Davis. The door chimed, signaling her entrance as she strode in.

"Hey." Rivers smiled. Her short blond hair stood on end as if she'd been running her fingers through it again, and various colors of acrylic paint dotted her arms. Such an adorable artsy girl. "How does this look?" She held a large, brightly-colored abstract painting against the front wall.

"Nice." Nodding, Star struggled to lift her lips upward.

"What's wrong?" Rivers lowered the piece of art to the ground.

"I—"

"Did I hear a customer?" Davis approached from the back studio. "Oh, it's just Star." He made a goofy face with a dramatic huff. "And who's been feedin' you lemons?"

Star grimaced. Even when she kept her mouth shut, her expression said it all. "Does someone want to go to Hilton Head with me?"

Rivers stepped closer, concern creasing her brow. "Mrs. Kelly's son is still pushing her to move?"

"He's taking her to look at the place today. He actually had the nerve to say I wasn't needed."

"Brutal." Davis's forehead crinkled.

"I'm going to check the place out for myself."

Davis thumbed toward the door. "Hilton Head is two hours away, and that old Bug you drive's not about to win Talladega or anything."

"My car can make it." She hoped.

"Make it to where exactly?" Rivers asked. "There's more than one retirement community in Hilton Head. Several actually."

Shoot. Had Paul said a name? She couldn't remember.

Davis pointed a finger at her. "Could it be that you need to stay in your own hula hoop?"

She nailed him with a harsh stare.

His finger drifting down, he offered a sheepish grin. "Or maybe research Hilton Head retirement communities on-line? Read the reviews?"

A weary groan worked its way through her lips. "I'm just so frustrated. Mrs. Kelly even offered to let me live with her. The setup could've been perfect for both of us."

"I know it's disappointing." Rivers touched Star's arm, her expression hopeful. "What about the apartment above the studio? It'll be vacant soon."

Star's gaze whipped to Davis. "But you live there. Where are you going?"

Glancing around, he rubbed his neck. "Actually, I'm taking over as house parent for the men of Re-Claimed for a while."

Had this change at the sober living house been announced and she'd missed it? "What happened to Kevin?"

"It's still hush-hush, but he finally has a special woman in his life." Davis shrugged his muscular shoulders. "There may be wedding bells in his future."

Something about this plan gnawed at Star. "Good for Kevin, but is that what you want? Will you have time to study for your seminary courses between working here and dealing with the residents at night?"

"One day at a time." Davis's voice was strong and calm.

Too calm for Star's taste. "I'm sick and tired of one day at a time. I wish I had even a hint of my future."

Sympathy laced the look Rivers directed at Star. "Why don't we go create something in the back? Cooper's out running errands. The gallery's quiet."

"I don't feel like painting." She didn't need anyone's pity.

"How about you teach me to slap some mud on that wheel?" Davis nudged her shoulder. "I'm itching to get my fingers dirty. It looks fun."

"Using the pottery wheel is harder than you think." She narrowed her eyes at him.

"Not for a manly man like me. Let's go." Davis locked elbows with her.

Any other guy, she would have balked—maybe even snatched her arm away. But Davis was funny. He felt...safe.

In the back studio, Star scooted away from him to grab ten pounds of clay. She placed the bulky mass on the counter that ran along the far wall.

Davis watched her. "Why are you putting it up there?"

"We need to wedge the clay."

"That sounds freaky. Wedge it where?"

Star chuckled. "Wedging means to compact the clay and get the air bubbles out. There are a few techniques to do it. One is the cone method, and another is the cut-and-slap method."

Laughter bubbled from Davis, brightening his blue-gray eyes. "You've got to be joking. Cut and slap, all the way, baby."

"You're such a kid." And fun to be around. She'd never had a guy as a friend. It was kind of nice.

They spent the rest of the afternoon messing around with the wheel, creating various bowls and vases, discarding a few, but all with a hefty dose of laughter.

~~~

Laughter streamed from the door ajar at the back of the gallery, piquing Paul's curiosity. The sound couldn't be coming from the Ogre, aka Star. But that's where the owner, Rivers, had directed them. Once he and Mom had finished their tour of Sparkling Pines and eaten lunch, Mom had insisted they rush back and check on her help/friend/stray-human.

Frustration simmered in his chest, and his jaw clenched, setting him up for the start of a tension headache, which, when added with the presence of Star, would likely turn into a migraine—again. This whole trip home to check on his mother seemed to be one colossal pain because of her. Mom hobbled with her cane beside him, and he did his best to take slow steps. It was hard to move at such a sluggish speed, but he'd have to learn patience if he was going to be a caregiver when he moved back.

Without announcing their entry, Mom pushed through the doorway dividing the gallery from the studio, and Paul followed. An immense grin lifted Star's pinked cheeks, and shiny strands of her hair framed her face. She sat behind what looked like Mom's pottery wheel close to a stocky man. Really close. Which was none of his business, of course, but for some reason, the muscles of his torso coiled tight and squeezed.

The man glanced their way and stood, smile lines crinkling his temples. "Well, Mrs. Kelly, aren't you lookin' prettier than a speckled pup in a field of daisies?"

Speckled pup? Seriously? Who was this guy?

"And healthier than the last time I saw you." The bulky guy sidestepped the equipment and made his way across the concrete floors to reach them. "I'd hug you, but Star was teaching me to make treasures from your mud."

Star's narrow gaze landed on Paul, analyzing and probing as if waiting for him to say or do something wrong. Her disdain for him funneled between them in an almost palpable force.

"This must be your son." The man's voice pulled Paul's attention back.

"I'm Paul Kelly." He gave a nod of his head in lieu of offering to shake the man's muddy hand.

"Davis." Though inches shorter, Davis made eye contact with Paul and held it. "Good to meet you. I hope you'll join your mother and our crew for Bible study tonight."

Several unsavory Southern sayings popped to the tip of Paul's tongue, but after five years with his ill-mannered employer, he'd learned to think before he spoke. Mostly.

Okay, not during the past couple of days with Star. "I don't think—"

"Paul." His mother took hold of his arm. "Please, come

meet everyone at my new church."

"You changed churches?" What else hadn't Mom told him?

"It's a community church. Cooper will be there. You remember, his grandmother lived next door. Maybe others you remember."

More people with problems. How many strays would she adopt if he didn't move her soon? And he'd rather eat his shoe than "meet everyone" or go to a Bible study.

He let his gaze slide to Star. The smirk on her face indicated she enjoyed his discomfort. What had Mom told Star about his past?

"Sure, Mom. You know I'd do anything for you." He'd check out this church and these people before he left. And maybe see exactly what this Davis fellow was teaching. He didn't want some scam artists milking his mother's savings.

Chapter 8

"Why'd you have to invite Paul?" Star shook her head and groaned while she helped arrange the chairs of the church's classroom into a circle. Davis preferred an open setup where everyone could face each other rather than having the teacher in front of lined rows.

"I invite everyone I meet to Bible study. Should Paul be disqualified because you don't like him?" Davis's gaze held a challenge. "Seems the man needs all the Jesus he can get if he has to contend with the wrath of Star."

"Not funny." She huffed.

"I'm serious. If you think he needs to repent of something, he can't do that without help from the Big Guy, can he?"

Davis's words made sense, but another groan escaped her. "Why do you have to be so good?"

"Not me, but the Father's Spirit living within me, lest I should boast."

She had to laugh. "Boy, you know you boast. How you're the best driver, how you're a great cook, how you got the best dance moves. I've even seen you flexing your 'guns' in exercise class."

"Guilty." He chuckled. "I may boast about my dance moves, but I don't boast about being *good*."

"Who's got dance moves? I used to love to cut footloose." Mrs. Kelly shuffled in with Paul at her side. Again, he looked about as stiff as his starched button-down collar, but a smile lit his mother's face as if she were remembering better days when

51

her body hadn't been contorted by arthritis.

"Welcome." Davis made his way over and took her hand with a grin. "I do admit to cutting loose on the dance floor now and then."

"Wish I still could." Her expression turned wistful.

"I bet you used to bust a move." Davis shook his head.

Paul cleared his throat, his mouth pinched. His gaze collided with Star's, and for a moment, she thought she recognized a hint of grief there. But she wouldn't feel sympathy for him. His misery probably only stemmed from the fact that he'd been coerced into attending tonight.

Turning his attention to Paul, Davis offered his hand. "I'm glad you made it."

With a small, rigid nod, Paul accepted the handshake, clearly *not* glad.

Star plopped onto a folding chair across the room. She waved at Mrs. Kelly, then dug through her purse, not really looking for anything but needing an excuse to ignore *him*. Fortunately, other participants began arriving and taking their seats. Just not any beside her, so Paul and Mrs. Kelly came her way.

Lord, help me.

Mrs. Kelly sat one chair away and indicated for Paul to take the vacant spot in between them. He glanced around for another choice, but the other seats were quickly filling.

With a sigh, he consumed the space next to her.

Good garden seeds. Now she had to rub shoulders with him the entire hour. This would be sixty agonizing minutes. What else could she look for in her purse? She glanced down and remembered her Bible and journal. She'd focus on that. She took the highlighter and pen she'd clipped on the journal cover and opened it to a blank page.

Keep reminding me about grace and mercy, Lord.

"It's about time to start." Davis surveyed the room. "Let's open with a prayer. Would someone like to lead it?"

Beside her, Paul's legs stiffened. She dared a peek his way. His whole body and expression congealed. Was he that afraid he'd be forced to lead a prayer?

"Sorry, we're late." Cooper Knight rushed in with Rivers behind him. "I got caught up talking in the hall."

"Uh-huh." Davis's voice teased. "Being late means you get to start us off with prayer."

Cooper's dark eyes smiled. He removed the hat and pushed back his messy-but-cute mop and took a seat beside his wife. "Let's bow our heads, then." A hushed stillness came over the room. "Father, thank you for life and breath and grace and joy today. Fill your servant Davis with Your Spirit and Your Word. Open our ears and hearts to hear. In Jesus's name."

"Amen," the group chorused.

"And now, my captive audience, aka seminary student-Guinea-pigs—no offense—we will begin where we left off in the book of Acts, chapter fifteen." Davis opened his bookmarked Bible.

The crinkling of pages filled the room as the group turned to follow along. Others pulled out their phones to use the Bible app, but Star loved the feel, the sound, and the smell of a real book. Especially her Bible. Despite the fact that she still struggled to find her way around it. Rivers had taught her a couple of children's songs that helped her memorize the book order of the Old and New Testaments.

Star found the New Testament and hummed the tune in her head until she reached Acts, thankful it wasn't far into the song. The last thing she wanted was Paul judging her.

"Look at verses thirty-six through the end of the chapter."

Davis read the passage aloud. "Okay, so, we're back with Paul, the man with first-century theology credentials out the wazoo—"

Star and others in the group snickered at Davis's use of slang.

"Oh, sorry, folks." Davis made a goofy face and scanned the room. "I'm low on the social graces totem pole, as some of you already know. Anyway, this apostle Paul fellow had been *the man* back in the day. Best teacher. Best rule-follower. He was so self-righteous, he had his own Christian extermination plan until God lit him up—literally—and showed him the error of his ways.

"Now, here's reformed Paul having a throw-down with his best buddy, Barnabas, over taking a young man named John Mark on a mission trip. I mean, what's up with this argument? Seems to me Paul is still struggling a bit with works-verses-grace, but I could be wrong. What do y'all think?"

A long, awkward silence filled the room.

"There are no right or wrong answers on this one, people." Davis extended one hand. "Throw me an opinion."

Beside Star, Paul fidgeted with his fingernails, and his knee bounced. Was he ready to leave? Did he suffer from social anxiety?

She would've been uncomfortable in a group like this just last year. And it was awkward that no one seemed to be jumping in with an answer. Maybe she should try. "I think you could be right about him still struggling with trying to be good enough to get to heaven."

"No." Paul sat forward in his seat, his fingers gripping his knees. "Things are too critical when you're on a mission trip to carry dead weight. You need partners you can count on because those kinds of journeys can be the most moving, faith-building times of a Christian's life. Or they can become a dark night of the soul that will strip away a lifetime of core beliefs."

Star turned and gawked at the man. Of course, he'd taken the opposite opinion from hers, but where had that vehemence come from? What was his deal?

~~~

Why couldn't he keep his thoughts to himself? Paul held in a scoff. Probably his years in seminary coming back to haunt him. He didn't dare look at his mother, because Star's gaping mouth said enough. He hadn't meant for his words to come out so passionately, but they spewed like steam from a pent-up geyser he didn't realize still existed inside him. It seemed as if this Davis guy had stalked Paul's past and tailor-made this lesson to provoke him.

"Good points. Anyone else?" Davis nodded, unfazed, or else he had a great poker face.

"I think you're both right," Cooper said, his tone conciliatory. "No one can serve their way to holiness. Isaiah said our righteous works are like filthy rags. So, only Christ's blood cleanses us. But when choosing a personal ministry partner, you have to pray for wisdom."

"Amen to that." The Davis guy butted in. "Most of you know we had one of our own members learn the lesson that a hard head makes a soft tail. And my buddy, Angelo, won't mind me telling you that orange ain't the new black. He's gonna be serving hard time because he fell into temptation, and he sure regrets it."

"He does." Cooper nodded. "Angelo is ministering to other prisoners now, but his actions caused a lot of hurt, not only to the hearts of those close to him but to our ministry and the church as a whole."

Paul's thoughts couldn't help but drift back to his time in

Africa. He'd nearly drowned in the wake of the devastation when his mentor's moral failures had been exposed. But the missionary, Dr. Jones, hadn't just betrayed Paul, he had shattered the hearts of many others.

"That's exactly what I'm talking about." Paul couldn't seem to keep his mouth shut. "One person's actions can injure hundreds of innocent lives. As a pilot, I have to realize that my every move in the captain's chair isn't just about me. I have a responsibility for all the souls on board and those on the ground below me."

"Oooh, great analogy with the pilot stuff." Davis locked his gaze on Paul. "We needed to hear that. Because despite the rumors, ignorance ain't bliss."

Pilot stuff? Paul studied Davis. Though rough around the edges, the guy seemed sincere enough, and he was open to a discussion with varied opinions. Even if all of this Bible study was still nonsense.

"Yeah, but"—Star lifted her Bible from her lap—"this whole book is about a perfect yet loving God building His church out of jacked-up human beings. And if God wasn't willing to give up on Paul, then Paul shouldn't have been so quick to hate on John Mark. Maybe the guy had a reason to go home—like one of his parents was sick or something."

The words slammed into Paul, and fire crept up his neck. Had Star heard he'd made it home from Africa just in time to see his father die? That must be why she wouldn't quit needling him about his mother. He swallowed the bile rising in his throat. How dare she?

What a low blow. He couldn't sit here another second beside this woman.

He turned and gave his mother a head nod toward the door, then mouthed, "Let's go."

56

Chapter 9

"No one set up anything to hurt you, sweetie. Star and Davis wouldn't do that, especially at Bible study." Mom hadn't stopped insisting on the truth of those words since they'd left the church. "Please don't rush off upset."

"My boss is going ballistic anyway. I'll come back for your surgery." In his childhood bedroom, Paul finished packing and pocketed his passport. He was ready to leave. He'd drive to Jacksonville tonight and fly standby on the first flight he could finagle to London. He didn't mind staying in the airport all night if he had to. The sooner he got out of here, the better.

"I'd rather wait until near Christmas to have the surgery. Dr. Johnson said that would be okay." Her eyes pleaded. "Once I'm well, I could consider a move to Sparkling Pines."

"Why wait three months?" Was this another excuse, or was she considering the move? Though the extra time might give him time to find a contract pilot to take his place while she recovered.

"Those cottages have a lot less square footage than my house. If I decide to move, I'd have to figure out what I'd take with me. Three months will give me time to think more about things."

And more time for Star to sink her hooks into his mother, if Mom was even seriously considering Sparkling Pines. "Are you going to tell your aide to start looking for another job?"

"You're wrong about Star." The wrinkles in Mom's forehead drew together. "If you could get to know her—give her a chance. She's a sweet girl—"

"Then she'll want what's best for you."

"But if we wait until Christmas, she'll have more time to figure out the future God has in store for her."

He let out a quiet sigh. Now Mom was bringing God into the equation. Again.

"It'll delay the inevitable."

"No." Mom's voice was firm. "You have no idea what is inevitable. I'll pray about it."

"But—"

A knock at the door interrupted his response. Frustration built in Paul's chest. If Star had followed them home after church, she was about to get an earful. "I'll get it."

"I can, honey. Wait."

Paul ignored her and raced down the hall. Since she couldn't keep up, he easily outpaced his mother through the house and flung open the door. "What?"

Instead of Star, Davis stood on the front porch steps, arms hanging at his side. "I wanted to check in. I thought one of y'all might be sick when you left so quickly."

"Sorry. I thought you were someone else." Relief and a hint of disappointment tugged at Paul. He didn't normally relish confrontations, but something about Star had him aching to at least defend himself.

"You thought I might be your mama's friend, Star?"

The guy had a lot of nerve to show up here. "You mean my mother's aid."

The man's brows pinched. "They're friends first."

Paul didn't have time to dissect what kind of relationship Star had with his mother—or this guy. He wanted to get on the road. "We're fine. I need to go back to work tonight."

"Is that your pilot gig?" Davis didn't seem to be able to

take a hint to leave, or he was purposely avoiding it.

Paul forced an amicable tone. This man was his mother's friend, after all. "Yeah. The boss doesn't give much downtime or take excuses."

Davis's head bobbed. "The army was that way too. Where's your home base?"

"London." This guy was former military? He didn't look very disciplined.

"Bro, I don't think you're gonna make it to work on time tonight."

An unexpected laugh slipped from Paul. "Probably not, but I'm about to head to Jacksonville and find the next flight out. Where were you stationed?"

"Afghanistan, mostly. Sometimes out in the belly button of nowhere."

"Been to places like that in Africa."

"With your job?" Davis's probing hit another nerve.

"Before it." Paul's jaw tensed. Did the guy already know or not? "I was a missionary in Africa."

"Noo waaay." Davis drew out the words, and his eyes rounded.

The surprise looked and sounded legit, which should have made him feel better, but instead, a knot formed in Paul's midsection. "Yes, way." He sounded like a preteen, but the guy's shock was offensive. Why was it so hard to believe he'd been in ministry? Not that this guy's opinion mattered. Or anyone else's.

"Sorry." Davis's chin dipped. "You just look so…" His gaze traveled as if looking for a way not to be insulting. "Not like someone who'd live out in the savanna or something."

"Looks can be deceiving."

"Ain't that the truth?" Davis gave Paul's shoulder a light

punch as if they were best buddies. Which they weren't. "Why'd you give it up?"

"Why'd you leave the army?" Paul leveled a gaze on the man. Two could play at this fishing game.

"IED explosion." A faraway look fell over Davis. "Lost a buddy. I got off easy. A few burns and hearing loss."

"Sorry." Not what he'd expected. He figured the guy was dishonorably discharged if he'd been some kind of addict or alcoholic, but he shouldn't be so quick to judge. Maybe the addiction came after the injury. He'd heard veterans often suffered from PTSD.

Outside, frogs chirped loudly. Odd for this time of year, but it soaked up a bit of the awkward silence.

"You know"—Davis's gaze brightened—"it was hard times, but God worked it for good. I believe God's purpose in the desert times—in the struggle—is for us to know Him more."

Now the ridiculous preaching again. "How was God working for good when your friend died? It doesn't sound like things worked out well for him."

"He was a man of faith and knew where he was heading."

Paul couldn't stop the eye roll or the scoff. "Figures you'd say something like that."

Shaking his head, Davis's gaze turned sympathetic. "I don't know what happened to you, but it seems like you're all sails and no anchor." He scratched his chin before continuing. "In pilot terms…maybe all wings and no rudder? Or would it be, all wings and no landing gear?"

"Enough. I get it." Paul held up one hand. "I'm fine. Thanks for coming by."

"I may have the brains of a houseplant, but I think you're in need of prayer."

"I tried that. It didn't work out. I'm done." The guy was still in that naïve stage. Probably needed his fantasy to deal with the trauma he'd been through.

The wind kicked up, rustling the moss in the trees, and the air smelled of rain. He should have checked the weather earlier, but he'd been so frustrated.

"Look, Paul, I've learned something over the past two years." Davis wasn't letting it go yet. "Prayer is not telling God what we want like He's our personal vending machine. Prayer is asking God *what He wants.*" The guy's gaze held a challenge. "As the Brits say, those ideas are as different as chalk and cheese. We say as different as night and day, but maybe as different as bread and a stone works better. Or as different as a donkey and an octopus or—"

"Got it." Paul stuck out his hand for a handshake, hoping to end the conversation. "Thank you for checking on us. I need to leave now."

Davis squeezed Paul's hand, his grip tight. "You may've given up on God, but I feel in my spirit that He's still pursuing you. He loves you, and He's got better things in store for you when you really *let Him own you.*"

Fire rushed to Paul's face, and he released the handshake. "You don't know me." No one was going to own him, once he freed himself from Kenneth.

Davis's head bobbed. "I do know our plans aren't always His. Close that old chapter you wrote, and let Him write the next one."

Paul stepped inside and shut the door, careful not to slam it since Mom had probably been listening. Where did that guy get off? The muscles in Paul's neck spasmed. The sooner he got out of here, the better.

~~~

Exhaustion gripped Star as she made her way to Mrs. Kelly's, probably for the last time. Not keeping her mouth shut last night had blown up in her face. She should have known better. Thunderstorms had rattled the windows overnight, but it had been tears and anxiety that consumed her and kept her awake—all of her emotional armor had been stripped away.

Now she'd need to find a new job because the part-time one at the gym wouldn't cut it. Painting or construction cleanup paid well, but she knew how risky that could be for a woman alone. A few years back, a friend of hers who'd worked construction cleanup had been raped and left for dead in an empty house. She wasn't taking that kind of risk. Maybe she could work out something waitressing at lunchtime. But how would she serve God there? Usually, people were in such a hurry. She'd just do the best she could.

Lord, I'm willing to go where you send me.

Oh, and please help me with my mouth.

Early morning mist still hung in the air when Star parked the car in the drive, acutely aware that Paul's rental car was nowhere to be seen. Had he gone out to buy groceries already? She read the index card she'd written the night before.

If anyone among you thinks he is religious, and does not bridle his tongue but deceives his own heart, this one's religion is useless.

This was a verse she'd memorize. And she'd force herself to apologize to Paul, even though she hadn't been quite sure why expressing an opinion different than his made him so angry that he'd walked out in the middle of Bible study.

As she exited the car, Mrs. Kelly flung open the door, fully dressed, and makeup applied. "Hurry! I need to talk to you."

"Okay." Star put some pep in her step, despite the fact that she was about to get fired. "What's going on?"

"Did you ever find your passport?" Mrs. Kelly asked when

Star reached her.

"Yes, ma'am." Not sure why she still needed it. The only thing Vince had been good for, other than the exercise certification, had been paying for her passport. Before he'd shown his true colors, she'd agreed to travel to the Bahamas with him to get married. Thank God they'd never gone.

"If you're still willing to be my travel buddy, go pack your bags." Mrs. Kelly's mouth cocked into a sheepish grin

Nothing was making sense. "Where's Paul?"

"He had to get back to work in London." Her smile faltered, but she waved off the comment.

"He left?" There had to be more to the story than that. Mrs. Kelly was deflecting. "That seems kind of sudden."

"You know, he's always on call, and the whole trip here was unexpected." Her face brightened. "Like the one we're about to take to Ireland."

"Take when?"

"If you can pack quickly, I found some last-minute openings with the travel company I've used in the past. We can fly out this afternoon."

"Today?" A giddy feeling rose in Star's chest. They were really going out of the country. Today.

"In a few hours. Rivers agreed to watch Phoenix. Do you have warm clothes, a raincoat, and a suitcase?"

Yikes. She didn't have much. Star ran through her small wardrobe in her mind. "I'll see what I can borrow from Rivers."

"I have an idea." Mrs. Kelly held up a finger, and her hazel eyes shone. Like a happy version of Paul's eyes. "Let's see if Gabby has what you need at Re-Claimed's thrift store."

"I can get by with what I have." And she wouldn't owe more money to anyone. The last thing she wanted was for Paul to think she'd ripped off his mother. No matter how long it took, she'd pay Mrs. Kelly back every penny of this trip.

"I've been meaning to make a donation to Re-Claimed. What better way than to support the store?" Now her gaze pleaded. "Come on. I'll feel better knowing we're ready for the weather there. Ireland can be cold and rainy. And I'm all packed."

Star's mouth fell open. "Did Paul see that?"

She shook her head, and her brows dipped. "No. And I don't plan on telling him about any of this."

At least his lack of calls and visits would help them sneak across the globe undetected. "Let's hit the road, then."

Chapter 10

No one respected a slow lady and her cane.

The Jacksonville airport buzzed with activity, and Star's adrenaline roared as rude people rushed to get around Mrs. Kelly. If someone scrambling past them, not paying attention to anything but their phones, knocked Mrs. Kelly down, they'd get an earful. Star could imagine Paul suing her if his mother broke her hip. Maybe even jailing her. Especially on this trip since he'd had such strong opposition to the whole shebang. Plus they were going without telling him.

Rolling both sets of luggage, Star led the way to the baggage counter and heaved Mrs. Kelly's bright red suitcase onto a scale when directed, then her own smaller bag. While Mrs. Kelly checked in, Star looked at the weather on her cell. The satellite showed a few hurricanes swirling over the Atlantic. Seemed the fall tropical storm season had finally kicked up. Their first flight would land at JFK in New York, but they might not make their meeting with the tour group in Ireland if they encountered delays. She'd keep that information to herself. No need to be a Debbie Downer for her gracious employer, but already the overnight storms had rocked Florida with tornadoes causing numerous flights to be canceled.

Once they'd finished at the counter, Mrs. Kelly grinned. "We made it. Now, we just have to get through security and find our gate."

"Security, huh?" A trickle of perspiration pricked her palms.

She'd be flying on a plane. Soon. A swoop of excitement converged with a hefty dose of fear in her chest. This was so crazy—actually traveling over an ocean. Maybe it was the suddenness of such an adventure swept up with the idea of her first plane ride, but Star's pulse quickened while her insides shook. What would it be like thousands of feet above the ground in a giant metal tube?

Lord, help me.

They made their way through lines and rows until they neared some gates with uniformed officers. People began taking off belts, shoes, and jackets. They emptied their pockets into plastic trays.

Good thing her own boots and jacket weren't a big deal. Star checked out Mrs. Kelly's tennis shoes. The transition would be difficult with arthritic hands and knees.

Once their turn came, she pointed to the bench. "You sit, and I'll get your shoes."

"You are such a blessing." Mrs. Kelly gave Star a side hug before she sat. "I thank God for you every day."

Warmth slid over Star as she knelt, untying and removing Mrs. Kelly's shoes. "I'm the one who's blessed." If only Paul could see how fortunate he was to have a good mother.

They passed through the weird scanner, picked up their personal belongings, and put their shoes back on. After accomplishing that chore, they hurried—as much as they could considering Mrs. Kelly's cane—toward the assigned gate.

Finally, they made it to the sitting area, which looked nothing like a gate, but the chairs in their section had all been taken, so they waited in seats across the way. They settled in, though they shouldn't be here long if the flight to New York left on time.

"Would you mind getting us a couple of lattes?" Mrs.

Kelly stifled a yawn. "I need a burst of caffeine to keep going."

The trip hadn't even started, and Mrs. Kelly was tired already? "Do you feel bad?"

"No, sweetie. I didn't sleep much last night." Her mouth curved into a smile. "Too excited."

"Okay, I'll be right back." Coffee did sound good. Until she saw the long line.

By the time she received their order and walked back to the waiting area, passengers had begun gathering their carryon bags and standing near the gate.

Mrs. Kelly stood holding her cane in one hand and waving with the other. "They've boarded the first class. We're about to be on our way."

Star's heart slammed into her chest. She was getting on a plane. A loud whoop slipped from her. "This is so cool."

A man from the front of the line turned at the sound.

Not just any man. Her mouth dried.

It was Paul.

Dressed in the same clothes as the night before, only now instead of starched and wrinkle-free, his shirt hung crumpled and untucked under his jacket. A duffle bag was slung over his shoulder, and from the looks of his hair, he'd used the thing as a pillow and forgotten a brush.

Of all the flights in the world, why this one, God?

Eyes searing, he left his position in line and stormed their way. When he reached them, he cursed under his breath, and his face turned a dark shade of red, reminding Star of molten lava. He was surely about to explode.

"What are you doing here? You better not be—"

"That. Is. Enough. Paul Randall Kelly." Mrs. Kelly's spine straightened, and her chin lifted. Using all three names had never been a good sign from a parent. "I am going on a vacation. It's my life to live as I see fit, the same as you do with yours. You go on back to your work, and I'll take care of my business." Mrs. Kelly's tone left no doubt she meant her words to be final.

Star swallowed hard. She'd never seen Mrs. Kelly angry, but the woman seemed to have reached her limit.

"Yes, ma'am." Paul's stance softened.

At least he respected his mother. For the most part.

He stood silently for a long moment with his fingers steepled below his chin. "I guess I'll swap my flight when we get to New York and go with you." He turned his attention to Star. "You won't be needed."

It all slipped away. The plane, the flight over the ocean, the green, green land of Ireland. Why had she let herself believe?

Of course, he wanted to get rid of her. She could imagine how he saw her—*former addict, trailer trash*. She wasn't fit to be with people like Mrs. Kelly. Like him.

And really, she couldn't blame him. Mrs. Kelly was too kind to see it, but Paul knew. Paul had taken one look at her and known Star Youngblood wasn't their kind.

"Star is going. That's not negotiable, either." Mrs. Kelly placed one hand on her hip, but she smiled. "I'd love to have you come along as well, Paul, if you can behave. I'll call the tour company and let them know before our next leg."

Star's entire body trembled in the tension. Should she just leave, let Mrs. Kelly and Paul have this time to themselves? Except, Mrs. Kelly wanted her along.

Someone needed to care for Mrs. Kelly, and Paul had been gone so long. Would he actually be helpful?

Star held in a groan. Selfishly, she wanted to go too. She'd never left the States. Never been out of the South. So she moved along with them in the line. When they reached the ticket agent, Mrs. Kelly went first, handing her ticket to the woman, then hobbling toward the door.

Lips pressed tight, Paul waved a hand for Star to go ahead. As if he were a gentleman.

He didn't hold her back, didn't stop her. So she walked on.

Once they boarded the plane, Star followed Mrs. Kelly down the narrow aisle. The cabin reminded her of a clean version of a Greyhound bus. Airlines didn't leave much room for the regular passengers. It was tight in here. Panic rose up to grab her throat, but she forced the feeling down, determined not to let fear rule her.

Mrs. Kelly kept going until they reached the back of the plane. "Finally," she huffed. "I must've gained weight, or else these aisles are shrinking." She squinted at her phone, where she'd stored the itinerary. "I like to sit on the outside of the row in case I need to go to the ladies' room."

"Of course." Star nodded. "I'll sit wherever."

"Sit by the window. I'll help Mom." Paul's breath warmed Star's cheek. "Apparently, crazy coincidences aligned when my flight got canceled last night. I'm assigned the last seat available on this one." He grunted. "On this row."

A lump formed in Star's throat. She didn't believe in crazy coincidences anymore. Their meeting had been orchestrated by unseen forces. She just had to trust that the unseen Someone she loved and served would look after her.

~~~

Paul got his mother settled, pushed his duffle overhead, and took his seat. It seemed everything in the world worked against him and his overall flight plan for his life. His boss, his mother's health, *and her help,* the airlines being overbooked, even the weather... How much more screwed up could things become? His gaze met Star's as she tried to buckle her seatbelt.

Her soft brown eyes opened wide, but her mouth pressed tight. Was she scared?

He glanced down, where she still struggled. Her fingers shook. "Let me help." He touched her hand, and she stilled.

"Okay." The word came out breathy, and her hand felt clammy beneath his touch.

He slipped the buckle in place then studied her. "You've flown before, right?"

Her lips pinched harder, and she shook her head.

"Never?" Incredible. How could Star help Mom when she looked so terrified she might bolt any minute and demand they open the emergency exit?

"No." The clipped word shot across the small space between them.

He leaned close and whispered, hoping Mom wouldn't hear. "Why are you going if you're scared?"

"This trip means so much to her." Her gaze traveled to his mother, whose face positively shone with excitement.

The sight gutted him. He should have known about Mom's dream to travel to Ireland. He was her only child. He should have talked to her more often. And really listened. Instead, he'd been all about working to save money to come back home to her. With Mom's declining health, he understood, in some ways, why taking this trip now was important to her. She might never get another chance to travel if her health deteriorated even more. His chest hurt thinking about that.

For him, though... The timing didn't fit the blueprint he'd made for their lives. Or for his dream of being his own boss, free from the tyranny of people like Kenneth or the mission board. Free to help Mom.

But this girl—this woman, Star—had been willing to drop everything at the last minute for Mom. Not that Star had much going for her, but maybe she did care for Mom. Or maybe she was just really desperate for love.

Or more likely a scam artist hoping to make a score off a nice lady like his mother.

The whine of the engines told him they'd leave on time, at least for this flight. And being in the back meant no one could push their socked feet through the armrest like the guy behind him had on the flight to St. Simons. A bit of good news.

Announcements crackled over the speakers, but Paul's attention fixed on Star. As if connected, he sensed her tensing in her seat. Her knuckles whitened where she grabbed hold of the armrest.

"It's going to be fine." He kept his tone calm. "Thousands of flights go off without a hitch every day."

She stared at him but said nothing. Her solemn eyes spoke volumes. The girl was terrified.

Not able to stop himself, Paul took her hand and squeezed. "Breathe in deep. Hold it."

She complied.

"Now, blow it out and repeat."

Her hand felt soft in his. He hated the way his pulse quickened at the touch of her skin. At her nearness. At the way her brown eyes focused on him as if searching for strength.

The plane taxied then lifted, and she gripped his hand. Hard. Man, she was strong. He sure hoped his circulation returned in time to save his fingers.

At least this was a short flight. "Maybe you could take something to calm your nerves on the flight to Ireland."

Scoffing, she rolled her eyes and jerked her hand away. "I'm not going to *take something*."

"What? People do…" Oh, right. She wanted to stay sober. "You don't even drink?"

Her jaw hardened. "No. And I don't think it's the flying that's bothering me."

Heat rushed to his face. "So, *I'm* bothering you?"

"No. Sorry. I didn't mean it that way." She released a long exhale, then glanced over to his mother. Once she seemed certain Mom was preoccupied with a magazine, Star continued. "I have baggage from my childhood that kicks up some claustrophobia now and then. It's been a while, but that feeling of being trapped hit me out of left field."

Claustrophobia? Sounded miserable. "These cabins are pretty tight. I'd much rather be in the cockpit." He tried to force a compassionate smile.

She bit her lip for a second. "Do you love flying?" Her gaze brightened a bit. "Seems like a cool job."

"It can be fun. Beautiful even." He shrugged. "Or the work can be hours of boredom interspersed with moments of stark terror."

A chuckle parted her full lips, which gave him way too much pleasure, but maybe they could at least be congenial until this crazy trip ended.

"I take pride in doing quality work." He grimaced. "I guess that's part of why I haven't made time to come home, even though I should have."

"I want to be like that, too—well, without the *ignoring people in my life* part."

Now he found a laugh of his own escaping. "Point taken."

The plane dipped with a bit of turbulence, and both of Star's hands dug into his arm. "What was that?"

"Just a little bump in the road." Between the work he'd seen evidence of around Mom's house and her fierce grip, he didn't doubt Star had the physical strength to help his mother.

"Bumps in the sky?" Her eyes were wide, but her lips

turned up at the corners. "Who knew?" She let go and leaned back in her seat.

The disappointment when she released him struck like an unexpected bird in an engine. He needed to stop being ridiculous and shift his focus to something else. He listened to the plane and tried to estimate their altitude and speed. The weather cleared, and the flight seemed to be going as it should.

His thoughts drifted back to Star's admission of claustro-phobia, and his curiosity got the best of him. "Did you get stuck in a well or something?"

"What?" Star's brows drew together.

"The fear of closed-in spaces. What happened?"

All emotion drained from her face. "My stepfather used to lock me in a closet at night." With that, she sank deeper into the chair, crossed her arms, and closed her eyes, their conversation apparently over.

He was too stunned to speak. He couldn't pull his gaze away from her pretty, young face. He'd cared for abused children at the orphanage in Africa. While obtaining his Master of Divinity, he'd counseled adults who'd been neglected or abused. Sadness flattened him as if he'd fallen out of the aircraft without a parachute. Why was he so dimwitted? He'd been cruel to her, and she'd been battling that kind of past.

He should have been kind. He should have recognized that kind of pain in Star.

Chapter 11

The plane whined, shuddered, and descended. Star opened her eyes but kept her arms firmly crossed. She refused to act like a baby and grab hold of Paul again. Already, she'd embarrassed herself and confessed a lot more than she'd intended.

Probably her anxiety speaking. Because no matter how reassuring he'd been on this flight, the majority of the time she'd been around Paul Kelly, the man had displayed the personality of a Billy goat. A mean Billy goat like the one her sister once nursed back to health. The noisy creature had been a busybody and incredibly demanding, getting into everything. One change in its daily routine and the animal went ballistic, trying to head-butt anything that moved.

Another loud noise clanked in the plane, and they suddenly bumped what she prayed was the ground, leaving Star's stomach a hundred feet behind. She stared out the window at the landscape whizzing by.

Wow, this was fast. How these machines worked, she hadn't a clue, but she breathed a sigh when the plane slowed near the terminal.

A chalky fog surrounded the JFK runway. Beyond the airport, the landscape looked as if there might be water on the horizon. Maybe the ocean? She could look up the geography once the staff allowed everyone to turn on their phones.

This leg of the trip had passed quickly. By the time they'd been served chips and drinks, then had it cleaned up, the pilot had announced their descent.

How long would the next flight imprison her in these small quarters? The muscles in her chest tightened. Maybe she didn't want to know.

And she hated herself for being the slightest bit comforted that Paul would probably be with them. But he *was* a pilot. Being comforted by him made sense. He'd know what to do in an emergency. At least he could fly the plane if something bizarre happened like in a couple of movies she'd watched.

He and Mrs. Kelly had fallen asleep after their snacks had been cleaned up. No wonder Paul had since he'd been up all night.

She stole a glance at him.

His eyes remained closed, his chest rose and fell slowly, and the tension had left his brow. She couldn't help but admire the strong cut of his cheekbones. And the nice angle of his chin. And his lips.

Too bad she couldn't paint like her friend Rivers, because the sleeping Paul made a striking picture.

As if he'd heard her thoughts, his lashes fluttered and opened. He'd caught her gawking like a creeper. His lips quirked into a puzzled smile.

Cheeks flushing, Star quickly tore her gaze back to the window. An announcement started, and she pretended to be absorbed while the voice asked for passengers to stay in their seats until they reached the gate. Most people seemed to ignore the announcements during the flight, while she'd strained to hear them. This time wasn't much different. People unbuckled and gathered their belongings.

Paul made no attempt to move until the pilot announced they'd arrived. It figured that he'd be a rule-follower. He probably made up rules just for fun.

Mrs. Kelly woke and clapped her hands together. "We're

here! Next stop, Ireland."

Sucking in a deep breath that oozed resignation, Paul turned on his phone. "Mind if I leave you, ladies? I need to change my reservation from London to Ireland as soon as we land. And get a message to my boss."

"Don't take too long," Mrs. Kelly chided as she turned her body toward the aisle to let him pass. "We'd hate to leave you."

"Right." He scoffed but aimed a smile at his mother. "You already tried that."

Mrs. Kelly's jaw dropped. "I asked you first, but you said you—"

"I'm kidding, Mom." He bent down and kissed her cheek. "Can you get me added to your tour?"

Emotion welled up in Star's chest at the tenderness Paul showed his mother. The love, the respect. Could this be his regular personality? Or was the anxious, badgering Paul the norm? Could he be putting on a show in public like her stepfather and Vince had?

"I'll call my travel liaison right away." Mrs. Kelly pulled out her phone and searched for the number.

He pinned a snarky look at Star, but his lips twitched into a teasing smirk. "Think you can find the next gate?"

And he was back to being a jerk. She leveled a no-nonsense gaze on him. "I'm not a man, so I'm not too proud to ask for directions if I get lost."

"Okaay." He leaned close to Star and lowered his voice barely above a whisper. "There's going to be a mass of humanity here from all over the world. Keep a close watch on your purses, and once you find the gate, stay put until I find you."

"I don't need you to mansplain." Just because she'd never flown didn't mean she'd be an easy mark. Like she was some country bumpkin because she'd never left the United States.

His fingers slid across her forearm. "I didn't mean—"

She crossed her handbag strap over her chest. "Nobody will be stealing anything from me."

His hazel eyes narrowed as he studied her. "Then keep an eye on Mom's purse."

"I will." Her jaw tensed.

"Good." He opened his mouth to say something else, then shut it.

The aisles cleared, and after one more glance her way, he grabbed his duffle bag and took off to try to change his reservations.

Star plodded behind Mrs. Kelly as they slowly made their way out of the plane. If he managed to come with them, she'd have two weeks to figure who the real Paul Randall Kelly actually was.

~~~

After half an hour arguing with a ticketing agent, Paul gave up trying to switch flights and paid the exorbitant rate to buy a last-minute seat on the one with his mom. In London, it was the middle of the night, so he couldn't call his boss to let him know about this unplanned vacation, but he sent an email.

And that would go over like a UFO buzzing the White House.

His stomach growled, and fatigue weighed his steps. The all-nighter waiting out the thunderstorms had caught up to him. Once he reconnected with Mom, they could get some dinner, then he could sleep more on the next flight.

Unless he'd need to comfort Star again.

The memory of her soft hand in his zapped warmth through him. He had to admit that being needed had been a little satisfying.

But that was ridiculous.

Yet, something about her gritty authenticity combined with her raw vulnerability made Star such an enigma. A puzzle to be solved. A much too attractive riddle. He needed to keep his emotional distance. And pry his mother away. Stray humans didn't fit his agenda.

He walked briskly until he spotted the pair. He zigzagged through the throng of passengers milling about until he stopped in front of his mother. "I hope I can join the tour because I have a ticket to Ireland."

"Oh." Mom's brows edged toward each other. "We haven't gotten an answer yet. Maybe because of the time difference." She sniffed, then sneezed three times. "Excuse me."

"Bless you," Star chimed.

Paul checked his front pocket for a tissue but found nothing but his passport. "I can always get my own hotel reservations and rent a car to follow y'all." He shrugged. "I'm used to driving on the other side of the road."

"That might work." The strain on her forehead eased, but she sneezed again. "There must be perfume or cleaning fluid irritating my sinuses. Goodness."

Star dug a small pack of tissue from her purse. "Here. Take these. I can get more if you need them."

"Perfect. I'll reimburse you."

"Oh, no." Star shook a finger. "I owe you for the clothes and this trip."

The clothes? Was Mom having to dress this woman? He wanted to inquire, but his stomach protested. "We have time to eat."

"Could y'all bring me a cup of soup and a bottle of water?" Mom leaned back in the chair. "I think I'll rest a spell."

If she was tired now, she'd really be tired when the tour started. "Are you sure you should go on—"

"I'm saving my energy, Paul." She sniffled and swiped her nose with the tissue. "Y'all go eat somewhere. Take your time."

As if he wanted to go to a sit-down meal here. With her. He turned to Star. "What are you hungry for?"

"I'll get a cup of soup too." She twisted a piece of her hair and chewed her bottom lip as if something troubled her.

"I know a place that's pretty good for airport cuisine." He waved her forward and walked toward the bistro down the terminal.

She followed without speaking, her subtle gaze taking in the travelers from all corners of the world.

When they reached the restaurant, a line snaked out of the entrance. Paul sighed. Apparently, word had gotten out about the good grub. "Want to wait or try somewhere else?"

"Doesn't matter to me as long as they have soup for your mother." Her tone was matter of fact.

Most women he'd been on dates with had definite opinions of what they would and wouldn't eat. "Is there anything you don't like?"

Her shoulders lifted in a shrug. "If it's clean and edible, I eat it."

"So you're not a vegan or paleo or on some other fancy diet?"

"Do I look like I need to be on a diet?" Her fists popped to her perfectly proportioned hips.

Paul scanned her form but immediately wished he hadn't. "No." Nothing wrong with Star's figure—at all—but he didn't need to dwell on that. "Let's try the deli counter. I bet they have soup."

"You're the airport expert." Sarcasm dripped from her

words, but her lips twitched as if holding back a smile. And they were cute lips.

"Follow me, then." They retraced their steps to the deli where there was a small line, but at least this one was moving. "You know, Mom would be better off with a heart-friendly entree or a salad."

"She *asked* for soup." Star pointed at the menu. "Chicken noodle. Perfect if she's catching a cold."

"Just because she sneezed doesn't mean she has a cold." What was she, a doctor now?

"I haven't heard her sneezing around her home." The undercurrent in her words made it obvious that he'd know if he visited more often.

"Which is where she should be now instead of here," he mumbled under his breath.

"And she will be in two weeks," Star snapped back.

Clearly, he'd not spoken low enough.

Her attention turned back to the menu. "These prices are like the movie theater on steroids."

Sticker shock at the airport never got old. "I'll buy. Order what you want."

"I'm fine." She pulled her wallet from her purse and retrieved two twenties.

"I'll at least get Mom's food."

Not arguing, she stuffed one of the twenties back in. Obviously, she thought he owed his mother dinner even though he'd probably lose his job for the impromptu time off. How in the world had his mother gotten into this tour so quickly, anyway? "Mom must've been researching this trip for a while to get things together this fast."

"She's been talking about it for months." Her gaze pinned him. "Hoping you'd agree to go someday."

He ignored the barb. After all, dumb idea or not, he was going now. "But what about you? Didn't you have a schedule to work around?"

Her look shouted *you're-an-idiot-Paul.* "I work for your mom so…"

"Yeah, but what about other commitments?" He raised his brows, wondering if she'd get his drift.

"I graduated from the sober living ministry if that's what you're asking. I still see a counselor once or twice a month and attend meetings." Now annoyance laced her tone.

"But no special guy or siblings who'll miss you?" He knew he was reaching—okay, prying—but he had a right to know when it came to his mother.

Her gaze dropped, the shake of her head barely perceptible. "I haven't seen my sister since I was sixteen. No other family. No guy." Her glistening eyes lifted to meet his. "And I'm not looking for any. I just want some normal."

A knot twisted in his chest at her admission. Life had dumped a lot on this girl. Unless she was running a scam on him. "What does normal look like to you?"

"A quiet life where I do my job, go to church, make a few nice friends." The hope in her eyes when she gazed at him pinched at Paul.

Wasn't that what he wanted, too, sans the church part? "That sounds nice, but I suspect *normal* is a fairy-tale."

"For once, I agree with you." She gave him a sad smile. "But God is good, and He'll be with me wherever I end up."

"How do you—?"

"Can I take your order?" a dark-haired woman behind the counter practically yelled.

Paul stepped in front of Star. "I've got this round. What'll you have?"

The *you're-an-idiot* stare returned. "A bowl of soup for your mom and one for me. Two waters."

He placed the order along with his own and reached to his back pocket for his wallet. Nothing.

He felt his shirt pocket. Just his passport. He turned in a circle feeling his other pockets and scanning the floor.

"What are you doing?" Star's forehead scrunched.

Could his week get any worse? He mumbled a curse. "My wallet's missing."

Chapter 12

"I'll get the food so you can retrace your steps." Star pulled out the credit card she'd just spent a year paying off and handed it to the cashier. But Paul couldn't help that his wallet had been lifted.

"What a load of garbage," Paul muttered an expletive and ran his fingers through his hair while he scanned the crowds walking by.

"What about when you changed your reservation? Could you have left it there?" She pointed at the duffle bag over his shoulder. "Or tucked it into your carryon?"

"I'll meet you back where Mom's sitting." His forehead scrunched so hard he reminded her of a Chinese Shar-Pei.

Paul took off, walking at a fast pace. In fact, she'd seen slower joggers.

The food came, and she navigated her way through the crowded airport, watching the directional signs and keeping her purse close in front of her.

She found Mrs. Kelly talking to a thin young man sitting next to her. Tattoos covered his arms, and his face twisted more than Paul's had.

"Hey, I found soup." Star opened the bag and offered Mrs. Kelly the cardboard bowl of chicken noodle. She nodded to the guy in the other chair. "Hi."

"Thank you, sweetie." Mrs. Kelly smiled, but her necked craned from side-to-side searching the area. "You seemed to have lost my son."

"Bad news." Star grimaced and took the one open seat next to Mrs. Kelly. "His wallet went missing. He's looking for it."

"Oh, no." Mrs. Kelly's posture wilted. "He'll be out of sorts."

"No kidding." She hadn't meant to say that out loud. "Here's your spoon. I can eat quickly and try to help him."

"No. Paul will know what to do." She opened her food. "He's so careful and structured, which makes him a great pilot, but when life throws him a curveball, he gets..."

"He gets what?" Angry? Violent? Star imagined Paul putting a fist through a wall or something worse. Things like her stepfather used to do.

"He gets disappointed in humanity. In God." Mrs. Kelly's eyes glistened with tears.

"God didn't lose his wallet." Star huffed. "He did. Or some slimeball stole it."

"You'd be surprised how tender Paul's heart is."

Tender? Star clamped her lips together. That description sure didn't fit the man she'd been around the past few days.

"This soup feels so nice on my throat." Mrs. Kelly smiled. "Thank you."

"I hope you're not getting sick." Star opened the container and scarfed hers down. At least it tasted good for the price.

"Where'd you find that?" The guy on the other side of Mrs. Kelly looked at their containers.

"Go that way." Star pointed. "Pass the restrooms, then look left. It's just a counter where you order. Good enough, but expensive."

He gave a knowing look. "Everything in an airport is."

"My first time," Star admitted.

"My first since I left the army." The man's jaw clenched.

"No luck, of course." Paul appeared in front of them,

looking more haggard than when he'd left the restaurant.

A bit of sympathy sliding over her, Star stood and offered her seat. "Sit by your mom and eat. I'm finished."

"Have my chair." The young man pushed to his feet with a bit of a struggle, then stepped forward with a limp. "I think I'll check out that soup, too."

"Thanks." Star put the lid on her empty container, but a sudden impulse assaulted her.

Pray with him.

What? She'd never felt this kind of urge. She stood staring at the guy.

Pray with him.

Was God sending her the impulse?

God, I want to serve you, but I'm not comfortable with that. Yet.

Still, the pressure remained on her heart.

"Um, hey, what's your name?" Star forced out her words.

Brows lifted, the guy gave her a curious look. "Erik."

"My good friend, Davis, had a traumatic experience in Afghanistan. An IED. Sorry if something happened to you like that."

Swiping a hand through his hair, he made a slow nod. "Same thing. They brought me back to the States in a medevac. I haven't flown since."

"And you're going to Ireland?" That didn't make sense, but who knew.

"Nah. I want to check on a buddy who's still in Germany. I came to the airport early, hoping I could get my...stuff together. I've been walking around, trying to..." He motioned toward Mrs. Kelly. "She had a nice face, so I sat here to rest."

Star smiled at him. "She does have a sweet spirit about her. Maybe God led you here."

The guy didn't speak, he just waited as if he needed more.

A lump formed in Star's throat. This wasn't comfortable. At all. But she'd give it a shot. "Um, I'm new at this, but I could pray for you. Or with you? If you want."

Tears welled up in his eyes, and his chin quivered. "I'd appreciate that."

"I'd like to join you." Mrs. Kelly set her food aside, stood, and hobbled the few steps to stand beside them.

Star's stomach flipped. So she was really doing this? Here and now. In the middle of the airport.

It's all You, God.

She offered her hands like they did at the sober living house when they prayed. Erik and Mrs. Kelly took them.

"God, thank you for the good stuff. For waking us up today. For food and shelter and life and Your Word." Star swallowed and took another breath. "Sometimes, junk happens, and evil tries to suck the hope out of us. Please, God, don't let it. Give Erik courage and comfort. Calm his anxiety. Hold Erik in the palm of Your hand, and let him know that he's safe there. Please, give Erik exactly what he needs at exactly the right time. Be with him and help him encourage his friend in Germany. In Jesus' name. Amen."

"Amen." Mrs. Kelly squeezed Star's hand.

"Amen." Erik's posture relaxed, and a small smile lifted his lips. "I needed that more than you'll ever know. Thank you. I'll go try that expensive soup now." He turned his attention to Mrs. Kelly. "I hope the trip to Ireland is an answer to your prayers."

~~~

Paul hadn't been able to tear his gaze from Star while she prayed with the tattooed dude.

Did she know this guy? Was she legit?

Once the man walked away, she and Mom took their seats.

Mom patted Star's knee. "That was sweet of you. I should've thought of it myself. He looked so nervous."

"I felt awkward, but I couldn't ignore the nudge. And I tried to ignore it." Star chuckled. "Well, it felt more like a shove or a push."

A memory struck Paul like a slap across the face. Those times at the orphanage when he'd felt led to share the gospel or pray with the children. Almost like a direct command, a thought or word would pop into his mind of a specific need or hurt in their lives. And it had usually been right on target.

No.

He wouldn't go down that rabbit hole again. There had to be a reason other than *God nudging him.* His training in counseling must have triggered his subconscious. He must have noticed something in their body language or expressions that led him to know their needs. It couldn't have been a supernatural Force, especially a supposedly loving One. Because if it was God, why would He let everything in his life fall apart like it had?

"Aren't you going to eat?" Mom pointed at the bag containing his turkey wrap and sweet potato chips. "It'll be a while before you get any decent food."

"I'm not that hungry." Losing his wallet soured his stomach. "I need to get on my phone and cancel my cards. Where are we staying? I'll need replacements."

"Our first day is in Ennis at The Jewel of Ireland Hotel."

He pulled out his cell and got started with the annoying process. At least he had a list in his phone for this kind of emergency. Of course, he'd never needed it before.

Thirty minutes later, his credit secure enough, he opened the food. The turkey wrap felt dry and tasteless in his mouth. He took a sip of his drink to force it down. "Was your soup any good? Because this is terrible."

"Delicious." Mom and Star both spoke at once.

Figures. He threw the sandwich back in the bag and opened the chips.

A woman at the gate announced the loading of the first class and anyone who needed a little extra help. "Mom, you need extra time, and you have a cane, so take advantage. Go get your seat."

"Really? Should I?" She took in the idea. "It would be easier."

"That's why they offer. Go." He shooed her forward.

"I guess we'll see you on the plane." Her expression hopeful, she nodded.

"Let's do it." Star offered Mom her arm, and they made their way to the gate.

He finished the chips and tossed the bag away. Once they finally announced his section, the ticketing agent stopped him. "Sir, the flight is full, and there's no overhead space left. We'll need to check your carryon. At no cost to you."

"It might squeeze under my feet."

She looked over the bag. "Sorry."

Man, he hated checking luggage, but Mom and Star had checked theirs, so he'd be waiting anyway. He sighed, turned over his duffle, and headed down the jet bridge.

Stuffiness hit him when he entered the plane. A man milled in the aisle, adjusting something in the overhead bin, which did look pretty cramped. A full load.

A honking nose erupted every few minutes as he waited. Someone blowing their nose? If so, they had a really bad cold.

Paul spotted Mom and Star on the end of the center row at the back and lifted his hand in greeting. He reached his place across the aisle. Right in front of the bathroom. About the worst seat in the house. And the honking nose volume increased. The sound came from a man in the middle seat next to his. A large lumberjack-looking man who reminded him of the cartoon character who used to try to beat up Popeye.

"Hello," the man spoke with a Russian accent. "Pardon my cold."

"Any chance you want to trade seats with my mother and her friend across the aisle?"

The man spoke in Russian to the woman beside him, then shook his head. "She likes the window."

"No worries." Paul took his seat. He didn't really need to sit by his mom, but the man's huge arm—and part of his body—covered the remote controls on the armrest that operated the screen on the seat in front of Paul. So he probably wouldn't be watching any in-flight movies.

"I can trade if you want to sit by your mom," Star spoke from across the aisle.

Tempting. He'd love to have a bit more room. Paul studied her expression. Brown eyes wide and clear, she appeared sincere. But this flight would be much longer than the last, and the thought of her sitting alone if they encountered turbulence niggled at his conscience. "I'm fine."

He leaned back and closed his eyes. Maybe he could sleep.

A second later, a little boy in front of him started crying. "I want out. I wanna go home."

Paul opened his eyes and craned his neck to get a glimpse of the kid. Brown hair, maybe three years old. Little arms and legs flailing.

"Sean, trade seats with Nana. You can see out the window," his mother pleaded.

The kid kept up the fussing during the flight announcements and the takeoff but finally quieted once they

89

got in the air. Paul let his eyes close again. Man, he was tired.

A nose honk and a horrible smell woke him minutes later. Had someone already gone in the restroom?

He glanced around to find nothing other than his seatmates eating something on brown bread that reeked of rotten cabbage, boiled eggs, and pickled herring.

Gross. He swallowed back a gag. How did they get that on the plane?

The smell must have rallied the little boy too. "I need out." His whine was stronger than ever.

"You have to stay in your seat, Sean. Remember?"

"No. No, no, no, no. I go potty." His frantic words seemed urgent.

"Are you sure? And you mean you need to go to the potty, please?"

Why would she bother with politeness when the kid needed to go?

"No!" Sean screamed. "I go stinky in my pants. My tummy hurts."

Another odor accosted Paul. Worse than rotten cabbage and boiled eggs ever imagined smelling.

"Oh, no, Sean." The mom rose up and out into the aisle with Sean. "Wait until we get to the potty."

"Hold me," Sean cried, arms up.

"Okay," the haggard mother lifted him gently.

But the pressure seemed to expel Sean's breakfast, lunch, and dinner.

Onto Paul's shoulder.

And again onto his lap and feet.

Paul froze, trapped between the sick boy and the mass of the Russian. Nowhere to escape.

Please let Sean stop puking on me.

Who was he talking to anyway?

"I'm so sorry." The shocked mother looked torn between cleaning Paul and getting to the bathroom with Sean, who was squalling, big tears running down ruddy cheeks.

"I'm fine. Take care of your boy." Paul tried to sound confident in his assessment.

As soon as the mom disappeared with Sean into the lavatory, a flight attendant rushed over. "Sir, how can I help? Do you have a carryon with clothes you can change into?"

"Had to check it. Full flight." Unable to stop the sarcasm in his tone, he raised his brows—the only part of him he wasn't afraid to move.

Another male attendant arrived bearing towels. "Come to the galley, and we'll find something you can change into."

Paul stood and followed them, ignoring his own urge to hurl what little he'd eaten in the past twenty-four hours. In the back, one woman helped wipe up what she could with napkins while the other searched for something he could wear.

"Hey, a passenger gave me this T-shirt, but you can have it." With a tenuous smile, the woman, a pretty redhead, held up the offering. The shirt pictured an ugly leprechaun wearing sunglasses and playing an electric guitar.

No wonder she didn't want the thing. "Thanks."

The male attendant pulled out a pair of shiny blue gym shorts. "The weather will be cold when you arrive, but these might do until you get your bag."

"Perfect." Paul forced his lips to curve upward. These people were doing their best in a bad situation, after all.

He just hoped this nightmare didn't get any worse.

Chapter 13

The ugly T-shirt hugged Paul's chest tighter than his own skin, but at least it didn't sparkle like the running shorts. On the bright side—if there was one—the shiny shorts had a small pocket for his passport. And neither item stunk like his clothes. Including his coat. The stench on the clothes he'd removed reminded him of the pig farm he'd visited once with his father. The most significant loss in his situation could be that of his jacket. The chilly, wet Irish weather would demand one, and he hadn't packed another.

He grabbed the garbage bag containing his contaminated mess and exited the bathroom.

"We can keep your dirty clothes back here until we land." The redheaded flight attendant's eyes widened as she took in the whole picture of him, but then she gave him a flirty smile. "You look...ripped in that shirt. Snazzy even." Her words carried a slight Irish accent.

"I look ridiculous, but thank you for trying." He set his soiled clothes on the ground.

She held up a small bottle of vodka. "Sometimes we use gin or vodka to wipe down biohazards. Or you might just want to drink it at this point."

"Not necessary." He held up one hand. "I doused myself in sanitizer while I was in the lavatory."

"Might I bring you a glass of wine?"

"Sure. Thanks." Maybe it would help him sleep. He made his way to his seat. The sweet smell of deodorizer hit him, along with the sight of Star and his mother, who had traded into his row. Now the Russians were willing to move, huh? But who could blame them?

"Oh, sweetie, are you okay?" His mother offered him a tissue. "Here."

"I'm fine." But he took the tissue just in case.

A muffled snicker slipped from Star. "Ready for St. Paddy's Day a few months early."

"You're hilarious." He slipped onto the seat that now sported a blanket draped over the top to cover the desecrated upholstery.

"Sorry." Her mouth cocked into a sheepish grin. "That had to blow. Literally."

"A regular comedian. You should take that show on the road."

"It's not funny. I know." She covered her lips as she held in a giggle.

"Yet, you're laughing."

"I brought your wine." The flight attendant hovered close. She held a small bottle and offered him a cup. "Let me pour it for you."

"Thanks." He definitely could use a drink. He held the cup, waiting for her to open the plastic bottle.

She unscrewed the lid and held the bottle over his cup. The plane jolted. The flimsy plastic bottle overflowed like a volcano spilling the cool, red liquid onto Paul's bare leg.

"I'm so sorry." The attendant's mouth hung open as she stared at his leg.

At least the wine missed the neon blue shorts. "I've got a tissue."

The flight attendant took the cup. "I'll pour a fresh glass at the back and bring it to you."

"I'll pass and wait for something clear, like ginger ale, when the drink cart arrives." He wouldn't chance staining this outfit. The alternative might be worse.

Star's chest shook, obviously trying to contain more laughter.

Paul bumped her with his elbow. "Who needs a trip to Ireland when you can be so easily entertained at another's misery, right?"

"I'll stop." Star squeezed his arm. "I'm trying. Sorry."

Warmth traveled from his arm to his face, but he did his best to ignore the sensation.

She let go, plugged in her earbuds, and switched on the screen in front of her.

Paul did the same. He changed channels until he found a documentary about Ireland and sank deeper into his seat. Maybe it would lull him to sleep.

Castles flashed across the screen. Star craned her neck to get a glimpse and then switched her remote until she found the same one.

He raised his brows and pulled out one earbud. "Are you mimicking me now?"

"I want to know more about where I'm going."

He closed his eyes and tried not to be pleased. *Time to relax now. Deep, stress-clearing breaths.*

A honk from across the aisle jarred him. The Russian blew his nose two more times. Sleep didn't seem to be on the agenda. Paul pulled out the other earplug, and another noise assaulted him.

A lopsided grin crossed Star's face, and she pointed to his mother. Mom's eyes were closed, but her mouth hung open, emitting a sound reminiscent of a foghorn.

"Her nose must really be stopped up," Star whispered.

"I've never heard her snore like that."

"Good luck sharing a room." He gave her a sarcastic smile now.

"I'll survive." She replaced the earbud and turned her attention back to the screen.

Paul did the same. Two documentaries later, the plane shook. Bordering severe turbulence. He pulled out his headphones.

Drinks spilled, and the flight attendants' trash cart rocked. They quickly rolled everything back to the galley.

Star's fingers dug into his arm. "This is a lot of bumps in the road," she whispered near his cheek.

"Turbulence is mostly a nuisance. Pilots generally worry more about fires, mechanical problems, or bird strikes." Of course, he'd seen some ugly weather over the Atlantic on the satellite.

An announcement urged passengers to fasten their seat belts. Flight attendants were told to return to their stations and buckle up. The pilot explained they'd encountered rough weather.

The shaking worsened. Paul focused on the airplane motion and tried to determine what actions the pilots were taking to respond. He listened to the sounds generated by the aircraft.

A baby cried, and a woman three rows ahead prayed aloud.

The plane lurched and dropped. A few of the overhead bins popped open, and bags fell onto the passengers below. Loose items shot up in the air. People shrieked.

In turbulence this severe, pilots struggled to read the instruments in the cockpit.

Then the plane dipped hard. Paul pictured the radar covered by an angry red storm and the pilots' fight to get control. His heart fisted in his chest, and he broke into a sweat. What if he died tonight? And wearing this hideous shirt? He didn't believe in God anymore, so what happened when he died? Would he just disappear into nothingness? Become one with the earth?

…for dust you are and to dust you will return.

~~~

How was Mrs. Kelly sleeping?

Anxiety swam in Star's chest. The plane seemed to be shaking apart. A man near the front hurled. Kids and a few women bawled. Even Paul looked frightened, and he'd taken her hand, holding on tight. Was he trying to comfort her or himself?

God, I'm scared. Her prayer changed to a whisper, as she raised up another desperate plea. "Help us, God."

Do not fear, for I have redeemed you.

Relief coursed through her body and ran down her arms and legs. God's word soothed better than any drug. No matter what happened, He was in control. She knew where she'd go when her end came.

Her thoughts drifted to the soldier from the airport. She prayed he wouldn't fly through this mess, and if he did, that God would give him comfort.

After minutes that seemed like ice ages, the shaking eased. Paul's grip loosened.

"We good now?" Self-conscious, she slipped her hand away.

"I think we've cleared the storm." He breathed a long exhale. "Must've been some heavy wind gusts."

"I saw hurricane watches on the weather this morning, but I didn't want to upset your mom."

One side of his mouth lifted. "So your first flight, and

you're willing to fly through a tropical storm? You must really want to see Ireland."

"Honestly, I didn't know anything about the place other than green beer, St. Paddy's Day, and Lucky Charms, but I'm sure it's wonderful."

"Really?" His brows scrunched into a disbelieving tangle. "Lucky Charms aren't actually…" He tilted sideways to look at her as if trying to tell if she was being honest.

She gave him the stink-eye and splayed the fingers on one hand. "I've been in exactly five states. Sorry, I don't know all the world like you do."

"Where'd you grow up?" Paul still studied her, his hazel eyes doing funny things to her insides that she struggled to ignore.

He was probably fishing for ammunition to get rid of her the minute they touched ground State-side in two weeks.

Whatever. She'd get axed no matter what. "Along the Gulf Coast. Mostly Mississippi, Alabama, Florida. We went over to New Orleans a few times with my mom, but it was hard to get around in the camper down there. The streets can be narrow and almost as bumpy as this plane ride."

"Camper?"

"Until the stepdad came in the picture, we lived in it." Pain ricocheted around her chest, the memories with Mom and her sister, Skye, stabbing at pieces of her heart. "Those were the good times."

"Living in the camper was the good part?" His voice rose at the end of the question.

As if anyone had control of what situation they were born into. He could think what he wanted with his uppity self. "Compared to after Mamma married the scumbag who sold the camper and kept the money, life was golden."

97

"Sorry." The single word left his lips with awkwardness, his gaze finally dropping.

Star's face scorched. "I don't need your sympathy." She closed her eyes and pretended she wasn't about to spend two weeks with Mr. I'm-better-than-you.

Chapter 14

What a nightmare.

Paul massaged his throbbing forehead. Meanwhile, his mother's snores competed with the Russian's nose-honking as the plane made its final descent. How had Mom slept through those massive storms? Just as well. No sense her experiencing the retching and terror with the other passengers.

A round of applause broke out when they touched the ground. At least the landing hadn't been too bad, considering.

He glanced at Star. Her eyes closed, lashes touching her cheeks, but there was no way she could be sleeping. Obviously, he'd upset her. And for some reason, hurting the woman tore into him like broken glass. No matter how much he wanted to get rid of her, he never meant to cause her pain.

Mom's breath caught, and she popped up. "Are we here?"

"We're in Ireland." He forced his lips into an upward curve.

"Wonderful." She clasped her hands together.

Star opened her eyes and turned her gaze toward Mom. "You slept hard. Are you feeling okay?"

"My throat's a little scratchy is all." She coughed as if to solidify the point.

The captain's announcements began. "Sorry for the rough patch. We hope you'll fly with us again. You'll be needing your Wellies and waterproof jackets today. The temperature is eight Celsius with light rain."

More rain. And cold. Paul looked down at his absurd outfit.

Maybe he'd prefer for the earth to swallow him up, after all. Of course, that was easy to think now that they'd landed on terra firma.

"What's eight Celsius in Fahrenheit?" Star directed the question to his mother.

"I'll have to look it up on my phone." She bent and reached under the seat to retrieve her purse with a soft groan.

Paul hated seeing her struggle. "It's about forty-six degrees."

"That's chilly." Star pulled her fleece jacket close as if she'd already stepped into the wind that tore across the Irish landscape. "Good thing I'm layered, and I have a raincoat rolled up in my purse."

"Good thing for you." Paul couldn't stop the sarcastic tone from tainting his words.

"Oh, sorry." Star popped a hand over her mouth. "But, you'll have something warm in your checked bag, right?"

"Warmer than this." He waved a hand over his get-up.

Star's lips pinched shut.

A line of passengers formed and moved toward the exit. Paul cringed when little Sean popped out of the row in front of them.

The boy chewed two fingers and stared at Paul, then spoke garbled words. Sean's mother pulled the fingers from his lips. "Now, tell the nice man."

The child's chin dipped. "I sorry I sick at you."

Paul couldn't help but feel bad for the kid. No one could control when a stomach bug hit. "It's okay, buddy. You couldn't help it."

With a sudden move, the boy flung himself at Paul, climbed into his lap, and pressed a sloppy kiss against his cheek. "You're nice."

"I hope I am." Paul chuckled and hugged the boy. "I try." And he hoped he didn't catch whatever caused the little booger to get sick.

~~~

What an adorable scene. Star couldn't believe what she was seeing. The kid had barfed all over Paul, and now he'd climbed all over him. And honestly the kid smelled like a porta-potty after an outdoor rock concert.

But Paul held the boy as if the situation—or *the stank*—didn't bother him at all. Well, except the part when she'd laughed at him.

Star shuddered to think about what her stepfather would have done. He'd have cussed the kid out and then knocked him into the next row. Just for starters.

Was Paul for real? After he'd shown his backside at the hospital, she'd considered him like the other beasts she'd known.

"Tell the nice man bye-bye." The boy's mother reached for him and pulled him into her arms. "We're really sorry. Let me give you my number so I can pay for the dry-cleaning." Her smile seemed a little too flirty for Star's taste. "Or I could buy you dinner, depending on where you're headed in Ireland."

Paul held one hand up. "I'm fine, thanks." He kept his attention locked on the boy. "I hope you feel better, Sean."

"Sir, your clothes." The male flight attendant squeezed through the aisle and stretched to hold out the tied-off garbage bag.

"Thanks." Paul took the bag and set it on the ground with rigid movements.

At last, their turn came to squeeze down the aisles and exit the plane. Stiffness ran through Star's legs. No telling how bad Mrs. Kelly's felt after the long ride, and she hadn't gotten up and moved around during the flight like the doctor recommended. Of course, the storm's turbulence prevented most movement on the flight.

Star kept her pace slow and listened while Mrs. Kelly talked about their itinerary.

Paul switched on his phone, and a series of chimes began. He kept his gaze glued to the screen as they made their way to the baggage claim area of customs.

"A lot of messages already?" Worry covered Mrs. Kelly's expression while they waited for the bags to circle on the conveyor belt.

"Umm-hmm." He gave a single nod and seemed to avoid looking her way.

Mrs. Kelly placed her hand on his forearm and rubbed. "Good news or bad?"

"The good news is Bill Gates is trying to reach me. The central bank of Nigeria keeps messaging, along with a man from Kenya about my deceased relative. And a long-lost friend wants to share their mega-jackpot with me. Oh, someone tried to use my stolen credit cards on a porn site and tried to buy a phone in Kentucky."

Star couldn't stop a chuckle. "Your lucky day."

"Just keeps getting better." His gaze slid her way, and something in his hazel eyes tugged at her heart.

"Any other bad news?" Not that it was her business.

He opened his mouth, closed it, then pointed. "Is that Mom's red bag with the pink ribbon?"

"That's it." Star charged toward the stream of bags. Apparently, Paul did too, because they plowed into each other. Paul caught her shoulder to steady her. His grip combined strength and gentleness, a touch unlike any she'd known.

"Sorry. I got it." They spoke in unison.

"I'll get it." A hint of a smile tugged at his lips. "I'm sure you're Wonder Woman and all with your aerobic workouts, but I still enjoy being a gentleman."

Wonder Woman? A gentleman? Heat rushed to her cheeks, and a bit of goofiness started in her midsection. Why would she feel this way? This was Paul Kelly, after all.

She shrugged and slipped from his grasp. "Okay, but it's gone back into the tunnel now."

"I'll grab it on the next round." His gaze dropped.

"I'll wait with your mom." And away from Paul. She turned and scooted her way through the crowd of passengers.

~ ~ ~

His boss had already replaced him. Paul swallowed down the bile rising in his throat and a few obscenities he wanted to shout. But he wouldn't ruin Mom's trip.

After all this time without taking personal leave, all this time neglecting his mother, living his life to satisfy the man's every whim, his boss dumped him. Very similar to the way the missionary board had dumped him when he'd only told the truth about his mentor. He was sick of getting screwed over.

Another reason he'd wanted to be his own boss. Freedom. That might not happen now. At least not as soon as he'd planned.

Pressing his lips shut, he retrieved his mother's bag, then delivered it to her and watched for his own. Getting out of these clothes rated first on today's to-do list. Already he'd received a number of strange stares. And a man in the crowd tried to hand him a business card with a phone number written on it. Paul pretended not to notice, keeping his focus locked on the conveyer belt. He stayed away from Star too. She'd taken a position in an opening on the other side of the procession of bags. She seemed too curious about his messages as if she could read the bad news through his expressions.

Too bad he couldn't read her.

He made some discreet glances her way. Who was this woman?

Though she'd shown some fear on the plane—which was reasonable for a first-time flyer in a tropical storm over the Atlantic—the angle of her strong chin displayed no such emotion now, despite being in a foreign country for the first time.

So she said.

She wore no makeup that he could tell and had twisted her long hair into a messy bun, but still, she was pretty. Not a glamorous pretty like Francesca. Just natural. The men around her took notice—except the one who'd tried giving him the business card. But she didn't give any of them a second glance. Or a first that he'd observed.

Her gaze collided with his, and Paul's face warmed. Caught.

Covering quickly, he raised his brows, held up his hands, and mouthed, "Any luck?"

She shook her head. People around them had thinned to only a few. Most passengers had already claimed their suitcases and moved on. Only four bags circled the belt now, none of them his, and apparently not Star's, either.

"Wonder what's taking so long?" Mom rolled her suitcase closer.

"No clue." But a sinking feeling made its way through Paul's midsection. "I better go check with the airline."

Twenty minutes at the customer service counter and a mini-stroke later, Paul received his answer. How in the world had they lost a bag he'd checked at the gate?

A sarcastic smile lifted Star's lips when he approached her

and Mom. "They're lost, aren't they?"

"You're quick for a first-time flyer," Paul scoffed.

Chapter 15

"Oh, no." Mom's face crumpled, and tears filled her eyes. "I'm so sorry. Our first stop will be to buy y'all something to wear."

"The stores aren't open this early." Paul tried unsuccessfully to keep the flatness from his tone.

Worst day ever.

Okay, not the worst. Losing his father had completely devastated him. Leaving the children in Africa...also life-shattering. And, as much as he wanted to throw a fit and blame Star—or even his mother—for this irresponsible trip and everything that had happened because of it, the tears in Mom's eyes kept his mouth clamped. Seeing her cry broke his heart.

"It'll all work out, Mom." Except, of course, his lack of employment.

His attention turned to Star.

Shoulders shaking, she bent over. Laughing again. At him. "Oh my goodness," she practically roared.

"What the...?" Paul bit his tongue, though his face roasted like fire. "Not that funny anymore."

"I know, but..." Gasping for breath, she waved him off. "It's just, this trip has been so crazy, I thought, I *have* to find a tackier outfit than yours, no matter what."

"As if that's possible," he grumbled and tightened his grip on the stupid garbage bag that held his desecrated clothing.

"The feat will take colossal effort, but I'm always up for a challenge." She laughed harder.

"As soon as a store opens, you can have this one. Sooner

if you don't stop laughing at me." Paul was tempted to strip the shirt off right there and hand it to her, no matter how frigidly the early-morning Irish chill swept through the automatic doors. "Better yet, you can have what's in this garbage bag."

"Now, Paul." Mom neared and touched his shoulder. "Star's suitcase was lost too—"

"Oh, I'll find something uglier, and I dare you to do the same." Star leveled a hard stare at him, a mischievous glint sparkling in her eyes. "And I'll win. To prove I'm serious, I'll trade shirts with you."

Paul tried to rein in his imagination. "And how are you going to go about trading clothes in the middle of the airport?"

Mom cleared her throat and shot him a pointed glare.

"I'd go in the bathroom, take mine off, zip my coat, bring it out, wait for you to switch. Then I'd go put on your raunchy rock-and-roll leprechaun."

He pulled his gaze from her honey-brown eyes to glance at the blue sweatshirt beneath her fleece. It'd be warmer, still too small, though. But why would she want to play games with him? No matter how much irritation brewed inside his soul, at the moment, the idea intrigued him. "No trade, but I accept your challenge to find a more obnoxious outfit than this. Then you have to wear it an entire day."

"You're on. If I do find one, then it's your turn again." She stripped her fleece jacket from her shoulders and offered it to him. "Here. You wear this outside. I have a Columbia rain jacket rolled up in my purse."

"What? I'm not making you freeze out there."

"Okay, take the rain jacket." Star scoffed. "I'll live."

"You'll get wet." He might look like an idiot, but he was still a gentleman.

"Suit yourself." Star reached for his mother's suitcase handle.

"I got this." Paul caught Star's hand.

She held onto the handle. "You find a taxi. You're the experienced traveler, plus you have that bag of grossness you're carrying." She eyed his trash bag.

"I can rent a car and drive us."

"Without a driver's license?" Her brows lifted in another challenge.

Crud. Nope. He'd forgotten that scrap of woe. His fingers still lingered on hers, a maddening warmth surging up his arm. But she did make more sense. For once. "Okay, but wait here. And watch your purses."

"Fine." Star slipped her fingers into her pocket and turned her attention to his mother. "We'll wait."

Mom's gaze bounced between them. She said nothing, though, seemingly content to let them duke it out.

"I'll be right back." Paul took off toward the group of drivers lingering near the rental car window, hoping to catch a good fare. After a bit of haggling and explaining his tale of misery, he found a young Croatian driver willing to give them a reasonable price.

"You lock arms with Mom. The weather will be a mess out there." Paul took the suitcase before Star or the driver could catch the handle. He didn't have any cash to tip the guy, after all.

The driver's gaze zeroed in on Star, his eyes roaming. "Your first trip to Ireland, beautiful ladies?"

Paul's pulse kicked up. Maybe he should have chosen a different driver.

Star motioned toward Mom. "She's been looking forward to this tour for some time. We've got the whole agenda mapped out."

Star owned some street smarts, at least, evading the question and letting the guy know they'd studied the route.

"It's a magical place for love." The driver glanced at Paul then returned to gawking at Star. "Is this your honeymoon?"

"Sort of." Star again evaded. Fluttering her lashes, she flashed a silly grin Paul's way. "Captain Buttercup totally surprised us. Right, snuggles?"

Snuggles? Captain Buttercup? Paul forced his lips into a smile. "More surprises to come, snookums."

Mom chuckled. "Shall we start the adventure, love birds? I have the directions ready on the map in my purse."

Satisfied that the driver was duped, or at least muddled enough not to try to rip them off or keep flirting with Star, Paul led the way outside. Heavy wind and blowing rain greeted them. The cold drops slapped against Paul's arms and legs and soaked into his shirt.

Star held an umbrella and helped Mom into the back seat of the gray sedan while Paul lifted the one suitcase between them into the trunk, along with the garbage bag. When he finished, Star had taken the front seat for some reason, so he sat in the back.

And they were off. To whatever pandemonium awaited.

~ ~ ~

Star shivered inside and out. The stocky driver gave her the willies. Thank goodness Paul and Mrs. Kelly had picked up on the creepiness too. Over the years, she'd made a habit of taking shotgun so she couldn't get locked in the backseat of some psycho's vehicle. And she could watch where they were going. And figure out something to use as a weapon if needed. All she had in her purse right now was an ink pen, but it could work in a pinch. She switched on her cell service and studied the

GPS long enough to memorize the way. Then she'd turn it off and keep an eye on the road signs.

At a roundabout, she questioned the guy about a turn to let him know she'd be on guard. The man chattered on in his strange, thick accent about why he'd left Croatia for a job in Ireland. His country was beautiful, but he often had been paid late for work, if at all. He and his cousin had moved.

"People try to rip you off." Star nodded. She'd been there. "Happens everywhere."

"Even in the US, eh?" He shot her a glance.

"Oh, yeah. I got canned at this snobby hotel because some rich guy kept hitting on me."

The driver's gaze flitted to the rearview mirror. "Did you not defend your wife?"

Star shook her head. "That happened before I met Captain Buttercup, but my boyfriend at the time took up for me. He got fired too."

"Which boyfriend was that, sugar lips?" Paul called from the back.

Sugar lips?

"You don't know him." And she shouldn't have brought up such a heartrending memory.

"I might, cuddle bug. What was his name?" Paul's syrupy sweet tone held way too much curiosity. Especially with the subject of Blake.

She didn't want Paul Kelly poking around in her past.

The driver laughed and waggled his brows. "I think someone is jealous."

"Nothing to be jealous about." Star spun around to face Paul. "He's dead."

And that shut him up.

Shut everyone up. She hoped for the rest of the drive.

Chapter 16

Please let this ride be over. And soon. Paul let out a quiet groan amid his shivers as they drove slowly through the quaint streets of Ennis. Between the awkwardness after Star's blunt announcement about her dead boyfriend and the crash of pouring rain, they'd ridden the last fifteen minutes without talking. Even the creepy taxi driver clammed up. Mom looked to be enthralled in the scenery, despite the thrashing water streaming down the windows. He could use a double shot of expresso this morning—or a half-day nap.

At last, the driver pulled onto the brick drive of a vine-covered building and stopped in front of glass double doors. The Jewel of Ireland Hotel. The place looked nice enough, but no awning waited to keep them dry. Probably too windy in Ireland to keep one.

"Here we are." The driver stated the obvious.

"I'll get the bag while you walk Mom in." Paul readied himself to get even more drenched.

"Who would be paying the fare?" The driver turned and shot a look Paul's way.

The guy wasn't even getting out? What a loser.

"I've got it." Mom retrieved a wad of Euros from her wallet.

"Here." Paul slipped the agreed-upon price plus tip from her, then motioned for her to put the rest back.

"This should cover it." He handed the money forward. Letting his mom and Star pay his way irked him. He'd never been a freeloader. Even when fundraising for mission trips, he'd worked odd jobs to help defer his own travel expenses. Maybe his replacement cards would arrive at the hotel in a day or so.

The driver counted and pocketed the payment, then locked his gaze on Star. He offered her a card from his console. "If you need another ride or anything else."

The words had barely left his lips when—looking fierce—Star narrowed her eyes at the man, shooting the kind of daggers with her eyes Paul had been on the receiving end of a time or two. Completely ignoring the phone number offering, she barreled out of the car and dashed around with the umbrella to help Mom exit the backseat.

Like some cartoon character now himself, steam tore through Paul's chest, up to his cheeks, and out his ears. This guy was a piece of work. "I'll take care of my wife's needs. Pop the trunk, so I can get our bag."

Even if he didn't want Star working for his mother, he respected her tenacity. No one intimidated her.

More rain pelted him at the back of the car. Already, Mom's suitcase would get wet. He rolled it as quickly as possible around the car to the entrance.

Inside, Star and Mom stood on the black-and-white tile floor in front of a mahogany check-in desk. Paul waited, dripping on the entrance rug. Even at this ugly-early hour of the morning, a bellman should be along any second. He could request a towel to dry himself. Or four.

The lavishly decorated lobby boasted antique furniture atop Turkish rugs. Warm flames flickered in a fireplace dividing the sitting areas. Europe did have its niceties. The quaint towns and ancient history provided many hours of distraction while traipsing around the continent with his boss.

Ex-boss.

"Sir?" A burly gray-haired man wearing black pants with a black vest over a white shirt approached. A questioning stare raised bushy brows as he took Paul in.

"I messaged about getting a room, but haven't heard yet." He pointed down at his wet getup. "There was a mishap with my luggage, my clothing, my wallet—basically a mishap with everything along the way."

The older man leaned close and lowered his voice. "Been enjoying the craic at the pub all night, have ye? Perhaps a bit much Irish whiskey for an American?"

"No, look…" Paul bit back the frustration raging to spew out.

"Now, now, I've slunk out and carried on with the lads having a pint too many and come home —"

"I did not. Have not." Of course, he must appear to be a crazy drunk dragging in from the street after a night on the town. "My mother and her friend are checking in." Looking past the man, Paul called to his mother. "Mom, I have your bag here."

She turned to face him. "Oh, Paul, you're soaked to the bone."

"I'm fine." Other than he'd probably be hypothermic soon. "Can you check on my reservation while you're at it? I didn't want to mop the floor with myself."

"Pardon me, sir." The bellman's voice became formal again. "I've made a pig's ear of welcoming you. I'll gather your mother's luggage. You must be in tatters from your perilous journey."

"I'd love a towel and a place to buy dry clothes."

"Dunne's and a few other stores open at eight, but it's only half six yet. You've not a stitch?"

"Nothing. The airline lost my luggage, and a kid threw up on my clothes." He held up the garbage bag.

Mom and Star left the counter and shuffled over, both donning guarded expressions. They must have more bad news.

"What now?" Paul groaned.

Mom coughed a few times, then cleared her throat. "Our room will be ready in a few hours, but they won't have one for you unless someone cancels. They're calling other hotels to check availability. No luck so far, but they assured me they'd keep at it."

A few hours for Mom? Nothing for him? Paul's stomach churned. He doubted even the supposed luck of the Irish would be with him today. Or the rest of this confounded trip.

~~~

God, we could use a little bit of blessing soon, please.

Star said a silent prayer for Mrs. Kelly's sake. There was no way the sweet lady would have fun unless Paul could be at least semi-happy. And he looked anything but at this new announcement about the reservations.

They were all exhausted, and he had to be miserably wet and cold. If only he'd taken her jacket when she'd offered. Of course, he was way too stubborn to accept.

Even if the guy was unlikable—mostly—she needed to find a way to help him. He *had* been slightly nice, taking up for her with creepy-taxi-guy. Which was decent. During the plane ride, he'd demonstrated patience. Not many guys would have. Probably a show for his mother, but still.

Paul's shivers drew her attention. And the way the goofy T-shirt clung to his dripping wet self. A muscular self.

Okay, Star, back to finding a solution for those shivers. He needed to dump those wet clothes and warm up. Too many times, she'd been caught in the elements, and she knew how dangerous hypothermia could be.

Star turned to the bellman and gave him a pleading look. "What about your lost and found? Would there be something Paul could borrow temporarily? Or one of the hotel staff's uniforms? Anything? He's freezing."

"Nice thinking, Miss. I'll take a look. Meanwhile, I'll store the lady's bag until room three-thirty-three is ready for you." The man seemed anxious to scurry away. Probably because they were all stuck sitting around in the lobby for a while, it seemed.

"Good thing he's a big guy." Star pondered aloud.

"Why is that?" Paul gave her a quizzical look.

"His lisp. It sounded like he said tree-tirty-tree."

Paul chuckled, lines crinkling his temples. In a nice way. Too bad he didn't smile like that more often. "It's not a lisp."

"What is it called, then? A speech impediment?"

"A thick old Irish accent. They don't pronounce the h's when they put it with the t."

"Oh. Huh." She laughed. "So I'm staying in tree-tirty-tree. That's kind of fun to say."

"Yep. And tanks for good tinking, by te way, with te lost and found." Luminous hazel eyes bore into her, their depths causing a little swirling storm of their own in Star's tinking.

Heat crept over her cheeks. Was he being nice again? What game was he playing? "Whatever's in their lost and found has to be better than what you're wearing."

"A man can dream." Paul gave a shivering shrug, his gaze still glued on her.

"What if Paul stayed in our room just for tonight?" Mrs. Kelly touched Star's arm.

Star jolted. She'd almost forgotten where she was, why, and the fact that Mrs. Kelly stood beside them. She must be delirious, getting caught up in Paul's gaze this way.

"There are two twin beds," Mrs. Kelly continued. "Maybe there's a chair I could sleep in."

Maybe this was jetlag. She'd heard of the condition. And what was Mrs. Kelly suggesting? Paul in their room? But she was Paul's mother, after all. The sleeping arrangement wouldn't be weird. For them.

Star took a step back. Maybe she should have left the airport when Paul had told her she wasn't needed.

"Mom, I can find something." Paul shook his head. "An Airbnb. I've heard the college kids couch surf these days."

No way.

Paul Kelly did not look like the couch-surfing type. Probably more a five-star hotel type. It wasn't fair to put him out.

"I've slept on the floor most of my life," Star found herself blurting. "I can sleep beside your bed, Mrs. Kelly, and Paul can have the other twin for tonight. No biggie."

Mrs. Kelly wrapped warm arms around Star's shoulders. "You are such a delight and a blessing."

The words sank deep into Star's heart, warming her from the inside out.

But Paul's shivering mouth fell open. "You've slept on the floor most of your life?"

Star's abs tightened, squeezing at memories of dark times bubbling up from the past. Black nights. Alone. Frightened. Tender bruises and burns. Creepy things crawling against her skin.

She definitely had jetlag. Or she was just plain crazy to reveal so much in front of Paul.

Chapter 17

Star turned at the tap on her arm, and Mrs. Kelly pointed down the hall. "I see a ladies' room. I think I'll freshen up. How about you two?"

"Sounds good." Star welcomed the opportunity to escape Paul's scrutiny. She removed her coats and offered the fleece to him. "Put on this jacket until the bellman gets back. I'm praying he has something warm for you soon or you'll have hypothermia."

"Praying's not going to produce clothes from thin air." Paul rolled his eyes.

"Nothing is impossible with God." Star repeated the mantra she'd learned from her year in the sober living home.

Lips pressed into a frown, Paul shook his head. "That's a load of—"

"Here you are, sir." The bellman appeared with a large shopping bag. "You won't believe the luck. I've found just the yoke for the weather. It's a men's large size, and we were to have it donated to the charity shop today. And I'll trade this one for the nasty sack, and take the mess to wash."

Paul made the swap, opened the bag, but his expression remained flat. "Thanks."

"You're welcome. I've placed a hairdryer in the washroom. We'll have you settled in as soon as possible. In the meantime, we're delighted to offer you a full Irish breakfast." With a slight nod, he excused himself.

"Let's see it." Curiosity itched within Star. What had some

hotel guest left behind?

"You're gonna lose your little contest."

"No way!" Star grabbed the bag and ripped out the clothes. Holding them up, she couldn't stop a snort. Neon orange lightning bolts striped the aqua retro wind jacket and pants. A plain white tee to wear underneath. She'd seen pictures of women in the nineties wearing similarly-fashioned wind suits, but those paled next to this gaudy atrocity.

Paul shook his head. "Can't catch a break."

"But, Paul." Mrs. Kelly stepped closer and touched his cheek. "You'll be warm, so this…this outfit is an answer to prayer."

"Your God sure likes to humiliate me." Paul scrubbed his fingers through his wet hair.

"That's not true, Paul." Mrs. Kelly's voice faltered, and tears coated her eyes.

"Hey," Star gave Paul's arm a shove, "I can still beat you." Maybe. It would be tough though with that ensemble.

Paul leveled a weary stare her way. A stare so disillusioned and worn down that it tugged at her heart.

She shifted her gaze to Mrs. Kelly. Pain etched the older woman's face. Drastic measures had to be taken for her sake.

Determination rose up in Star's chest, and she fisted her hand. She had to liven things up on this trip and steer Paul back to the Truth for Mrs. Kelly. Because somewhere along the line, Paul had lost his faith, and it was obviously breaking his mother's heart.

Star scrambled to find the blessings in their situation, the way she'd been taught by her therapist. "We need to think about the positives, like how we survived Mr. Stranger-Danger-Taxi-Driver. He was a creeper-and-a-half. Plus, the plane made it through all that bad weather safely."

Mrs. Kelly nodded. "My suitcase made it here. We can give thanks for that."

Star gave him her best challenging smile. "So go put on your swag, and we'll be first in line for the full Irish breakfast I heard about. Then we'll go shopping, Captain Buttercup."

One side of Paul's mouth tugged at the silly term of endearment, and he rolled his eyes before snatching the clothes. "I'll meet you in the dining room."

Minutes later, Star and Mrs. Kelly had been seated, orders taken, and fresh coffee poured. The delicious taste matched the amazing aroma. Star took in the room as she sipped. The hot liquid soothed the bone-deep chill of the wet weather. But this hotel, this restaurant with its white tablecloths and formal waiters, the tall windows and chandeliers… She'd worked in a few upscale places but never in a million years imagined being a patron in one. A lump caught in her throat. Through her time at Re-Claimed, where she'd met Jesus and Mrs. Kelly, her entire life had been transformed. Before that, she'd lived in utter chaos.

God searched her out when she'd been trapped in a dark pit. He'd provided for her. A verse popped into Star's mind, and she spoke it aloud to share the moment with Mrs. Kelly. "He lifted me out of the slimy pit, out of the mud and mire; he set my feet on a rock and gave me a firm place to stand."

"Don't even start with the snarky laughter." Paul slipped into the chair between Star and Mrs. Kelly. "What were you saying?"

The bright blue actually looked good on him. Probably anything he wore looked good on him. She couldn't dwell on that fact. And she wouldn't dare laugh at him right now. "I had a verse pop into my mind." She repeated it for Paul. "I honestly have no clue where it came from in the Bible. It's weird, but

Scriptures just pop in my head since I became a Christian this year."

"I love that verse." Mrs. Kelly dabbed a napkin to her lips. "I'm so proud of you."

The words snuggled around Star's heart like a thermal sleeping bag on a cold night of camping.

"Psalm forty." Paul studied his coffee, his voice flat. "Have you ordered?"

Obviously, he'd once known the Bible. Really well. While she had only just read the book for the first time. What had happened to him? "How did you—?"

"Two full Irish breakfasts and a porridge with fruit?" The waiter arrived with a full tray.

"I hope it's okay, Paul." Mrs. Kelly gave him a wary gaze. "We ordered a full breakfast for you. The porridge is mine. Sticking to the cardio diet, sadly."

"It's perfect, Mom." He set a napkin on his lap while the waiter laid their plates in front of them. "I'm starving."

Whew. At least he didn't complain about the food. Though, he'd had plenty of reasons to complain over the last twenty-four hours.

Mrs. Kelly said a quick and quiet blessing. Probably hoping to keep the peace.

Star stared down at her overflowing plate. Sausages, fried eggs, mushrooms, grilled tomatoes, and a round, black hunk of something resembling sausage. Star dug into the eggs first. The protein should give her an energy boost, and with a big breakfast, maybe she could go without eating lunch. No need to spend more money. She wanted to keep good records of exactly what she owed Mrs. Kelly.

Once she finished the eggs, she moved on to the sausage.

"The black one is blood pudding," Paul spoke between

bites.

Weird. "What's that?" Star kept at the rest of the food while waiting for the explanation.

"Sausage made from pork blood, fat, and a cereal."

Star swallowed a mushroom. "Aren't there verses about not eating blood in the Bible?"

"Some consider the ordinance to be due to the idol worship and traditions of the pagan culture, so they ignore it." Paul kept his focus on his plate. "Others abstain."

"That's so confusing." Star cut her tomatoes into smaller bites. "I'll skip eating mine since I don't understand."

His gaze lifted, hazel eyes a churning sea of deep greens and browns. And suspicion. "But you'd eat it otherwise?"

"I don't waste food for no good reason."

"It doesn't"—he made air quotes—"gross you out?"

"When I'm hungry, I eat what's offered." And she'd known hungry.

"Huh." He held her gaze another long moment before scooping up the last bite of eggs from his plate. His piece of blood pudding sat untouched as well. "So there's nothing you won't eat?"

"Not so far."

Was the arch of his brow curiosity or challenge? "Would you try the Scottish dish called haggis? We might be able to find some in Ireland. It's made with —"

"Paul." Mrs. Kelly frowned. "I'm still eating."

"I'll eat what they put in front of me on this trip unless it violates my conscience." Star shrugged. "Being picky is a luxury, and I've not had many of those in my life."

"Sorry." The shift in his tone—from challenging to soft, caused her cheeks to ignite. "That must've been hard." His gaze roamed her face, increasing the burn. "But, on the bright side, your flexibility makes you the perfect person to travel with. You don't care what you wear, what you eat, or where you sleep."

She couldn't help but laugh. And savor a bit of pleasure at the strange compliment. Maybe savor the pleasant lift of his lips. "I never thought of my past that way. You've found another blessing to be thankful for."

~ ~ ~

Finding a *blessing* hadn't been his intention. Man, the girl had been brainwashed.

Paul scraped the last of the relish from his plate while fumbling for a polite response. The observation about Star had tumbled from brain to mouth without a whit of restraint. Maybe the turbulence rattled a screw loose up there.

And what exactly had she lived through? The protective-warrior-woman, then a verse-quoting, tenderhearted Christian offering her jacket, and then a vulnerable girl with some kind of difficult past. Or was this all an act? A play for his sympathy?

A slew of guests entered the dining room with the host. He seated them at two tables of eight.

A man followed, a bit of a five o'clock shadow, thirtyish, a couple of inches shy of six feet. He made his way straight toward their table. "I hear you're the Kellys. I'm Colin Murphy, your guide. Glad you made it."

Mom grinned. "We're so happy we've arrived in time for the orientation meeting this morning. We've had quite an adventure already."

After wiping his mouth with his napkin, Paul stood and extended his hand. "Paul Kelly."

Colin scanned Paul up and down before a firm shake. "Aren't you all dressed up like a dog's dinner?"

Smart-aleck. "Long story."

Colin's gaze fell to Star. "Is this lovely lass your wife?" His fingers released Paul's, and he offered his hand to Star.

"No." Paul and Star spoke in unison. Their eyes met.

"Star is my mother's…" He cleared his throat, wishing he'd never started that sentence.

"Friend," Mom said quickly.

Technically, Star was Mom's employee, but whatever.

An awkward grimace clouded Star's features. Slowly, she lifted her hand to Colin. "I'm Star Youngblood."

A huge grin covered Colin's face. "Single, are you?"

"Yes." Star's voice came out hesitant.

Colin lifted Star's hand to cup it between both of his. "You'll be beating the lads away with a stick, I imagine. If you need assistance, remember, I'm the one who looks like Brad Pitt with shiny black hair and blue eyes. We'll all meet upstairs after breakfast."

"Got it." Though her cheeks reddened, Star smiled back at the weasel.

Fire seared Paul's neck. *Brad Pitt, my foot.* Would she actually buy that load of bunk? The situation shouldn't needle him, though. Paul ran a hand through his hair and sucked in a breath. Maybe Star would fall for the guy and move to Ireland. Then he wouldn't have to feel guilty about her losing her job.

Chapter 18

Three cups of coffee and a full stomach later, Star traipsed behind Paul, who walked arm-in-arm with his mother, helping Mrs. Kelly wind around the maze of halls to reach the meeting room upstairs. Thank the Lord for the elevator.

Navigating Ireland would prove a true challenge for Mrs. Kelly. More than Star had realized. Honestly, it was probably a good thing that Paul had come along. She'd noticed a gentleness in the way he handled his mother. He hadn't been nearly as impatient as she'd expected. Her stepdad would've already blown a few gaskets, probably—no, she wouldn't think about him. Or Vince. Wouldn't allow memories of those losers control over her.

At last, they reached the room designated for the tour orientation. A few butterflies took flight in Star's midsection. Part anticipation, part intimidation. What would the other travelers be like? Rich? Educated? She couldn't imagine hanging out with these people and feeling like she belonged to their group. She'd never even finished high school, for goodness's sake.

She would never be an equal. As Paul kept reminding her, she was only the help. Unwanted help. They stepped into the room, where a dozen people already waited, mostly middle-aged or older, dressed in preppy-looking slacks and collared shirts or nice sweaters.

The guide, Colin, stood just inside. A grin spread across his face as he spotted them. "Welcome, welcome, Kelly family."

"And welcome to the lovely Star." His gaze landed squarely on her, and he winked.

Her cheeks heated at Colin's attention. She'd never gotten comfortable with flirting. She didn't trust strange men's forwardness, no matter how friendly or good-looking. Surely that was the way her mother had fallen into the trap.

Maybe ten more tour members filtered in, chatting and introducing themselves to each other. Star inhaled deeply, then blew out a shaky breath, hoping to drive away the tension gathering inside her chest.

A couple that looked to be in their late fifties made their way to Mrs. Kelly and Paul. They wore nice jeans, matching blue tennis shoes, and identical blue sweatshirts that read *Reunite Global.*

"Hello, I'm Morris Donovan." Smile lines crinkled near his graying temples as he shook Paul's hand, then motioned with his head toward the tall brunette beside him. "This lovely lady is Linda, aka My Rib."

Chuckling, Linda took Mrs. Kelly's hand. "His eccentric way of saying I'm his wife. You get used to him. Eventually."

"I'm Priscilla Kelly. This is my son, Paul, and my friend, Star."

They all shook hands and exchanged nice-to-meet-yous.

"What does your shirt mean?" Star couldn't help but ask. She glanced at Paul and could almost feel his eyes aching to roll.

Morris Donovan pointed at the writing. "I work for an international Christian ministry organization. When we started packing, we realized most of our sweatshirts and fleeces are from work. We don't need a lot of cold-weather clothes in Florida."

Star returned a smile, thankful that other Christians would

be on the trip. "What do you do?"

"We help—"

"Circle up, lads and lasses." Colin clapped his hands. "We are to begin with some extremely fun and exciting mixers. And if you don't think they're extremely fun and exciting, remember it's always polite to agree with your guides, lest you find the bus has left you one early morn." His voice was teasing, his accent charming.

"First mixer, you must line up by your birth date, not counting the year." He held up one finger. "But wait, here's a kicker. You may not speak."

Several in the room murmured or groaned, but Colin continued. "I'll be watching, and there will be prizes for those most enthusiastic in these challenging, yet extremely fun and exciting, games. So, on your mark, get set, go."

Motion started in the room, the dozen or so people scrambling around holding up fingers and trying to communicate with sign language. Mrs. Kelly hobbled around with one finger held up for her January birthday. A sour look pulled at Paul's lips, but he held up eight fingers and took a few steps, surveying the room.

"Why are you just standing there, Star?" Colin whispered loudly. "Everyone else is enjoying themselves. Except perhaps your friend Paul, who, despite his festive outfit, looks like a bear with a sore head."

A laugh slipped from Star at the fitting description. "I'm waiting until they get organized. Then I'll jump in."

"Surfs up." He caught her elbow and nudged her forward. "Flash those fingers and join the craic."

Star slid her arm away but continued on toward the front of the group and signaled the third month for March. Others signaled for her to stand in a certain place in the lineup. Oh boy, she could already tell who would be the bossy bodies. A blonde in an expensive-looking red top, maybe fifty, took over and waved each person into place. Finally, she signaled they were finished.

Colin pressed a button on his phone. "Fastest yet."

The blonde cheered and applauded. "Yes!"

"Well, isn't she a gas?" Colin grinned. "And a wee bit competitive. We'll see how she does on the next game."

Great. Another game. Star played along through each silly activity and pretended she was comfortable. At least she had to look happier than Paul.

"And now our last game, my competitive crew." Colin clapped his hands together. "The name game. Make a circle facing each other." He moved to stand next to Star. "Find out the name of the person to your right and give them a nickname. Something that begins with the first letter of their name to help us remember them. For example, this pretty lass's name is Star. But I dub her Shining Star."

Star's cheeks burned, and her pulse kicked up a notch.

"Now it's your turn for Paul at your right." Colin pointed and raised his brows.

Oh, why did she have to be standing by him?

A nickname for Paul? A nice one? Words like Prickly Paul, Proud Paul, and Pushy Paul flitted through her mind, but he'd just get crankier. She chewed her lip as he stared at her.

"Come now." Colin nudged her. "You can do it. Don't be shy."

"Perky Paul," Star blurted. "No, wait." He wouldn't like that, either. "Perfectioni—"

"Perky Paul it is. And his outfit agrees." Colin winked at her, but Paul's expression stilted. "Now, it's your turn for your mother."

Paul seemed to force a smile his mother's way. "Patient Priscilla."

"Come now. Your mother must be patient for sure with a strapping son like you, but how about something more personal for the rest of us."

The corners of Paul's mouth dropped, but his mom held his gaze, eyes wide and pleading. "Pretty Priscilla."

His mother reached up and hugged him. "My sweet boy."

Paul's face reddened, but the group gave a collective aww.

"Now it's my turn." Mrs. Kelly pivoted to Mrs. Donovan beside her. "Lovely Linda."

And everyone's attention turned. Thank the Lord. Star released a quiet sigh. Paul would surely be upset with the nickname. And with her. What else was new?

But she couldn't ensure Mrs. Kelly would have a nice trip if she kept upsetting him. She'd have to pray harder to keep her tongue under control.

~~~

Perky Paul, my foot.

Paul struggled to cap the steam gathering in his chest and avoided glancing toward Star while Colin continued torturing the tour members. Lovely Linda dubbed her grinning husband Mighty Morris, and so it went on down the row with the ridiculous, annoying nicknames. Now, every day, all day, these people would forever be repeating Star's infuriating slam.

Once the group ended that emasculation, Colin began again. "Very well, all we need are our buddies for the trip. I have assigned them at my whim, whilst you were enjoying the craic. *What is craic*, you may ask? In Ireland, it is many things, but some are good times, entertainment, gossip, news, and fellowship if you will."

"So no one thing?" Star asked.

128

Curiosity forced Paul to look her way. Her brow furrowed with genuine wonder. Or nosiness. Or, more likely, annoyance with the entire Irish country for not being more specific.

"Nope, we Irishmen like to keep you guessing." Colin winked at her. Again.

Paul's fists curled at the corny spectacle.

"Now for the buddy assignments."

Not Star. Anyone else but her. Except maybe the bossy blond. Most of the people on the tour appeared to be fifty or over, other than himself, Star, one married couple, and the teen grandson of one of the men.

"The buddies cannot be someone in your party. It must be someone you just met today."

Whew. No Star.

"Paul, you are buddies with Morris Donovan. Mighty Morris, that is." Colin continued with the assignments.

He took in the tall man with graying hair. At least Morris was tolerable.

Colin had almost finished assignments, and Star had yet to get a buddy. If Colin assigned himself to Star... Heat stung Paul's ears.

Wait. Why would he care about that? The setup would be perfect. Unless the guy was a real creep. How well did the tour company check out their people? Star was young and came up hard, from the sound of it.

"Star, you will be a buddy to our young Wise Will."

Wise Will looked more like Wishing-He-Were-Anywhere-Else-Will. The boy, maybe eighteen, lifted his gaze at the announcement. Star waved and offered a pleasant smile. Wise Will lifted his index finger and made his first semi-positive expression. The kid had to be thanking his lucky stars. Still in her early twenties, Star was no doubt closest to his age. And pretty. A man, no matter how old, would have to be blind not to notice that much. Despite being up most of the night, her face shone with a natural beauty—her complexion flawless with her straight brown hair falling down around it. And partnering with the teen would be safe for her. Probably. Maybe.

Would it?

Star's gaze turned his way, and her light brown eyes met his. There was a softness there. Her brows lifted. "Sorry about the name. I couldn't think—"

"And first prize in the games goes to Mighty Morris." Colin whisked a hideous green shamrock top hat from a bag and presented it to the winner.

Thank goodness. Paul held in a chuckle as Morris donned the ugly hat and smiled. At least someone else looked a bit ridiculous.

"The prize for the non-winner, aka loser, goes tooooo"— Colin grinned and pulled a small wooden leaf from his bag— "Perky Paul. It's a Christmas ornament to offer you some cheer."

Great. Paul took the "prize." The leaf shaped like a piece of holly had been painted green with red berries. It read Dingle on the left side and Berries on the right. "Nice." Paul held it up, and the group chuckled.

Colin's lips quirked into a cocky expression. "Ah, yes, it 'tis."

What a smart aleck.

"And it's time to go, lads and lasses. As we exit, I'll hand everyone a transceiver with an earpiece to wear for the tour of Ennis. Make sure you have on your walking shoes."

Lingering while his mother chatted with one of the other women, Paul tried to gather his composure. Just the thought of the walking tour twisted a knot in his stomach. He'd have to stay close to Mom to make sure she didn't fall.

"Interesting prizes, huh, *buddy*?" Morris clasped Paul's elbow as he passed. "I think we're in for some fun on this trip if my knees hold out."

"Exactly what I'm worried about." Paul nodded. "Europe's old streets can be treacherous. Not to mention the wet weather making them slick."

"Worry much?" Morris's tone was teasing, but his gaze looked sincere. Compassionate even.

"About Mom, yes. She has rheumatoid arthritis."

"My wife and I traverse much worse in our mission travels, and we have our own health issues." Morris shot a glance toward Mom. "Older generations have to embrace adventure, too, even if there's a slight chance of danger. If we don't, we're not really living, are we?"

Something about the man's views made sense. For some people. Paul couldn't embrace that for his mom. Morris and his wife had each other, but Mom was all alone. His throat tightened. Except for Star. But he'd be home soon.

Sooner than he'd thought, maybe.

"But there's no sense throwing caution to the wind. Tempting fate." Paul kept his voice low. "Doesn't there come a time to take life easy?"

"Is that what you'd do in her position?"

The question frustrated Paul's confidence. What would he do?

Chapter 19

Ennis: National Award Winner Tidy Town.

Star smiled at the sign as they finished touring the old, narrow streets. Brightly colored buildings stood cheery, despite the cloudy weather, and trees dotted the green river running through the adorable town. She took in the sweet song of fiddles playing from within the pub they'd stopped beside, perhaps the same tunes as they had for hundreds of years before.

"Y'all go ahead with the others for lunch in the pub. I'll go with Will to the Chinese place down the street." Star gave a wave toward Paul, Mrs. Kelly, and Will's grandfather. "I love Chinese food."

Not exactly true, but she didn't hate it. And she wanted to go to the little stores she'd spotted next to the Asian fast-food place where Will had been trying to convince his grandfather to eat. The menu was probably cheaper than the pub, too, and maybe didn't smell so much like Guinness. Not that beer had been her drug of choice, but still. There'd be a lot of temptation on this trip. Why not skip one?

"This tour's going to be lame," Will mumbled once the others went inside. The wind whipped his shaggy auburn hair. "Looks like a nursing home set the trip up for their patients." His chin tipped, and he glanced at her. "Except for you, I mean."

"They aren't that old." Star chuckled. "Besides, people are all the same, just some have lived longer. Mrs. Kelly is really cool. And fun to talk to." Not her son, but whatever. "Paul's not that old."

"Is he your boyfriend?" The thin teen had a dejected expression Star recognized all too well. The I-don't-know-where-I-fit-in look. She'd been there.

"Nope. My boss's son."

"Good. Cause he looks like he's been sucking on Sour Warheads his entire life, even though he's dressed like he's going to a rave at a ski lodge."

That brought up another laugh. "Give him a break. Some kid threw up on him on the plane, then the airline lost his luggage." Of course, he'd looked sour before the incident.

"Gross. That would be a bummer, I guess." Will pointed. "This is the place."

"Any reason why you didn't want to eat at the pub?" Star took in the menu on the glass window.

"Who knows what those Irish dishes have in them. Could be cow brains or something."

Star held in a scoff. As if the kid knew the Irish-Asian restaurant ingredient list. After scanning the menu posted by the door, she pulled some cash from her purse. "Will you get me two eggrolls and tea while I run in the sporting goods store across the street? And maybe the gift shop next door."

"Sure." He took the money, looking a little anxious.

"I'll be fast. Get a table, and I'll be there before you know it." She gave him a hard stare. "Don't leave this place, or else." She didn't want to be responsible for losing her buddy on the first day.

Her threat seemed to settle him down. He probably hadn't traveled outside of the US, either. Once he went inside, she booked it into the store. Earlier, she'd noticed exactly what she needed, so it wouldn't take long.

Fifteen minutes later, she'd made her purchases. Not as cheaply as she'd hoped, but wasn't that the story of her life? Back in the restaurant, bags in tow, she found Will in the corner booth of the brick-walled restaurant. Several food containers sat discarded and empty, but he still munched on eggrolls. Teen guys sure could scarf down some grub.

"Hey. You didn't eat mine, did ya?" Star nudged him before she took the other side of the booth.

"Thought about it." He smirked. "Not much for you to eat, though."

"I had that huge Irish breakfast, so this'll do." She unwrapped an eggroll and took a bite. Not terrible. Crunchy enough.

"You're here with that lady and her son?" Will spoke through bites.

"Yeah. I'm her aide back in St. Simons. I help her around the house and stuff."

Will's dark eyes lit up for a second. "I went to St. Simons with my parents once." Then he shrugged one shoulder. "When they were still together." His mouth clamped shut before his attention returned to his food. Will wadded up some remaining paper into a tight ball and took his trash to the garbage.

Clearly, he had parent baggage. She got that.

Star hurried to finish her eggroll and catch up. "Ready to go back to the others?"

"Not much choice, is there?" Walking back toward the pub, he seemed to fold in on himself.

"We can choose to enjoy ourselves."

"Right." A sarcastic laugh came with the words.

God, is this an open door? Is Will why I'm here? Because I sure don't know what to say.

Nothing came. They walked without speaking on the busy sidewalk, small cars zooming by until they neared where the dark wooden doors of the old pub stood open, awkwardness bouncing between them. Taking a deep breath, Star reached for Will's shoulder and gave it a light pat. He stopped and turned her way.

"My parents wouldn't have won any awards. In fact, they probably should've been institutionalized or jailed or something, so I know how family junk hurts."

He eyed her, seeming to size up the truth of her admission. "My parents pretty much dumped me on my grandparents once they divorced."

"That stinks." Star nodded. "Your granddad seems nice, though."

"I guess." He sighed.

"Where's your grandmother?"

"Died a couple of years ago."

"I'm sorry." That had to be hard, but at least he still had someone who cared. "There was a time I wished for someone—anyone—I could've escaped to."

"That bad?" He really studied her now.

"Worse. I was on my own after my mom died. My stepdad was a psycho. "

"How old were you?"

"Sixteen." There was movement in the pub entrance, and Star turned to find Paul only a few feet away. How much had he heard, and why was he just standing there staring at her? "Paul, is something wrong?"

Paul shook his head. "I finished lunch, and I was coming outside to see if I had better service on my phone, but y'all were in a conversation. I...I didn't want to interrupt."

"Thanks for going with me." Will offered a half-smile

before he slipped past Paul into the pub.

"I enjoyed it," Star called after him, wishing they could have talked longer.

Paul always seemed to get in the way.

~~~

"Sorry." Paul gave Star a sheepish look. "I was trying not to interrupt, but it seems I did anyway."

She lifted one shoulder to secure the two shopping bags hanging from her arm. "You couldn't help it."

"That was kind of you."

"I like eggrolls. No biggie." She avoided looking his way.

"I meant talking to him about your past." And now he'd admitted his eavesdropping.

Her teeth caught her lip for a moment before she spoke, capturing his attention. "I hear that's what the bad stuff is good for. Helping others." Now her soft gaze met his, looking hopeful that he'd agree.

Because that's what she'd been brainwashed into believing. She was about to start the religion talk. He wouldn't fall into that trap. "Can I ask how your mom died?"

"Hung herself." The words came out barely louder than a whisper, but the weight of them slammed into Paul as if he'd leapt from a cliff and hit shallow rock.

"I'm sorry. I shouldn't have pried."

"You didn't know." Her soft answer drew him closer.

He longed to offer comfort—draw her to his chest and hold her.

But that would be ridiculous. They didn't even like each other, did they?

Instead, he touched her shoulder. "Losing my father devastated me. And I wasn't as young as you were. I can't imagine."

136

Despite the cheery Irish tune filtering from the pub's open doors and people milling around the quaint town, silence ballooned between them. Paul fumbled for something else to say. "My dad died of an infection after the flu. The doctors fought it. My dad fought it." They'd prayed. He'd prayed. Oh, how he'd begged God for help.

Emotion clogged Paul's throat. "Nothing worked. And I'm not sure how you can believe that the bad things life dishes out have any meaning to…" He shouldn't have started that sentence. He pressed his fingers to his temples, tension building in his head at the memory.

"I bought you something." Star shoved one of the shopping bags into his hands.

"Me?" Why would she? It must be something hideous.

"Yes, you." A flicker of a smile played on her lips.

Definitely something embarrassing. He opened the bag and found a pair of gray jogging pants—normal jogging pants—and a nice black sweatshirt. "But why? Why would you buy this?"

"The store was nearby, the clothes were on sale, and you needed them." Her brows raised, and she gave him a once over. "Besides, you know, you do look pretty ridiculous."

"You shouldn't—"

"Shining Star, we missed you at lunch." Colin bounced out of the pub and straight to Star. "And you missed some great grub. They even have bangers and mash here."

A laugh bubbled from her, and it was a sweet tinkling sound like a wind chime in summer. "Well, since I have no idea what that is, I didn't miss anything."

"It's just mashed potatoes and sausages that remind me of hotdogs. They serve them a lot in England." Paul dismissed the silly banter because the other shopping bag on her arm had

137

captured his attention. He couldn't seem to control himself. He had to know. Who was this woman, and what was she up to? "What else did you buy?"

Mischief danced in her eyes. "That's for me to know and you to compete with. Tomorrow."

Unexpected pleasure at their little game plowed through Paul, but he battled the indulgence. He didn't need to get sucked into any more emotions regarding this woman.

Chapter 20

Why would Star be so kind? Maybe she was trying to manipulate him into letting her keep her job. Paul strode down the carpeted stairs into the hotel lobby. He'd barely had time to change into the new clothes before the group lined up near the door, waiting to board a bus. He was thankful for the gift. He still carried the obnoxious coat, though, in case of rain.

Star stood a few feet ahead of him with Morris and Linda, looking as though deep into conversation. What could they be talking about? He couldn't imagine them having much in common.

This woman stirred so many questions.

Paul's gaze rested on her. She still wore the same outfit, her hair still twisted into a messy bun. A few loose strands lay against her slender neck.

And he couldn't seem to tear his gaze away.

His thoughts traveled to Star's disclosure about her mother's suicide. How horrific that must have been. Trauma like that could break a person. He couldn't imagine losing a parent that way, especially his mother, especially at such a tender age. Maybe he could understand why Star had wanted to numb herself.

If only Mom had hired someone more normal—more businesslike—for him to fire. Not a young, vulnerable woman with a tough past. And so stinking pretty.

No. He couldn't get caught up in feeling sorry for her. Or any of the other bizarre sensations that staring at her neck stirred up. Really, he didn't even know if what she'd told him held any truth. The whole thing could be manipulation. He needed to focus on something—anything—else.

He had to think about what was best for Mom. Where was Mom anyway?

A familiar sneeze and cough pulled his attention to the left. Mom rested on a chair nearby rather than standing in line. Exhaustion wore on her face, her eyes red and drooping. Maybe she was sick. Or this trip was too much on her, exactly as he'd predicted. And the black skies outside warned of more rain. The tour of Bunratty Castle and grounds might give her pneumonia and do her in.

Paul wound his way around the sofa to kneel beside her. "We should stay here and rest, Mom. It won't hurt to miss one part of the tour, and they serve dinner at the restaurant attached to the hotel."

"I've been looking forward to the castle and the medieval dinner. I'm fine." She wiped her nose with a tissue. "Just allergies or a little cold. Don't be a worrywart."

"Mom, you could have the start of the flu, and we lost Dad to—"

She caught his hand and gave him a tender look. "I took flu and pneumonia shots already this season. I'll see a doctor if I'm actually sick."

"Or go home?" He felt like a beggar on his knees, but he didn't care. His mom was all he had left in this world.

"I bet you know how to find a good doctor here or in London where you live."

As if London were next door. "Promise to tell me if you feel bad."

"The line's moving. The bus must be here." Mom slowly pushed to her feet.

And she didn't promise.

"I can't wait," Mom said. "I've heard great things about the castle dinner from my friend Beth."

Well, if Beth said the castle was great, it was worth risking life and limb, apparently. Paul held in a scoff and followed her out. At the mini travel bus, he helped her up the steps.

Colin greeted them and motioned to the right front seat. "I've saved Mrs. Kelly, otherwise known as Pretty Priscilla, a place up front to herself. She can stretch out in comfort. Once everyone's on, we'll do our buddy check."

Mom waved him off. "You didn't have to—"

"Don't fight it." Morris shook his head. "He saved one for me, too, because of my bad knees. Might as well enjoy."

"I give." Chuckling, Mom sat and stretched her legs. "May as well."

Paul rolled his eyes. If only he could convince Mom of anything that easily. He continued toward the back of the bus to find an open seat. There was a place by Star, but did he have to sit with her? What was the touring-with-your-mom's-help protocol? Pretty help, at that.

Glancing up at him with those honey eyes, she smiled and motioned with the curl of her finger for him to sit. Though his breath caught as if he were freefalling from thirty-five thousand feet, he obeyed. It seemed something curled around his heart as well.

"I'm so glad the clothes fit. You look better. Almost relaxed." She gave a half-laugh. "Almost, but not really."

"Thanks, I think." He glanced down at himself, pleased to be in casual, non-hideous, attire. "How much do I owe you?"

"Don't worry about it."

"No, really. How much?" He didn't want to be in her debt. Especially since he was the one who would be causing her to

141

lose income. He didn't have a wallet right now, but maybe his credit and debit cards would be delivered to the hotel tomorrow. And luggage would be nice too.

"Not tell-ing." Her voice had a singsong tone, and she leveled a snarky-yet-cute gaze at him.

His thinking fogged when their eyes met as if the lobe of his brain in charge of speaking had been struck by lightning. As if there was no pilot in the cockpit anymore. Paul swallowed hard, trying to regain the ability to speak. "Well, I'm buying you something next," he blurted, then shrugged. "When I get replacement cards."

He pulled his gaze toward the window, desperate to regain control somehow. Thick, angry clouds hung suspended above the town's roofs. "Looks like we're in for another storm."

~~~

A niggle of worry danced across Star's heart as she stood beside Mrs. Kelly.

"I'm fine staying at this pottery demonstration until it's time for the castle tour and dinner." Under the thatched roof of a small stone cottage on the grounds of the Bunratty Castle, rivulets of water streamed from Mrs. Kelly's raincoat onto the concrete floor. She coughed a couple of times, then cleared her throat. "You and Paul go tour the folk park without me."

"I don't know." Star hated to leave her, but she'd like to see the historic village. The group had been given a couple of hours to tour on their own. Glancing at Paul, she hesitated, guilt and indecision welling up in her chest.

Paul's attention seemed to be somewhere else. His gaze darted everywhere but toward her, and he ran his fingers through his damp hair. Maybe he was upset he'd had to put the ugly jacket back on. Why in the world did the man have to be so uptight? He looked attractive, no matter what he wore. Too much so. It annoyed the stew out of her the way he got under her skin.

"I'll stay with Priscilla if you don't mind Will tagging along with y'all." Will's grandfather volunteered. "I'd just as soon not walk the slippery trails in the rain."

Mrs. Kelly smiled up at him, then motioned toward the potter setting up for the demonstration near the front of the room. "I'd love to have company, but will you be bored watching a potter for so long?"

"Don't know much about it, but when my wife was still alive, I learned to appreciate watching others enjoy something." He gave a sad smile. "Wish I'd learned sooner. Besides, in the book of Isaiah, God is described like the potter, forming us as the work of his hand."

Star couldn't stop a chuckle. "I think y'all will get along fine."

Mrs. Kelly winked. "Indeed. We'll meet you at the castle for the tour before dinner."

"Come on, Paul." Star nudged his shoulder. "We're taking Wise Will to tour the folk park."

Will nodded and stepped closer. "Probably as boring as this."

Finally, Paul seemed to zone in. "Where's your grandfather from?"

"Originally, North Carolina, but we live near Jacksonville Beach."

"Nice area." Paul nodded. "Only an hour or so from St. Simons."

Will raised one shoulder. "The beach is okay, I guess."

"The beach is my happy place." Star motioned with her head. "Ready to go on an adventure?"

One side of Will's mouth lifted for a second. "I guess."

They spent the next two hours running from one stone building to another between showers, learning about Irish life years ago. She loved listening to the musicians who fiddled ancient Irish folksongs and touring the old farmhouses and shops, furnished as they would've been centuries past.

Will seemed more interested in finding out how to become a pilot. Paul's description of flying kept the two of them talking while Star soaked in every single morsel of history. She'd probably never travel anywhere like this again, and she wanted to absorb as much as she could.

Finally, they approached the enormous castle, which looked more like a fortress than the Disney palace she'd imagined. The rain had slowed to a drizzle, and the massive stone structure loomed before them, towers high and lofty against the gray sky.

"How in the world is Mom going to get in that monstrosity, much less tour it?" Scorn laced Paul's every word.

"Maybe they have an elevator?" Star prayed they did.

"Yeah, because those were common centuries ago," Paul huffed.

As they neared, a group waved from the top of the wooden deck leading into the castle. Star squinted to make out the faces and breathed a sigh. "She's already up that staircase."

"That's probably the first of several," Paul mumbled.

"Aren't you the downer?" Will smirked. "Maybe give your mom a little credit."

Star made a half-snort. Those statements seemed fairly ironic, coming from Wise-but-a-bit-whiny-Will.

Paul's lips clamped shut as they hiked up the wooden steps. Maybe he'd been right. The incline was pretty steep. Yet, Mrs. Kelly and Will's grandfather greeted them, both with huge smiles lighting their faces.

"We had such a lovely afternoon. How about y'all?" Mrs. Kelly wrapped Paul in a hug, then Star.

Paul and Will stared inside the dimly-lit castle, so Star answered for them all. "Amazing. I learned so much."

"Let's go learn more, then," Mrs. Kelly said. "The rest of the group are gathered inside with Colin."

More steps, stone this time, awaited them. Star's abs tightened as Paul took Mrs. Kelly's arm. Star followed closely, one slow stride at a time, hands ready to catch Mrs. Kelly if needed. God forbid. *Please keep her safe.*

At last, Colin led them into a huge banquet hall. Enormous antlers and tapestries and statues hung in the damp, cold room. Long wooden tables lay from end to end. Small rectangular windows provided very little light. Maybe living in a castle wouldn't be so wonderful.

A young woman gave the history with an accent so thick, Star had to strain to understand her. Something of Vikings and Normans and earls.

Once they'd finished looking around that area, they reached a small gap in the wall. A narrow spiral stone staircase. Star couldn't stop her gasp. A healthy sixty-something-year-old might struggle with these steps. Or even a thirty-year-old.

"Mom, wait." Paul took her arm. "This is too much."

"I'm fine." Mrs. Kelly grabbed for the metal handrail and took a slow step, then another. On the third, her cane hit the stair in front of her. She stumbled forward and dropped her cane, which clattered to the ground and down the stairs, where it landed with a clang.

Chapter 21

Paul caught his mother, narrowly stopping her from falling, and then holding her upright. "Mom, are you okay?"

Star rushed to pick up the cane and offered it to them.

She dared a glance at Paul, who stood between her and Mrs. Kelly.

If his dark gaze had been a fist, it surely would've punched her. "And this deathtrap is exactly what I warned you both about."

"I think I'll pass on the upstairs part." Mrs. Kelly offered a smile that appeared forced. Obviously, the stumble frightened her. She allowed Paul to help her back to ground level. "Y'all take pictures for me."

Star released a pent-up breath, sad but relieved that Mrs. Kelly realized her limitations. "I'll stay down here with you."

"Oh, no. I don't trust a man to take enough photos." Brows raised, Mrs. Kelly patted Star's arm. "I want details."

"I'm staying down too." Morris nodded toward Paul. "No sense injuring my knees the first day out. Linda can go with y'all, and I'll wait with your mother."

"Thanks." The word squeezed through Paul's pinched lips. He turned and began the ascent.

Still stinging from Paul's harsh words, Star followed. Her emotions churned with each step. Guilt that Mrs. Kelly couldn't go up. Remorse that maybe she should have talked Mrs. Kelly out of this trip. And if she allowed herself, a slight bit of wonder about the ancient structure. Who had passed through these stone passages—lived and died here? What had their lives been like?

When they reached the top of the castle, they walked out onto the structure, an open tower with stone walls. Wind swept up, thrashing her hair. A green, white, and orange flag whipped on a nearby pole. Star approached the rocky fence and looked over. The Shannon River wound through green pastures and round hills, creating an image so perfect she could see it every day and not grow tired. The sweeping view stole her breath away. The whole trip had pretty much deprived her of oxygen since she'd left the ground on that first airplane ride. She snapped photo after photo on her phone.

"Let me take your picture," Linda offered. "You two get together by the watchtower opening."

Star turned to find Paul standing nearby. His gaze dropped when her eyes met his. Her face heated, imagining such a photo of them. It seemed too personal. And just plain weird, considering their strained relationship. "You don't have to. I'll take some of the scenery."

"You look beautiful. Stand a little to the right." Linda nudged both of them until they were side by side.

Paul looked down at her without speaking, but his hazel eyes seemed to shimmer. No sign of the anger he'd displayed earlier. "May as well say cheeseburger in paradise."

"Cheeseburger in paradise?" The surprise of his sudden lightness caused a laugh to spill out.

"My dad always said that."

"Jimmy Buffet. Good song." She smiled up at him, diving deep into those pools of greens and golden browns, their depths as rich and beautiful as the Irish landscape. More oxygen deprivation. She might need to be resuscitated if this kept up. "Love me a cheeseburger."

"What's not to love?" Brows raised, he smiled back. A smile that lit his whole face, unleashing more warmth that traveled to a vicinity near her heart this time.

"That's so cute." Linda's phone clicked, breaking Star from what felt like some sort of hypnosis. "Now look at me and smile like that again."

Maybe it was the heights or the overwhelming history of the tower. Or could the altitude be different in Ireland? Because a peculiar flutter in her midsection joined the warmth and had her feeling dizzy. She'd heard of sickness due to heights, hadn't she?

"Want me to take it with your phone, too, or send it to you?" Linda asked.

"I'll give you my number when we have Wi-Fi." Star stepped away from Paul and took a deep breath. "I'll go back down now."

"Me too." Paul followed.

They wound back down to the main floor without speaking. Candles shone now, changing the atmosphere from dark and dank to cheery and warm. Romantic even, if someone were into that kind of thing. Pottery place settings lined one of the tables, and a harpist played near the center of the large room.

Within a few minutes, their group gathered in the entrance, and the castle closed to other tourists. Their own private group dinner. Nice.

"Greetings, clan of Colin the Handsome," shouted a blond man in a strange old-fashioned, green velvet costume. His pants came to just below the knees, and he wore yellow hose below. Several women gathered beside him in long colorful dresses with circular crown-like things on their heads holding back their hair. "Come in. My ladies will be serving you honey

148

mead while your scrumptious dinner undergoes final preparations."

"Here you go, my lady." A dark-haired young woman offered Star a pottery mug with no handle as they entered the banquet hall, then turned to Paul. "My lord." The actress's eyes twinkled when she gazed at him, setting off a disturbing and curious clench in Star's abs.

Star focused on the cup and took a sip of the drink. The sweet yet hoppy taste set off immediate alarms. "Whoa. What is this?"

"Mead made with honey." The woman pulled her attention back Star's way.

"And what else?" Star held her breath.

"It's fermented with our own secret recipe. The earl might slay me if I give it out." The woman pretended to be afraid.

Fermented? "It's alcohol?" Good grief. They could warn a person.

"Indeed. Warms the cockles of our hearts in this cold castle." A smile lifted the woman's full lips.

"I can't drink it." Star forced herself to hold the cup back out. She'd fought too long and too hard to screw up her sobriety.

"Here." Paul took the drink. "I'll take it. Maybe it'll help me sleep tonight."

Will popped up from somewhere behind them. "I'll drink anything you don't want."

The woman moved on, but not without winking at Paul.

"Good stuff." Will slugged back a gulp of his mead.

"Are you old enough to drink?" One of Paul's brows lifted.

"I am in this country." Will grinned for the first time since they'd met him. "Why don't you like it, Star?"

"I don't drink." She didn't mind sharing her story, but the

room was noisy and crowded. She didn't feel the urge to shout it out, especially when she still felt a little out of sorts from the tower. She definitely needed to look up altitude sickness in Ireland when she got back to the hotel internet.

"At last, I've found my king and queen." Another man in costume bowed before Will, then Star. "I have a crown and a throne for both of you."

"Me?" Star glanced around to see if another woman stood nearby.

"Yes, you, your majesty." The man introduced himself as earl Something-or-other and kissed Star's hand. "What shall we call you, my queen?"

"My name is Star."

The earl gasped, and a huge grin lifted his lips. "I've been waiting to meet Queen Star me entire life."

Anxious to be rid of the attention, she pointed at Will. "We call him Wise Will."

"Come, then, King Will the Wise and Queen Shining Star." He held out his elbow. "I'll show you to your thrones."

Who told him Shining Star? Her pulse ramped as the man led her and Will toward the banquet table. What did being queen entail?

~ ~ ~

And off they went. Paul's gaze followed Star to the head seat of the banquet table. A smile tugged at his mouth. She'd sure had a possum-in-the-headlights look when the earl had chosen her to be queen. He took another sip of the mead, and warmth flooded his chest. Not bad.

Other than the atrocious stairs, this whole day hadn't been bad. No headaches and he'd enjoyed touring the village with Will and Star. Will seemed to be interested in becoming a pilot, and Star looked like a kid meeting Santa for the first time, she'd been so enthralled with her journey through Irish history.

His thoughts drifted to the wind tousling her hair up on the tower, her honey eyes taking in the countryside. More heat flooded his chest, and something about the vision pinched a little. What was that?

"I hear you used to be a missionary."

"What?" Paul hadn't noticed Morris's approach.

"Your mom told me you spent time in Kenya."

Hearing the country's name brought back flashes of sweet children with bald patches on their heads and runny noses, flies swarming their thin bodies. Paul's throat tightened. What exactly had Mom told this man?

"That was a while back. I'm a corporate pilot now."

"My wife and I run a ministry, and we're looking for a pilot familiar with the ins and outs of mission work."

A bitter sigh released in Paul's chest. He knew the outs all right. "I gave up religion. And other fairytales too." Maybe that would change the subject.

"How'd you get into missions?" The bluntness didn't faze Morris at all.

Paul's memories journeyed back to his teen years when he and his father traveled to Haiti with the church youth group. The people and their smiles amid the poverty had attached themselves to Paul's heart. Over and over, Dad had told Paul how proud he'd been of him on the trip. Paul's eyes burned at the memory of his father. "When I was fourteen, I went on a mission trip. Young and impressionable, I decided that was what I wanted to do."

"And maybe that's how the problem started."

"What?" The man didn't make any sense. Morris knew nothing of his life.

"We should ask, 'What is He calling me to do?' Rather than

think, this is what I want to do." He shook his head. "It never works the other way around. You're swimming against the current."

Paul scoffed. "I'm not swimming at all anymore."

"From what your mom described, our ministry is different than the one you worked with." Morris put his hand on Paul's shoulder. "We strive to reunite the children in orphanages with a family member if they have someone. As you well know, many children are in orphanages because their families are poor and can't afford to feed or educate them. We teach the adult family members a skill to contribute to the communities with small businesses so they can keep their family together."

The concept did sound like a better plan, but that didn't mean he was interested in going back into that kind of work. Sure, he was unemployed now, but Mom needed him.

Where was she anyway? He surveyed the room and spotted her already seated with Will's grandfather at the banquet table. A wide smile covered her face as she laughed at something the man said. A strange awkwardness niggled in Paul's mind. He'd never heard Mom say anything about dating, and he couldn't imagine her with anyone but Dad, but she looked really happy talking with another man right now.

"Come sit and enjoy a glass of wine with our first course." The flirty brunette from earlier waved at him. Wine would be good. The day might've been okay, but this night was getting weird.

While the staff served food and wine, the entertainers sang and cracked jokes. The effort to make the dinner seem medieval included not giving anyone silverware, so the group navigated eating the ribs and chicken with their fingers and many napkins. No matter how hard he fought it, his gaze seemed to land either on his mother laughing it up with Will's grandfather or Star, whose face shone with wonder at the whole experience.

Both sights pleased and annoyed him at varying levels. How much longer would this thing last? He needed sleep. Or more wine. A costumed waitress neared, and he held up his mug for her to refill.

Then the room quieted, and the earl pointed Paul's way. "We've a villain in our midst. Men, bring him forward."

Two of the male actors appeared at Paul's side. "This way, rat," one said loudly, then whispered near Paul's ear, "Just go with it. All in fun, you know."

Grimacing, Paul downed his wine, then allowed the men to lead him to the stage. The night really needed to be over now.

They spun Paul to face the crowd, Star's gaze landing on him. She shook her head and mouthed something that looked like *sorry*.

Had she gotten him into this predicament somehow? He'd pay that stinker back if she had. The thought of teasing her stirred a bit of shyness inside him. And maybe pleasure too. He'd probably drunk too much.

"You've been found guilty," the earl proclaimed. "Of what, you ask?" The man made a silly expression as his eyes widened.

Paul shook his head. "No clue."

"That's what they all say." The earl rubbed his hands together. "You've been found guilty of trifling with the ladies."

A vision of Francesca and their night in Italy came to mind. *Thou shalt not commit adultery.*

Really, a Bible verse? Now? After all this time?

Even though he didn't believe the Scriptures anymore, maybe he'd been a little guilty of trifling with the ladies.

"You must move to the dungeon while we decide your

punishment. Beware of the large, hungry vermin down there."

The men led Paul off the stage into a stone pit but offered him another drink while he waited. "It won't be long. All in fun, mind you," they assured him again.

Fun. Yeah. "I'll take that drink."

Chapter 22

"Fetch the prisoner from the dungeon." The earl clapped his hands, and the two men escorted Paul back to the stage but remained at his side. "The king and queen have resolved to grant mercy on our villain. But first the scoundrel must"—the actor gave a dramatic pause, waggling his eyebrows, and Paul readied himself for more humiliation—"perform a melody of their Royal Highness's choosing."

Yep. More humiliation. Good thing he'd had a few glasses of wine.

"What will you have the scoundrel sing, Your Majesties? *Danny Boy? I'm a Little Teapot? Don't Go Drinking with Hobbits?*"

Paul groaned. Star and Will had to come up with better choices than those.

Star shot an apologetic look Paul's way, then leaned close to Will. They discussed back and forth, shaking their heads as they selected his penalty.

Finally, Star nodded, and Will smiled. Will stood and shouted, "Do you know *Don't Stop Believin'* by Journey? Maybe a little dance to go with it?"

Paul rolled his eyes. "Unfortunately." One of his boss's girlfriends had been a huge Journey fan and had played the group on the plane every flight. Plus, most every cover band in the world played that song.

"We've a treaty, then." The earl raised one hand high in the air. "Singing *and* dancing to *Don't Stop Believin'*. We will judge if your frolicking entails the proper amount of punch." Wiggling his hips, the earl turned in a circle, and the audience laughed. "Go forth, scoundrel."

The men nudged Paul forward and released him. He'd preached sermons in front of good-sized audiences and led kids' songs at the orphanage, acting pretty goofy while doing so, but that had been in another life.

Maybe he could admit it had been in a more enjoyable life.

At least he wasn't wearing his ugly outfit.

He took a deep breath.

Here goes nothing.

After belting out the first verse, he raised a fist. He wanted to be sure to give it the proper amount of punch so he'd be released from his misery.

The longer he sang and danced, acting completely ridiculous, the louder the crowd clapped and sang along with him. Finally, he gave it one last whoo-hoo and bowed. That had to be plenty.

Star jumped to her feet and whistled, and the rest of the room followed her lead, applauding and yelling.

Paul couldn't stop a snort. Shaking his head, he strode off the stage, directly to her. "Trifling with the ladies, huh?" He leaned close to her ear. "Are you sure you aren't doing a bit of trifling of your own, your majesty?"

A laugh tinkled from her as she pushed a loose strand of hair from her cheek, but it fell right back in the same place, capturing Paul's attention.

"It was Will's idea to pick you." Shoving her thumb toward the teen, Star asked, "Right? You got my back on this?"

Will raised his hands. "I think my queen is a trifler."

Unable to stop himself, Paul tapped her nose. "Payback is coming."

A blush crept across her cheeks, along with that loose

strand of hair. Paul fought the bizarre urge to tuck it back for her—to cup those pink cheeks with his hands and…

Whoa. He shook his head to free himself from the thought. She'd probably slap him silly anyway.

The wine was messing with his head. He should probably give up drinking too.

~~~

Two a.m., Ireland time. Paul shoved the covers off, grabbed a key and his phone from the nightstand, and tiptoed out of the hotel room. He'd given sleep his best shot, but the harder he tried, the more rest escaped him. His mother's snoring didn't help. Maybe if he sat in the lobby and read his email, he'd get tired.

He wound down the three flights of stairs. A few friends had told him tales of getting stuck in the elevators of older European hotels. In the lobby, he blinked. Hard. Three times. There she was. The queen, robed in the same clothes, teasing that sensation he'd attributed to the alcohol.

Was he dreaming?

Yet, there she sat on the couch, reading a book. She glanced up and spotted him. "Did I wake you?"

"I didn't know you'd left." His stomach clenched. He'd begged her not to sleep on the floor, but she'd refused and lain down on the other side of Mom's twin bed with a blanket. "I should've forced you into the bed."

"Um, no." She raised a brow. "I would've walloped you."

"Oh, man." He rubbed his head, felt the mess of his hair after tossing and turning for hours. "That didn't come out right at all." At least he'd guessed the kind of response he'd get for inappropriate behavior.

"I knew what you meant." She patted the couch and gave him a smile that stirred a startling and unfamiliar longing. "Sit."

Something weird in that honey mead, no doubt. "Did Mom's snoring like a crashing propeller plane wake you?" He sank onto the cushion beside her, all too aware of her proximity, and none-too-motivated to remove it.

"I thought she sounded like a dying rhino." Star chuckled. "She's clogged up, isn't she? But I think my being awake is because of the time change or something."

"That could do it." Although, as a pilot, he'd become accustomed to sleeping most anywhere.

"Or maybe it's the overwhelming excitement."

"Excitement?"

"I mean, I've never been anywhere like this, and probably never will be again, so I'm trying to soak in every moment."

"You don't think you'll travel overseas again? You're what? Twenty-three or something? Why would you say that?"

Her expression soured. "People like you wouldn't get it."

What in the world did that mean? He wasn't a snob. "People like me?"

"With money."

"My father was a veterinarian, not an oil tycoon."

Feisty brows rose above her soft brown eyes. "You grew up in a house your parents owned. I bet they bought your first car. Paid for college. You shopped for new clothes from the mall, not garage sales or thrift stores. You ate out at a restaurant once a week or more, right?"

Paul's throat tightened. Star hadn't lived that kind of life, from the sound of it. All things he'd taken for granted but shouldn't have. "Sorry. I don't think much about poverty in the US. It was easier to see overseas."

"I wasn't trying to make you feel bad, but you asked." Her chin cocked, and she leveled that challenging gaze on him. An intense gaze that was becoming so familiar. And intoxicating.

He needed to change the subject. "Reading something good?"

"*Mere Christianity*. Your mom gave it to me."

"C.S. Lewis." Used to be one of his favorite authors. Not anymore. Time for another change of subject. "Let's see. Instead of counting sheep, we could count what all went wrong the first twenty-four hours of this debacle." He lifted his fingers one at a time. "Had to pay to switch flights. Wallet missing. Storms. Crazy taxi driver. Rain. Mom almost—"

"Boy, your glass isn't even half-empty, it's shattered." Star grabbed his hand midair. "What happened to you in Africa? Why did you lose your faith?"

Pain like shards of glass pierced the walls he'd built around that part of his life. Dug into his heart and twisted. It had taken months to put himself back together—to create a new life. A process he'd be doing all over, thanks to this trip.

Now Star wanted him to dump all the agonizing ruins back out. Annoyance flared in his chest. "You're about as subtle as a rocket launcher."

~ ~ ~

At the harsh scowl Paul leveled her way, Star's pulse flew into overdrive. She released his hand. She hadn't meant to press him or to blurt that out, but his negativity drove her nuts. It was obvious from their day at the castle that he was able to enjoy himself, have fun even, when he quit trying to control every tiny detail of life.

But a scowl wouldn't scare her off. She'd been on the blunt end of much worse.

She softened her tone. "I just want to understand what happened." Understand him, too, for some stupid reason.

"Why?"

For Mrs. Kelly's sake? That had to be why she felt any concern for the man, but she didn't want to anger him more by admitting it. "Why not? Is it a secret?" She tried to look nonchalant.

His hazel gaze locked on her, intense and serious, then pulled away. He stared at the ceiling for a long moment. "I worked at an orphanage in Kenya with another missionary, Greer Jones, and his family. Greer was a mentor and friend— I thought. But I was fresh out of graduate school. Naïve. Too trusting."

"Been there, done that." Star gave him a knowing smile. "Not the graduate school part, but the other."

His brows and forehead loosened as if he believed she had. "I loved the children, the country, but I came to realize Greer wasn't the man he professed to be. Long story short, he was a…" Paul's lips pinched as he seemed to struggle for the right word. "Philanderer."

"A what? Is that someone who gives a lot of money to charity?"

"That's a philanthropist." Paul shook his head. "Greer was a womanizer. Adulterer. Maybe even a sex addict."

"You're kidding." Star sucked in a breath. "I've been around plenty of posers, so I guess it shouldn't surprise me. But, dang, why go all the way to Africa, in *literally* God's name, to pull that mess?"

"For real." Paul scoffed.

"So what happened once you got his number?"

"I confronted him about it. He denied everything, tried to make me think I was crazy."

"Oh, yeah. Liars are good at that." She shrugged. "Well, if I'm honest, drug addicts are good at that too."

He gave a gentle nod. "Anyway, his wife developed her third case of malaria. This time, while she was pregnant. While Greer went AWOL again, the disease really hit her hard. I

160

ended up running things and caring for her and their little girl. When his wife took a turn for the worse, and he still didn't come home, I called the mission board and reported him."

"You should have."

"One would think." The scowl on Paul's face returned. "They fired me."

"What?" Star shrieked, then covered her mouth. She didn't mean to wake up the whole first floor. "Why would they?"

"His parents were wealthy donors."

"So wrong." Anger burned through her like a cigarette on bare skin. "No wonder you're down on religion. I'd have been in Brokenville too."

Paul's head tilted, tentative gaze searching her face. "You agree with me?"

"I understand you." She tried to meet his gaze with compassion. "I don't agree about chucking God and the church out with those losers, though."

"And why not?" Sarcasm laced his tone. "I was trying to serve"—he made air quotes—"God, and that's the thanks I got. Why would I want to be around Him or the hypocrites in the church?"

"There are hypocrites everywhere. I'm sure they're in the grocery store where you shop, the airports you travel through, even the plane you fly, but you still go there." Star rested her hand on his. "Good and bad people are everywhere, Paul. I had a sucky childhood. The person who was supposed to protect me and take care of me didn't. It wasn't fair. But I've spent the past year learning, among many things, not to let bitterness rule my life. Because I'm pretty sure Jesus grew up poor, and I know he was beaten to a pulp too. If God's son had that kind of life, why would I expect some pie-in-the-sky existence?"

"And that makes everything okay with you?" From his tone, it was clear she was getting nowhere.

"Not okay." Star struggled to come up with an answer. What would Davis say? He always had the right words for this kind of situation.

Help me out, God?

She took a cleansing breath. "I have that peace that transcends understanding. Peace from God that doesn't make sense to people who don't have it, because I believe He loves me. He wants the best for me."

"I got home from the mission field in time to watch my father die." Paul yanked his hand away and sprung to his feet. "An agonizing death was best for him? And I didn't find any of your peace." He turned and walked back toward the hallway.

"It isn't my peace," she called after him. "It's God's."

But he disappeared around the corner.

Chapter 23

If the world hates you, keep in mind that it hated me first.

Heart racing, Paul sat up in the bed with a start. Who said that? Where was he?

He blinked in the hazy light. A hotel room.

He caught his breath and glanced around. The twin bed beside him stood empty but had been slept in. A suitcase lay on top of it. Mom's red suitcase.

Whew. He was in Ireland, and the words had only been part of a dream. An extremely vivid dream of flying back to Africa with a faceless man in the seat beside him quoting verses from the Bible.

Pain jabbed in Paul's temple. This trip might not kill his mother, but he seemed to be dying a slow torturous death. Dressed in his only set of decent clothes, the ones Star had bought him, he stood and made his way to the sink to mash down his hair and use the extra toothbrush Mom had found in her bag. Ah, some ibuprofen sat on the counter too. At least one thing was right with the world.

His conversation with Star rolled through his mind, burrowed in deep like a thorn and twisted. Annoying woman. And so blunt. His faith, or lack of, was none of her business.

But God chose the foolish things of the world to shame the wise; God chose the weak things of the world to shame the strong.

Blindsided by the thought, he choked on the toothpaste and coughed. He rinsed his mouth and closed his eyes. Was he going crazy? Maybe he had a brain tumor. Because he had no desire to revisit all the Scripture he'd learned during his early life and through college.

It was that weird dream lingering.

Coffee. He needed caffeine to snap out of it. He massaged his forehead and headed downstairs.

As he entered the dining room, the aroma of pastries and savory meats sent a loud rumble through his stomach. Really loud.

"You feeling okay, Perky Paul?" Colin greeted him with a cheesy smile. "You sound like a drowning bear with that gurgle."

"You've been around a lot of bears in peril?" Paul shot him a cynical glance.

"I've a large imagination."

"I bet." Yeah, like thinking he looked like a young Brad Pitt with dark hair.

Paul slipped past the guide to the table where Star and Mom shared a pot of tea. Star's hair hung in damp waves, and her face gleamed clean and fresh. She'd obviously gotten up and showered without waking him.

And he should end his study of her. "No coffee?"

"We wanted to try living like the locals." Mom grinned. "Tea for breakfast isn't bad. I even added a spot of cream to it."

After several years in London, he'd had his share of tea. "I'll stick with coffee." He took a seat and flagged down the waiter to place his order. And his stomach continued to protest noisily.

Star's gaze flitted his way, but she quickly turned her focus back to her cup, not saying a word. Maybe his behavior last night made her uncomfortable. Or the awkward sounds emitting from his midsection did. Great.

"Hungry?" Mom asked when they delivered her plate. "You can have some of mine until yours arrives."

They *could* hear his stomach.

Her porridge looked less than tempting. "I'll wait. Thanks." The coffee arrived, and he took a sip.

Mom waved her spoon at him. "I would've woken you, but you were sawing logs and talking in your sleep. I hated to bother you."

The coffee almost spewed from his mouth. "Talking?" And sawing logs?

His gaze traveled to Star.

Her lips pinched, and she still hadn't spoken. She focused on scooping her poached eggs on brioche toast and spinach salad.

A nice menu choice. She had good taste at least. "What was I saying in my sleep?"

Mom shrugged. "Most of it was garbled, but I think I heard you say, *Why? I can't. Who are you?*"

Steam rose to Paul's face, cheeks scalding like bare feet on hot blacktop. Even his subconscious was set on humiliating him.

"Pardon, miss." The older bellman from the day before strolled over, rolling an old suitcase. "Your bag has arrived, and I knew you'd want it right away."

"Amazing." She perked up with a stunning smile. "Did Paul's make it too?"

He gave a solemn shake of his head, his mouth turning down. "Afraid not. But I've picked up his clean laundry."

Paul's chest deflated. "Figures. How about an overnight package?"

"No, sir. But if you leave addresses of your next hotels and dates, I will forward your belongings."

Paul's head spun toward his mother. "Are we leaving today?"

She gave a slow nod. "I emailed the itinerary to you while we were at the airport."

"Your breakfast, sir." The waiter set a plate of scrambled eggs and smoked salmon before Paul.

"Thanks," he managed to grumble, then took a bite. He couldn't catch a break. The food tasted okay, but his stomach soured, imagining where his credit card replacements would land.

Star stood, and her jacket opened, revealing a gaudy green sweater. The ugliest rendition of a sheep he'd ever seen covered the center of the thing. Its eyes were crossed below a flamboyant paddy cap, and a green cud of shamrocks stuck out from its crooked yellow teeth.

It read *Kiss me. I'm Irish.*

Paul couldn't stop a snort. "That's the most atrocious thing I've ever seen. When and where did you find it?"

"I told you I'd win." Her mischievous gaze heated his cheeks in a completely different way. The warmth traveled down his neck to his chest.

"Oh, no way." He lifted his chin in defiance, and he couldn't stop a grin. "It's not over 'til it's over."

~ ~ ~

At least something brought the man out of his foul mood. Star rolled her suitcase into the lobby and took a seat on the couch while Paul went with his mother to retrieve her luggage. They'd be leaving soon, and Star had brought her purse down already.

She'd love to change into something else, but this hideous purchase she wore was the only thing keeping Paul's brows from staying knit tighter than the wool in her sweater.

166

Her mind tracked back to their conversation on this very spot the night before. After he'd stormed off, she'd prayed and imagined placing Paul before God's throne. There was nothing she could say to change him or anyone else. She knew that from sessions with her counselor and even AA meetings. She could only do her small part and leave the rest to God. That's where she found peace—realizing she didn't have to do—couldn't do—God's job.

The rest of the group slowly gathered. Morris and Linda smiled and waved.

"Get any sleep?" Linda left her bag with her husband and joined Star on the couch.

"A little. You?"

Linda yawned and shook her head. "Still adjusting, but I'll run on anticipation of all the sights today. First stop is the Cliffs of Moher."

"Oh, cool!" Star bobbed her head. "I'm bubbling over inside."

"If you consider that job we discussed for our nonprofit, you could go on some of the mission trips with us. See more of the world."

The couple had explained their organization and said something like you should come work for us, but Star figured people said things like that without actually meaning them all the time. "You were serious?"

"My receptionist's husband is being transferred. You could take her job."

Linda was nice and all, but there was no way they really wanted someone like her for an office job at a Christian organization. "I didn't finish high school and—"

"Look at Queen Shining Star tempting the lads with her festive jumper." Colin's deep, Irish voice interrupted, and he pointed her way. "They'd no doubt be happy to oblige a kiss."

Paul and Mrs. Kelly stood behind Colin, and Paul made a silly face of disgust at the back of the guide's head.

A laugh spilled from Star at the gesture. What a goof. "You're not going to keep calling me queen, are you? That's over."

"Fine." Colin winked. "I'll wager you prefer Princess Shining Star, anyway."

Warmth flooded her. "I've never been a princess, so…"

He offered a hand to Linda to help her up, and then to Star. "You are indeed royalty, and I won't let you forget it." He held her hand and her gaze for an intense second.

She couldn't stop a smile. He was kind of cute, plus the adorable accent. Light blue eyes and dark hair. Nothing like Brad Pitt, but attractive. "Thanks."

They boarded the bus, and people drifted to the same seats they'd taken the day before as if those were now their assigned places. Star hesitated before stopping at Paul's row. "Is it okay if…?"

"Of course, princess." His tone was playful.

"Shut up." She plopped down with a scoff.

"Yes, your majesty."

She slid a glance his way, much too aware of their shoulders touching. "Still not cool."

"Only Colin Pitt can flirt with you?"

"No. I mean… You know what I mean." She nudged him with her elbow.

"Ow. That thing's sharp." He made a production of rubbing his arm.

The bus motor started, and Colin announced the buddy check. Star and Paul waved at Will and Morris.

Once everyone had been accounted for, they rode out of

Ennis and into the Irish countryside of misty, rolling green hills. White farmhouses and sheep dotted the terrain.

Star pointed out the window. "Aww, I really want to hold a baby lamb."

"Ask Colin Pitt. I'm sure he'll make it happen for you, princess."

"Don't make me elbow you again, Perky." Star craned her neck for a better view. "It's so strange to be on this side of the road."

"You get used to it." The corners of his lips lifted into a smile that traveled up to his hazel eyes.

She could get used to that. His face took on a whole different persona when he let go of that chip on his shoulder.

"You want to trade seats?"

"I'll wait until next time." She shook her head. They'd have plenty of bus rides over the next two weeks. Would they sit together every time? So not what she'd pictured when she and Mrs. Kelly left St. Simons.

A few miles passed with only the murmur of conversations surrounding them, so Star pulled out a book.

Paul took immediate notice. "C.S. Lewis again?"

"Daily Reflection."

"Never heard of it."

"AA daily readings." She quirked a brow.

"Oh." His mouth formed a circle, and his gaze fell.

"Sorry if it's awkward for you."

"It's not awkward for me if it's not for you." He glanced back up at her. "Helpful?"

"They're short readings, and they keep me focused—grounded."

"Hmm." He nodded. "I heard you say you didn't finish school. How did you…? What hap—?" He held up one hand.

"Nothing."

Why was he curious? To make a stronger case for getting rid of her? Didn't matter. She was finished working for Mrs. Kelly, anyway. "I ran away when Mom died. My sister was leaving for college, and there was no way I'd stay with my psycho stepdad or go into a foster home. The alcohol and drugs dulled the stuff I couldn't handle emotionally."

The memories of that last day with her family slashed through Star like a serrated blade, tearing away the thick scars over her heart. Skye's screams when she found their mother. Her stepfather's curses. That dark, oppressive evil swirling in the house, thick enough to suffocate her. Emotion clutched Star's throat in a stranglehold and brought fresh tears to swim in her vision. That old anger and panic rose up in an icy wave, the nightmare that sent her looking to find relief in all the wrong places. She fisted her hands.

God, help me forget.

"I'm sorry." Hesitantly, Paul's palm covered hers, his touch gentle and warm. "I shouldn't have asked."

She glanced at him, and his eyes opened wide, the light filtering through the bus windows lighting up the amber flecks in the center of the green background.

He nodded, then squeezed her hand before letting go, allowing her the space to collect herself. They traveled the rest of the miles quietly until the bus made a turn, and the churning sea came into view. Waves crashed onto a rocky beach, so different from the level southern coastlines where she'd grown up.

"Are we here?" Excitement quivered in Star's voice.

Paul gave her a warm smile. "Close. Of course, a misting rain would start."

"It could be worse, Perky Paul." She nudged him with her

elbow, careful to be a bit gentler. "You need to live up to your title."

"Why?" He let his head fall back. "Of all the nicknames, why did you pick that one?"

"It was better than the others that came to mind." She couldn't help but laugh.

"Like what?" He huffed.

"Prickly Paul, Proud Paul, Pushy Paul. Maybe Perfectionist Paul."

"Is that what you think of me?" His brows pinched as if she'd hurt his feelings.

The man was a bit sensitive. "At least it wasn't Psychotic Paul or Putrid Paul."

"Oh, well, there's that." Another huff.

She didn't seem to be making things better. "I didn't have long to think, and when we first met..." No, going there wouldn't help either. "How about Prince Paul? You can be royalty too." She gave him her best smile, hoping to make up for insulting him. And she didn't like seeing that sad-puppy look in his eyes.

"I'll stick with Perky." His lips twitched to a half-smile, and he rubbed his forehead.

"Headache?"

"Yeah. I've been getting them a lot." He shrugged. "Just stress."

"One of my roommates was a massage therapist. I learned a few things from her that I've used during Pilates class cooldowns. If you turn the other way, I can give it a quick try."

His gaze bounced around the bus before submitting, as if she was going to stab him in the back or something. "Should I take off my jacket?"

"Yeah, and then close your eyes." Once he removed the

coat, she lifted her hands to the base of his skull, doing her best to ignore how nice his hair felt against her fingers. She pressed upward with her thumbs, applying pressure, then making small circles. Gradually she made her way down his neck, trying desperately to squelch the strange, toasty feelings expanding in her chest.

"Oh, you have the touch." Paul groaned. "I might never move again."

She had to laugh as he seemed to melt into a puddle before her. She reached his shoulders, her hands wearied, working out one knot after another. "Good grief. Are you always tense like this?"

"Only the last several years." His voice was breathy, barely audible.

"You need to get a different job or have weekly physical therapy. You're one giant knot."

"Lost my job."

"What?" Star froze.

Paul sat up straight and turned around. He pulled his arms back into his jacket. "Nothing."

"You lost your job? Because of this trip?" When he'd said his boss wouldn't let him off, she thought he'd been exaggerating. Of course, some of her employers over the years had been doozies too. Maybe she shouldn't be surprised.

"We're here." Face scrunched into a scowl, he motioned with his head toward the front of the bus. "Do *not* tell my mother."

And Prickly Paul was back.

Chapter 24

Why had he told Star about losing his job?

Paul stomped off the bus into the parking lot where the damp wind whipped up from the nearby Atlantic.

He could kick himself. She'd had him so relaxed, he'd melted into a soppy bumbling idiot. Heat sizzled through him at the thought of her touch.

Okay, that part had been kind of nice.

Really nice. And his head didn't hurt anymore.

Entirely frustrating.

Catching up with his mother, he placed his hand behind her elbow, anxiety thrashing in his chest. Her slow movements looked painful, she smelled of liniment, and she wore her arthritis compression gloves she normally preferred not to put on in public. "The asphalt's smooth here, but it's going to be slick and bumpy ahead, plus that's a steep walk in front of us." His gaze rose to the uphill path toward the cliff's edge, and his voice held a warning with the hope she'd change her mind.

"I'll be careful, but I'm going to see the cliffs. That's why I came." Mom took sluggish but deliberate steps down the slate walkway. She kept her gaze on the ground ahead until they reached a series of steps, then she looked up and out as the rugged cliffs came into view. They towered over cresting waves and against the low hanging clouds misting them.

"Oh," Mom gasped. "Bless you, Lord. It's so majestic." Her voice cracked. "I wish your dad were with us." She turned and patted Paul's cheeks, tears filling both their eyes. "But you're here, my sweet boy."

"Aww, Mom." His throat thick, Paul struggled for words. "I wish he could be here too."

"His grandfather, Paul Kelly, your namesake, proposed to Grandma Kelly somewhere in this area before they left for America. Your father wanted to bring me on an anniversary trip, but we put it off too long." Mom motioned toward the path of at least a hundred steps leading to the ledge of the cliff.

"I didn't know. Did my great grandparents live close by?" Maybe he'd heard the story of his ancestors growing up, but such things didn't interest young boys.

"Yes, near Galway. The country had such hard economic times during the famine and for years afterward."

"He might've proposed down at this level to save his future bride from falling to her death." Would Mom get his point?

She dropped one hand to her hip. "I'm going up there if I have to crawl."

"Wow." Star approached with Colin close at her side. Too close for Paul's taste. "I never in my life imagined such breathtaking beauty. God is an amazing artist."

Her complexion practically glowed, and her eyes shone. Seeing the cliffs through Star's earnest gaze brought a smile to Paul, despite the anxiety welling inside him. She was so full of life. And fire.

And blind faith…

Yearning rose up in Paul, and a picture formed in his mind—tenderly holding her close as she took in the view, brushing her long, shiny hair away from her neck, placing his lips against her cheek—

No. No. No. Not okay. He refused to go down that rat-crazy path.

He shook the image away. The story Mom had told him

about his great grandparents was messing with his head. That and the lack of good sleep.

The wind whipped to almost gale force, and Mom leaned close. Plowing forward, she pulled him along. "Let's get up there before a hard rain blows in."

As they began to climb the stairs, he blew out a frustrated breath. "Okay." He threw a glance back toward Colin. "You can go around us. We'll be taking it slow."

"Princess Shining Star and I will watch your back," Colin volunteered.

Annoyance churned in Paul's gut, and a loud rumble accompanied it. What was the deal with this guy?

And with his own stomach?

"I wish my mammy were here. I miss her dearly." Colin prattled on behind them.

"I'm sorry for your loss." Star's voice was barely audible in the wind.

"She's not dead, my pet. She and my da are living in London now."

My pet, my foot. Paul grunted under his breath.

Ten minutes and at least fifty harrowing steps later, they arrived at the top of the trail.

"Let me sit a minute to catch my breath." Mom eased onto a bench before even peering from the overlook. "Go ahead, then come back for me."

"I can sit with you," Star offered.

"Don't you dare." Mom waved them off. "I'll only be a minute, and I can see a bit from here."

"Not really," Paul grumbled. There were rows of people standing at the concrete guard fence.

Hesitantly, Star nodded and moved toward the ledge, saying something Paul couldn't make out.

Colin stayed at her side, laughing loudly. "You're such a gas, Princess Star. I'll catch up with you in a second." He took off down another path.

Whatever she'd said couldn't be that funny, could it? And didn't Colin have other tour members to giggle with?

The wind thrashed at Star's hair, and she struggled to keep it out of her face, which still possessed that sheen of wonder as she looked out at the majestic cliffs. Finally, she pulled a ponytail holder from her pocket and twisted the light brown strands up into a knot. Paul couldn't seem to pull his gaze away.

"A beautiful sight, indeed." Morris approached, his limp more obvious than the day before. "Both of the sights."

A haze in his brain lifted. "Both?"

"Your *mother's friend* and the cliffs." A sheepish grin covered Morris's face. "You seem to be more captivated by stars than heights."

Paul's face flushed. "She's in the way."

"That sounds like the wisdom of a much younger man." Morris's brows raised.

Paul's jaw tensed at the jab. Morris had no idea what he was talking about. "The tour guide is the one who seems to be head over heels for her."

"Maybe he knows a good woman when he sees one."

Star pivoted to look back over her shoulder, and her gaze collided with Paul's. A rush of warmth poured over him.

This is now bone of my bones and flesh of my flesh.

Not another Bible verse. Paul mashed his palm over his eyes, hoping no one could hear his thoughts.

"You okay?" Morris asked. "I was just observing. Didn't mean to upset you."

"I'm fine."

Around him, tourists snapped picture after picture of the

view. He might as well go join the throng. He made his way around them to look over the wall.

Morris followed and gasped, then blew out a low whistle. "For since the creation of the world God's invisible qualities — his eternal power and divine nature — have been clearly seen, being understood from what has been made, so that people are without excuse." He quoted the verse from Romans.

Not him too. Paul held in a groan. It was bad enough that his own brain was pumping verses out.

A light touch on his elbow turned Paul's head.

"I can't get enough pictures with my phone, it's so overwhelming," Star spoke above the wind's howl, her cheeks pink from the cold gusts. "Isn't it beautiful?"

Her eyes shouldn't draw him in the way they did. Shouldn't strike a match in his heart, igniting a blaze like a raging forest fire. Shouldn't rouse emotions he'd never imagined he'd have for a woman.

He tore his attention back to the waves crashing against the base of the soaring heights, the beauty even more staggering than he'd imagined. "It took millions of years and enormous force to create such erosion."

"That's what you see, Perky Paul? Erosion?" Her arms folded with a dramatic flair, but a smile lifted her lips, and her voice teased.

"Perhaps a catastrophic, earth-covering flood carved out these walls of splendor." Will's grandfather spoke from Paul's right. He and Will steadied Mom on either side as she reached the edge, her countenance invigorated despite the tedious walk up. "Perhaps the flood where only Noah and his family survived in the ark God designed."

Even him? If there was a God, He was enjoying a big laugh surrounding Paul with Christians to aggravate him.

But there wasn't, so the congregation of believers had to be a coincidence.

Right?

Doubt squirmed in Paul's midsection, but he smashed it down like a pesky insect. "Are you feeling better, Mom?"

"I am." She grinned. "And I want a picture of us. Will's agreed to take one with my phone." She let go of her cane and held out a hand to Paul. "Me and you, then me, you, and Star."

Star waved them off. "I don't need to be in your picture."

"Smile." Mom wrapped her arm around him, and Will stood on the bench she'd vacated for a better shot.

"Cheeseburger—" Paul stopped himself. The last thing he wanted to do was remind Mom that her husband was gone.

"In paradise," Mom's voice sang back as if she hadn't a care in the world.

Will snapped several pictures, then Mom motioned for Star. "I insist you join me, my princess friend."

Paul shifted his weight from foot to foot as Star wrapped an arm around his waist and stood close. A clean scent touched his nose like soap and fresh flowers.

Just shampoo from the hotel. Nothing to get all hot and bothered over like a preteen doofus.

Mom stepped away. "Take a few more of just the young people without an oldie messing it up."

Whipping his head toward his mother, Paul shook his head. "Aren't you Pretty Priscilla? You couldn't mess it up."

She grinned, and Will snapped more photos, so Paul turned back and pressed on a smile. Once they finished the photoshoot, they all stood quietly, taking in the scene. A nice bit of inspiration. A peaceful beauty. If only they didn't have to make it back down the mammoth hill.

Once the group had traversed various overlooks and up to

see O'Brien's Tower nearby, they started the downward trek. A cluster of teens ran the sidewalks, boisterous and careless. Worry churned in Paul. One reckless boy could kill a person in a place like this.

A few steps ahead, Star narrowed her eyes and scowled at the kids as they neared. "Slow down!"

At least her fire-breathing dragon skills proved useful for something.

One of the boys nabbed a girl's scarf and took off running with it—straight toward them, the kid's eyes locked only on the protesting female.

"Stop." Looking fierce, Star planted her feet, spread her arms, and set up her body as a shield.

"Look out!" Paul tensed, torn between keeping his mother standing and protecting Star from impact.

The crunch of the two bodies hitting the ground rivaled the sound of the bone-jarring tackles on an NFL football game. Star had to be hurt.

~~~

A torrent of excruciating pain blasted through Star's shoulder and down her arm. She knew this agony. Her shoulder had been dislocated a number of times growing up with her stepfather and that one time with Vince before Blake had kicked his behind.

Her mind knew how to put the shoulder back in place, and that the action would lessen the riveting waves of pain, but she also knew the tactic would be momentarily unbearable.

"Star, how can I help you?"

She forced her eyes open to find Paul hovering over her. And the teen scrambling back to his friends.

Had Paul left his mother alone? Turning her head, she tried to focus and spot Mrs. Kelly. "Your mom?"

"She's fine. Will and his grandfather are helping her down."

She let out a shaky breath. "Grab my right wrist, then slowly, but firmly, pull until my shoulder is back in place. I'll say when to stop." Or scream it.

"I can't do that. You need a doctor."

"Please," she groaned. "This has happened before." Back then, she'd taken something to numb it, though.

"But—"

"Just do it, or find someone who will." Moisture blurred her vision, but she felt Paul's fingers circle her wrist.

"Slow and firm, pull toward you." Her face was wet with both tears and perspiration as she braced herself for the pain to come. "Go."

He did as she asked, and she bit back a scream until her socket rested in the right place. "Stop." She heaved a breath. The pain diminished but wouldn't disappear for days, maybe weeks. And she'd need a sling. No drugs though.

And what about her job at the gym? They wouldn't want her now either. Nobody would.

Chapter 25

Three and a half excruciating hours later, the ride finally ended in the little town of Dingle. "Go help your mother." Star shooed Paul down the aisle of the bus. "I'll be along soon."

Star had gotten Paul to bind her jacket around her to keep her arm immobile, but the curvy roads still jostled, sending shockwaves of pain pulsing through her shoulder. Sitting by the window had helped since she could brace against the wall. The rest of the passengers exited, but she took her time. No use rushing to grab her bag and lug it into the hotel.

Once the bus emptied, she trudged down the steps to the sidewalk. Mrs. Kelly and Paul stood with her suitcase. Colin joined them. The group looked ready to gang up on her.

"Star, there's a doctors' surgery only four blocks away." Colin motioned toward the village's cobbled streets. "You should get checked out."

"Surgery?" There was no way anyone was cutting on her.

Paul raised a palm. "That's what they call the medical clinic."

It made no sense, but anyway, she wasn't going. "I don't need a doctor. This has happened before."

"Sweetie." Mrs. Kelly stepped close and lowered her voice. "I bought travel insurance, so it will all be paid for. I can text the information to file a claim. Please, let Paul take you to get checked out. So I'll feel better."

Star hated to upset Mrs. Kelly. "Fine. I'll go, but I don't need help." Her gaze darted to Paul and back.

"I can take—" Colin started.

"I insist." Paul stepped in front of the guide and rolled Star's suitcase over to him. "If our devoted leader will assist me in getting your things to your room and my mother settled in, I'll be back in five minutes, then we'll go."

It seemed there was no getting rid of Paul Kelly.

Two hours later, in a small exam room, a short, thin physiotherapist with an easy smile and graying blond hair introduced himself as Mr. Byrne. "I guess you're not too lucky in Ireland today, lass."

She couldn't even muster a smile. "My shoulder's popped out before. I'll be fine." This was all a colossal waste of time and money. Plus he might offer her something for the pain. As bad as it hurt, she didn't need to go down that black hole again.

"A lovely thought, but"—he looked at her over his wire-rimmed glasses—"since you're in my exam room, how about I take a gander?"

Paul bobbed his head from his seat in the corner. Why he'd followed her into the room, she had no clue, but it had been nice to have a little company during the wait.

A sigh escaped Star's lips. "Whatever."

"Anything below your festive jumper?" the doctor asked.

"Do what?" Star's mouth fell open. Maybe Paul being here was a good thing.

The doctor chuckled. "Don't think me a beast. I mean only to look at your shoulder, and your jumper is rather bulky."

"I'm wearing a cami." Star glanced at Paul.

Blushing, he stood, which was sort of cute, seeing him embarrassed. "I can leave."

"No need, if I'm only taking off the top layer." A smirk pulled at the corners of her mouth.

Paul slowly sat back down and stared at the floor.

"Allow me to assist you." The doctor helped her pull one arm from her sleeve. The other came out with a wince.

She sat in the cotton camisole, shivering as he began his exam, earning a sharp intake of breath. But she refused to cry. She'd been through much worse.

"I'd like to take an X-ray." The doctor continued his inspection down to her fingers.

"Of my shoulder?"

"Yes, and your arm. There's bruising and swelling."

"I don't know." She hadn't noticed her forearm being tender with the sharp shoulder pain, but it did look blue in the middle.

"It'll take five minutes. The aide will take you down the hall."

"You're here, Star." Paul tilted his head. "You may as well do it."

And this situation kept getting worse. A broken arm would mean a cast, which would put her out of exercise classes for six weeks. It'd knock her out of any kind of physical job, even waitressing. How was she going to make ends meet?

~~~

Paul looked both ways down the clinic hallway, seeing no one, but there had to be a men's room somewhere nearby. They'd been here a while now. He passed three closed doors until he found the one. Down the hall, voices caught his attention, and he halted.

"Lass, if you need help, I can get you somewhere safe," the doctor's voice.

"What?" Star sounded baffled.

"Your X-ray shows you've injured this arm a number of times. Old fractures healed over. Plus, the burn scars on your back. If your man is hurting you—"

"You've got it all wrong. I just met Paul recently. He's my employer's son. Those injuries are from when I was a kid. My stepfather."

"Ack. It sickens me that some men behave like animals."

"I figured out a way to put a stop to all that."

"Good. And you've soldiered on to become a decent young woman, I'm sure. We'll go back to the room, then."

Paul slid into the restroom, nausea creeping over him. He'd noticed the scars at the top of her back where the undershirt dipped, but he'd assumed they were acne pockmarks or something. When Star said her stepfather was a monster, she hadn't been exaggerating. He'd seen cruelty in Africa, but no place was immune to the evil in people's hearts.

How was a little girl supposed to defend herself against a grown man? Fury rose inside him and a fierce desire to protect Star from further pain. Sure, she wasn't his responsibility, but she'd be losing her job with his mother because of him, and she'd turned out to be a more decent person than he'd expected.

After all, she'd shielded Mom with her own body.

Minutes later, he traversed the hall again and found Star wearing the weird sweater again, along with a sling, exiting the exam room.

"Happy now?" She pretended to scowl, her nose scrunching in the most adorable way.

"Not happy, but I want you to get better. Is your arm broken?"

"No. Thank God." Her eyes narrowed. "Where'd you disappear to?"

"I needed to see a man about a horse."

"Good grief, how old are you, Perky Paul?"

"Old enough to know what's good for you." He gave her

a teasing smile.

The doctor followed her out, his serious expression catching Paul. "Take care of the lass."

"I will." He'd do his best anyway, even if he had to battle that strong will of hers. They continued to the checkout desk. "What's the diagnosis?"

"My arm has a deep bruise."

"The shoulder?"

She blew out a long breath. "He thinks I'll need surgery to repair it, but it'll be fine. It's gotten well on its own before."

Probably because no one cared enough to take her to the doctor. No one had protected Star. No one had been there for her. The realization seared through him. He'd love to take a blow torch to the man who'd beaten and burned her...see how the guy liked it.

"All finished checking out." Star's cheerful voice broke into his furious thoughts. "We can go back now and make it in time for the boat ride. See more of God's creation."

His jaw ground as he tried to compose himself. He would figure out a way to set things right for his mother. And for Star. Life hadn't been fair to him, but it had been particularly brutal to her. How in the world could she still believe in God?

Chapter 26

"More cliffs. So amazing." Star peered over the boat railing and took in the dramatic view. Stark, stony peaks dotted with green rose from the Atlantic. The briny smell of the sea enveloped her. "I'd love to visit one of those islands poking out under the clouds. I think the captain called them the Blasket Islands?"

"They're interesting, but aren't you dying to see Fungi, the celebrity dolphin?" Resting his chin on his fist, Paul studied her, his hazel eyes quickening her pulse.

"I grew up around the Gulf of Mexico, so I've seen plenty of dolphins." She made a broad sweep with her good arm. "This landscape is different from what I've known."

The boat glided gently along the sheltered bay, but the chilly wind swirled around them, sending a shiver through her.

"Your fingers are turning white." Paul straightened and put a hand over hers. "Scoot closer before you freeze."

Moving nearer to him, she allowed herself to lean into Paul's warmth, which felt particularly nice. Too nice. She shouldn't be having all this warm-gooey emotion over him. There was no place those feelings should or could go. The two of them were traveling different paths, plus the man sparked her unstable temper like nitro in a blender.

Yet, he'd invited, and she was cold. And being tucked close to him felt right somehow. The gusts picked up, rocking the boat as dark, angry clouds rolled onto the horizon. Waves crashed against the distant islands.

"I'm glad the captain had your mom sit up front."

"Me too. She's still sniffling and coughing. With this weathe. I'm scared she'll get pneumonia." His brows scrunched together.

Maybe he was thinking of how he'd lost his father to such an illness. Paul seemed to really care about his parents, despite her first impressions about him.

Star groaned. "If I'd had my wits about me, I would've insisted your mom go to the doctor too. I wasn't thinking."

"I should've thought of it." Paul shook his head. "At least she rested while we were gone, and now I know where to take her if she needs to go tomorrow."

Star glanced at the sling across her other shoulder. "A lot of help I'll be in this thing."

"But you have been." His grip on her hand tightened. "Good grief, you took a tackle for her, Star. I hate to think what condition she'd be in if you hadn't been close."

"I meant to block him, but my stance was off." If only she'd gotten the teen's attention.

"You were on the side of a cliff, Ms. NFL." His gaze locked on hers, flashing earnestness and maybe something more. "I'm thankful for you, and I realize how much you've been helping Mom this past year. The cooking and cleaning, the painting— yardwork even. I can't thank you enough." His gaze dropped and seemed to zoom to the vicinity of her lips.

Star's breathing stalled as her own gaze mimicked his, lowering, taking in the slope of his nose, the nice curve of his lips, a small scar she hadn't noticed on his chin. And back to his lips. A current zapped through her like lightning spearing a tree in a thunderstorm. What was happening to her?

Paul leaned closer. "Star, I—" The boat dipped into a large swell, and Paul grasped his stomach. "Oh, no."

"What's wrong?"

"I forgot to put on my Sea-Bands." His face paled, and he swallowed hard.

"Motion sickness?"

"Seasick." He pressed one hand over his mouth. "Happens every time. I don't know where my head was."

"But you fly planes for a liv—"

"That's different." He slipped away from her and scrambled up. "I need to get to the railing."

An instant later, he hurled over the side of the boat. At least they'd sat in the back. Star made her way to a crew member for help. The best they could offer was a motion sickness pill, water, and paper towels. Probably too late for that now.

Returning to Paul's side, Star handed him a paper towel, then wet another and pressed it against the back of his neck.

The captain's voice sounded through a nearby speaker. "We're turning back to harbor. There's a squall heading our way."

Paul groaned as they dipped into another swell.

"We'll be on land soon." She tried to sound confident. She sure hoped they would. She'd been around bodies of water her whole life, and that thundercloud raging toward them could be bad news.

~~~

"Sorry." Paul pressed his eyes shut before another round of sickness overtook him.

"You can't help it." Star's light touch against his neck was soothing. "Just hang on. We're almost back to the dock."

He couldn't be more humiliated. One minute he'd been in some weird trance, only inches from Star's lips, and the next, he was emptying his guts into the Atlantic. She had to think he was quite the loser. How many pilots did he know who couldn't be a passenger on a boat without losing their lunch? Zero.

After what seemed like a half-century of water torture later, his feet plonked onto the sidewalk. Wet with the pouring rain, but still solid land. "Terra firma at last. Where's Mom?"

"Colin's escorting her. He has an umbrella, and I asked him to hire a cab or something to take us back to the hotel. You gonna make it?" Star stayed at his side, checking on him when he should be making sure she and Mom didn't fall down on some slippery surface.

"I'll be fine. Soon." Except his stomach still quivered like a jellyfish on a windy beach.

"The schedule said our evening is free, so you can take it easy."

"You should too."

"We all will. We'll change clothes and maybe find a toasty fire in the hotel lobby…"

Despite his queasiness, the picture she painted warmed him as they fought their way through the downpour to the waiting car. Inside the vehicle, water dripped from every molecule of exposed skin and clothing.

"Did you at least see Fungi before the foul weather gave you a fright?" The driver glanced at them from the rearview mirror.

"I did." His mother nodded and twisted toward them. "But I was nice and dry in the captain's bridge, not soggy and cold in the back of the boat like these poor babies. I'm so sorry, y'all."

"Mom, you can't control the weather." Of course, they wouldn't have almost drowned while looking for a sea mammal, if she hadn't insisted on going on this trip. They had plenty of dolphins at home in St. Simons.

Love is patient, love is kind.

Not that again. Paul clamped his jaws together to keep from spouting out something inappropriate.

"I enjoyed the scenery. It's beautiful here." Star smiled at Mom. When Mom turned forward again, Star whispered and patted his leg. "We're almost there. I'll find you something dry to wear."

Oh, right. The limited wardrobe. He wasn't about to put on those shiny shorts. He'd rather make a kilt from a towel than don those ridiculous items again.

The driver looked their way. "You'll have a wash and a pint, and you'll be up to a bit of dinner and dancing at the pub before you know it."

Doubtful. Paul grimaced. The thought of beer sent another round of nausea through him. And food. He couldn't even...

Usually, his seasickness wore off pretty quickly. Unless... A vision of the little retching Sean from the airplane flashed through Paul's mind.

He better not have a nasty stomach bug.

Chapter 27

The cold tile floor of the hotel bathroom nudged Paul awake. Daylight streamed in from a window somewhere in the bedroom he hadn't really slept in. A decent bathroom, though. Until he'd arrived anyway.

The night had been long and miserable. A night so bad, he'd even appreciated the disco shorts as an alternative outfit at some point. At least the hotel had found him a reservation of his own, so maybe Mom wouldn't be overly exposed to the stomach virus he'd caught on the plane.

"Morning. How are you?" Star's voice crooned low and sweet, soothing the lingering nausea.

"An Irish Montezuma tried to kill me, but sadly I didn't die." Paul raised his head to find her leaning against the bathroom doorjamb, a post where she'd kept watch over him most of the hours since the return from the wretched boat trip in the monsoon. Despite her own shoulder pain, she'd insisted on tending to him, an act of compassion that had again challenged his first impressions of her.

"Your color looks better." She studied his face, then wet another washcloth and offered it to him.

He sat up, took the rag, and pressed it against his forehead. His stomach still felt as though it had been in the spin cycle all night, but finally, the rotating had stopped. "I think I'm going to live. Maybe even eat. Someday."

She knelt on the floor beside him, struggling with her sling to pour a cup of a sports drink. "Try some sips of this first,

Perky."

A smirk lifted the corners of her mouth. A cute smirk. Cute lips, too, actually. If only he could go back to that moment before he'd debased himself in front of her. There was no way she'd find him the least bit attractive after this demonstration of foulness. Not that he should want her to.

"You're good at caring for people. You should be a nurse. Or a doctor." He didn't want to sound sexist, after all.

"I've just taken care of a lot of drunk or messed up friends. And without graduating high school,"— her gaze dropped— "I don't think higher education is in my future."

"Hey." Paul lifted her chin with a nudge of his thumb. "I have full confidence you possess the tenacity to accomplish anything you set your mind to."

"For real?" Her eyes widened and coated with a sheen as they met his, a hint of sadness there.

Were those tears? "I'm positive." Something about this girl, her vulnerability beneath the fierce exterior, carved deep into his heart, his soul even.

Wait. When did he start thinking he had a soul again? He knew better. These mushy feelings were only hormones and nature and evolutionary genetics, right?

Of course, that was all. He'd been needy, she'd been there for him, and his natural instincts kicked in. "I desperately require a shower." He dropped his hand and worked himself to a standing position. Weakness swarmed him, but he managed not to sway.

"Are you sure? I'd hate for you to fall and hit your head. Maybe Morris or Colin—"

"No way." Definitely not Colin. Talk about a nauseating idea. "I can sit in the shower if it makes you less anxious."

"I don't know. Maybe if you promise to sip this drink

first."

"Your wish is my command."

She still looked hesitant to leave. Of course, the idea of her staying while he showered didn't repulse him. At all. The thought niggled in his mind. That would be nice. Better than nice.

Rather, clothe yourselves with the Lord Jesus Christ, and do not think about how to gratify the desires of the flesh.

What lunacy was overtaking him? He didn't even remember that Scripture being in the Bible. Where was it? The verse had to be in one of the epistles. Paul's letter to the Romans, maybe?

Didn't matter.

He shooed her toward the door. "Go rest or eat or something." While he regained his mind and manhood. "You've got to be exhausted and tired of me."

"Tired, but not of you." She pushed to her feet, too, and met his gaze. "I'll go change and find you something to wear in a gift shop. You can't get rid of Star Youngblood that easily."

"Good." Because suddenly, getting rid of her seemed like the last thing he wanted to do. Maybe she could stay in Mom's life—and his—without working for them. The idea oddly satisfied him. Surely they could help her find employment wherever he and Mom landed...after he found a new job himself.

Once she left, Paul turned and stared at his bleary-eyed face in the mirror. It was strange how his life had upended in such a short amount of time. Even though his body, plans, and belongings seemed to be up in flames, he was beginning to feel freer and more content than he had in London. He'd despised his boss, lived alone, and most nights ended up with a tension headache. Surely he could find something else, closer to Mom.

Not for as much money, but he'd be happier. Losing his job could be the best thing that ever happened. He glanced down at his damp T-shirt and the shiny shorts. He couldn't say the same thing about losing his suitcase.

~~~

Star tapped on Paul's hotel room door. She'd cleaned up as fast as she could and caught a ride to the closest clothing store, but it had been nothing like she'd expected and very expensive. She liked Paul—a lot more than when they'd first met—but she didn't have the kind of cash designer clothes required. The cheapest thing she'd found was a thirty dollar T-shirt that looked like it was supposed to be Star Wars-themed, but the writing was in Gaelic maybe, and the images were strange gray birds, one wearing a helmet.

Whatever. It was clean.

The door swung open, and Paul appeared, wearing a plush white hotel bathrobe, his hair still damp and curling up a little on his forehead. Cute. The smell of soap and clean linen drifted from him. More than cute.

Very attractive. Her midsection fluttered at the realization.

No way. Being attracted to Paul would be a definite crash and burn mistake. But yet…

He waited as though she were there to tell him something.

"You look better," she managed.

"Can't imagine worse."

She'd seen much worse—been much worse—but she wouldn't go into those old stories. His gaze held hers, smiling and warm. She stood there, face growing hot, but held in place, absorbing those flecks of green amid brown swirls. She could get lost in these eyes.

"Hey, sweeties." From down the hall, Mrs. Kelly's voice burst into Star's trance. "How is everyone this morning?"

"Better." Paul smiled at his mom. "Star is a *stellar* nurse."

Mrs. Kelly's laughter tinkled like the costume bracelet she often wore. A happy sound. "Silly, Paul." She turned her attention to Star.

"I'm good." Shuffling her feet, Star remembered to offer Paul the package she'd brought. "Here's a shirt."

His brows lifted as he chuckled. "What beastly treasure have you found now?" The bag crinkled as he dug into it.

"It's nothing. Just clean, and it was less—"

"How cool!" A huge grin lifted his cheeks, brightened his whole face. "Mom told you I'm a Star Wars geek?"

"Nope." She shook her head. "Just a happy coincidence, I guess. Of course, I had noticed you seemed to enjoy warring with me."

He eyed her. "It *is* fun Star warring, and maybe this is a sign. My luck is changing."

Mrs. Kelly clapped her hands together. "Not luck. It's because I've been praying hard for you. Do you feel up to going on the tours today?"

At that, Paul's grin faltered. "What are they?"

Mrs. Kelly pulled a printed paper from her purse. "A crystal cutting demonstration, lunch at a seafood restaurant, and"—she glanced at Star before continuing—"a tour of a distillery with a tasting, but we can stay here since both of you are under the weather."

"It'll be okay. I can handle it." Star lifted her good shoulder. "You shouldn't miss your tour because of me."

"I'd like to take a pass. Seafood and whiskey aren't on my stomach's to-smell list today." The expression on his face said just imagining the scent brought up a bad taste.

"What if I go without y'all?" Mrs. Kelly gave them a hesitant smile.

"No." Paul and Star spoke in unison.

"Yes." Mrs. Kelly pushed a fist to her hip. "Stop babying me. I'm a grown woman, and I can handle this. Besides, Bradford told me last night he'd be happy to escort me if y'all weren't up to it."

"Who?" Paul's brows were so tightly knit they could have switched places.

"Bradford Palmer." His mother huffed as if he'd spoken another language. "Will's grandfather. He's a very nice, Christian man. Attractive too."

"Oooh." Realization poured over Star. She'd noticed Mrs. Kelly and Mr. Palmer chatting. A lot. But she hadn't considered they might be… flirting?

Confusion cluttered Paul's expression. He opened his mouth, closed it, and repeated the action. Twice.

Star couldn't help but feel sorry for him. Knowing his mother might be attracted to a new man after all this time had to be freaking him out. Her muscles tensed, and fear for Mrs. Kelly's wellbeing kicked up. Would Paul blow up like her stepfather or Vince? Both men could put on a good show in front of others, but out of the public eye…

"There's a nice patio on the back of the hotel with tables." Star motioned with her head down the hall. "Great view of the bay. The sun's shining, the temperature's not bad. We could sit out there awhile, chill and relax."

His gaze bounced between her and his mom. Finally, he shook his head as if to clear the fog in his mind. "Okay."

Star breathed a cautious sigh. A single quiet word, *okay*, and he hadn't thrown a fit. Would that be the end of it, or was pent-up emotion simmering below Paul Kelly's surface?

196

Chapter 28

"Are you sure you're up for a walk, Perky?" A stream of sunlight broke through a huge puffy white cloud over Dingle Bay, sending Star's hand to her forehead to shield her eyes.

"I'm healed. And rather perky, actually." Paul's grin competed with the brightness, and he took a step down the path that circled the edge of the water. The nap he'd taken must have been a good one.

"A miracle after your night."

"I wouldn't go that far." He held a hand out to her. "Keep up, Wonder Woman."

Her pulse did a little two-step as she took his hand. She should ignore the silly sensation.

If only she could.

They'd come outside earlier in the morning to sit on the patio, but he'd looked puny. Still, he'd shared wonderful stories of growing up with his parents. Stories of sunny days fishing with his dad, rescuing animals with his mother and father, the way they'd adored each other. What Star wouldn't have given to have that kind of childhood. Maybe those experiences explained why the blow of his father's death had sucked the faith from Paul.

She hated what he'd been through. If only Paul could believe what she'd learned this past year. That God's ways weren't her ways. There was a bigger picture. She'd like to talk about it with him, but something inside her said *not now*.

"The beaches are so rocky and strange." She motioned

toward the muck and sand exposed by the low tide. Odd-colored seaweed and barnacle-covered shells poked up amid the stones. "I wonder if I'd ruin my shoes tiptoeing out there to collect some treasure."

"Treasure?"

"That's what my sister, Skye, and I called it when we'd find cool stuff in nature." She cast a wary smile his way. Would he get it? "Sand dollars, all sorts of rocks, flowers, leaves. Skye knew the name of every single one." Star pointed to a spot below them, where a large shell perched on a smooth stone. "I only remember a few names, like that one's some variety of the scallop shell. And talk about rescuing animals. She would've given your dad a run for his money. Mamma called her Elly Mae Clampett, whoever that is. I called her the critter whisperer."

Paul chuckled. "She should be a veterinarian."

"Maybe she is." Star shrugged.

"You don't know?" He nailed her with a curious gaze.

"After she found Mamma... you know, that bad night, I left through a window and took off. I wasn't about to stay with my stepfather or go into foster care. I was only sixteen, but Skye was leaving for college the next week, had a scholarship. I heard she moved in with one of her teachers until she left. She had someplace to go."

"What about your mother's funeral?"

"Couldn't be there. They'd catch me." She swallowed back the bitter memories. "Mamma knew I cared. I tried to protect her and Skye the best I could. Which was obviously not enough. I caught a ride down the Gulf Coast to start over." She shrugged. "It didn't turn out like I'd hoped, but I called the shots at least."

"Protect them? You were a child." His entire face screwed

into a frown.

"Don't look so somber, Perky. I'm still standing, and now it's all joy."

He shook his head. "With your shoulder injury, you may not be able to work at the gym you wanted. Your job with my mom is… Your past. How can you have joy?"

"I'll heal, and I'll figure out what God has for me next. Me hurting my shoulder didn't throw Him for a loop."

"Didn't you ever talk to your sister again?"

Of course, he'd ignored the God comment. "I called her, at first, but a lot of times I was drunk or high, trying to drown out the nightmares of grief and anger seething inside me. I guess eventually she changed her number or decided not to answer. I gave up. Life went on. I don't blame her. She cured animals, not people. She never trusted human beings much. Neither of us did."

His expression softened, and his eyes held hers. "I've been on the other end of that bullet."

A laugh burst from somewhere deep within her chest. "I did rip you a new one a few times those first days." Her hand popped over her mouth. "I guess I shouldn't use that phrase anymore. It's crude, and I—"

"You had a boyfriend?"

The big change of subject gave her a bit of whiplash. "Several. Why?"

"You said the last one died?" His voice softened, and his head angled as he took her in.

"Blake. Nice guy. Except for being a heroin addict. Tried to protect me in his own way. Died of an overdose."

"I'm sorry. That had to be tough."

"It was, but by that time I was at Re-Claimed, and I had good support to get me through it."

"And they matched you up with Mom?"

"That was a total God-thing." She shook her head. "I'd been in the hospital because some sleazeball tried to... Well, let's just say he tried to get the best of me, but I gave him a run for his money even though I got stabbed a little in the process. Gabby didn't want me to work at the thrift store yet because of my injury. Right around that time, your mom asked my friend Rivers if she knew someone who could stay with her because you were on her back to move. Everything fell into place."

"You were in the hospital? Stabbed a little bit? What's that mean? Did they prosecute that scumbag?"

She shrugged. "Nah. I took some extra Xanax for the pain and passed out. I guess that's when Blake found me and carried me to get help."

"No one pressed charges?" He scoffed.

She waved him off. "A fight between druggies. Police wouldn't be too interested. Anyway, when he took off, he had a few injuries to deal with himself." She sucked in a gulp of air and released it. Why had she told him that? "Sorry. I was kinda...rough back then." What would Paul think of her now that he knew she was *that kind of girl?* Her gaze fell to the ground. "You probably think I'm trash or something worse."

~ ~ ~

This woman. Her heart, her sweetness beneath the hard exterior, the protectiveness. He took in her pretty features glowing in the bright sun—features that had seen too much pain, too much heartache. He couldn't tear his eyes away from her. Her hair, her lashes...her mouth.

Paul swallowed back the ache tightening his throat and closed the distance between them. "You..." He caressed her cheek. "You are not trash of any sort. Don't ever think that.

You are a shining Star, dazzling in a dark world."

Her gaze lifted, honey brown and stirring up that warm gushiness inside him. "Whoa." Her lips lifted into a sweet smile. "You really know how to sweet-talk a girl."

"I mean it." He held her gaze. "You can trust me."

Other than the sounds of waves, wind, and birds, a quiet stretched between them. At least on the outside. Inside Paul, a storm of emotions roared. A hunger to take her in his arms, to protect her, to tell her he'd never let anyone hurt her again. To kiss her.

Dumbest idea ever. She'd slap him sideways. Or the feelings would be unreciprocated, and the rest of this trip would be super awkward.

Yet, she still held his gaze. He could drown in those eyes. "Would you want to...?" What was he thinking? Saying? Something stupid, that's what. "Want to keep walking?"

"Sure." Her gaze turned to the path. "Sounds good." Was that a hint of disappointment in her tone?

Probably only wishful thinking.

~ ~ ~

"Would you mind if Bradford and I skip out on the concert at the pub?" Mom practically strutted down the hall of the hotel toward the lobby where he stood. She wore a red silk top with dangly silver earrings and a matching necklace, not a hair out of place, and full makeup on. She'd even changed out of her drab comfort shoes into a pair of red flats.

Paul hadn't seen her so dressed up in years. The whole situation weirded him out. His mother attracted to someone besides his dad? "It's fine. But you'll miss the free dinner."

"We walked a lot today. We thought we'd eat dinner here, then sit on the patio and talk."

The same way he and Star had spent most of the day.

201

Again, too weird. "What about Will?"

His mother gave him a pleading look. "He wants to go hear the music. If you and Star could keep an eye on him, we'd feel better about it."

"We'll do it." Star appeared from behind them, smiling, her eyes sparkling even more than usual. She wore a pale blue pullover sweater that looked soft to the touch. But he shouldn't go there. Her hair hung down past her shoulders, shiny and fresh, with a sweet fragrance drifting to him.

Another thing he shouldn't think about. Sinking his fingers into her hair. His gaze rose to her face. Not much makeup, but a little pink lip gloss. He couldn't help but wonder... *No. Stop. Don't go there either.*

"Your mom was sweet to buy me these earrings." Star's voice almost sang in his ears. "Don't you love them?"

A long piece of silver hung from each of her earlobes. At the ends, a silver star dangled near her slender neck. Oh man, he was in trouble. "They're perfect." Like Star.

From the sitting area, Linda called Mom and Star over to show them something, likely another purchase from today's tour. Paul opted to wait near the lobby door, where a chill wind slammed through each time a guest entered. He definitely needed to cool off.

"You fancy her, don't you?"

Paul turned to find Colin standing at his elbow. "What?"

"You fancy Shining Star." Colin's chin jutted forward, a bit of a smirk quirking his lips. "You should. She's a keeper."

"Why would you ask me that?" As if Colin had a right to know his—or anyone else's—personal business.

"Because you seem like the kind of guy who might be mad about a girl, but instead of telling her, you'd become a cold fish and let her swim away to someone else."

How dare this guy presume to know anything about him? "And I suppose you seem like the kind of guy to be in line to scoop her right up, huh? Is that even ethical as a tour guide?" He spun on his heels toward the door. "Don't bother answering. I'll be waiting for the group outside."

Chapter 29

"You're not wearing your sling." Paul led Star toward the entrance of the pub so the staff could rearrange the room for the concert now that everyone had finished their dinner of fish and chips. How had he not noticed her missing sling earlier? Probably because he couldn't stop staring into her eyes.

Star gave him a sheepish smile. "I wanted to test things out. Maybe my shoulder's better, and I can dance."

Dance? He wasn't really into dancing. "Great. Now I'll have to worry the entire night about some Bozo spinning you around while you go Riverdance. Or something equally dangerous."

"Then you better be the one to dance with me, Perky." Her teasing gaze plunged deep into his heart, releasing a torrent of fire that swept up to his face.

Star giggled, a melodic sound to his ears. "Are you blushing?"

Was he? He fought the urge to touch his cheeks. And hers. How embarrassing. "I'm only thinking you'd probably insist on leading, then you'd get hurt, and I'd be to blame."

"Your brain sure wants to borrow tomorrow." The chairs had been set into rows facing the stage, and Star sank into one. She pinched her lips and then patted the seat next to her. "Chill. Enjoy tonight."

Like a puppy, he obeyed and sat. He actually felt pretty good now. And relaxed, considering the worry over her shoulder and the fact that his mom was on a date with a virtual stranger while she still sniffled from a cold.

The rhythm of a drum began, the lights dimmed, and the group quieted. Colin and Will slipped into the aisle and took seats on the other side of Star. Of course

"Back in the land of the living, you are." Colin directed the statement at Paul.

"Yes, Master Yoda," Paul mumbled.

Snorting a little, Star nudged him with her knee, rather than her sharp elbow. One benefit of her nursing a bad shoulder. "Be nice."

A male dancer, clad in black pants and a plain white T-shirt, took the stage. His feet tapped, creating a fast beat. The man jumped, kicked, and twirled in the popular Riverdance.

What would Star think of twinkle toes up there? Paul peeked a side glance her way. Her eyes glittered as she stared toward the young, muscular man.

Humph. Probably the first time she'd seen the traditional dance. Paul sat up taller in his chair and crossed his arms, tightened his biceps. Just a little. Maybe he should dance with Star.

To keep her safe.

He glanced at Colin. The lout was gooey-eyed watching Star take in the show.

The crowd cheered at the stomping finale, and Star let out a loud whoop.

Good grief. It was just tap dancing.

"Wasn't that amazing?" Star's warm breath tickled Paul's ear.

He gave a slow nod. Sitting next to her had been amazing, anyway.

A small group of men with instruments took the stage, playing the traditional Irish tunes with a fiddle, accordion, flute, and guitar.

She nudged him with her knee again as they played. "This may sound weird, but the sound of the fiddle reminds me of Cajun music."

"It does have a similar quality." Facing her, Paul smiled. Her eyes still glittered, like a constellation of her own.

He barely noticed the band finish, but a soloist and guitar player took their place. The woman sang a sweet, hauntingly soulful tune in Gaelic. Star's hand slipped over his, clasping his fingers.

He turned and glanced her way.

"So beautiful," she mouthed.

Oh, those lips.

Yes, beautiful.

~~~

The night, the music, the look in Paul's eyes as he gazed at her… Star let that warm feeling unfurl and envelop her entire body.

It was all so magical. Like something she'd see on a rom-com or one of those poor-girl-becomes-a-princess movies.

And for one night, maybe she could be that princess.

When she'd taken his hand, she hadn't been thinking, only enthralled with the music. But he'd held on, caressing her fingers gently with his thumb. Such a tiny movement, but oh, it turned her inside out.

She'd probably revert to a poor girl with a pumpkin if she allowed this to go on. And yet, they walked hand in hand toward the small dance floor.

"Have you claimed the first dance from our fragile bird, Perky Paul?" Colin winked Star's way as they neared where he stood by the bar.

"I have." Paul whisked past the guide, rolling his eyes, until they reached a relatively clear corner of the floor.

"Don't get wild now." He placed a hand on the small of her back and whispered. "You've got to protect your broken wing, little birdie."

"You goofball." Laughing, Star smacked Paul's shoulder.

"Ouch," they said in unison.

Paul's brow raised. "Another reason not to hit or elbow me. And I'm not the one who started the goof—"

"Shh." Star pressed one finger over his lips, partly to quiet him, and partly to keep herself from planting her own lips on his. She breathed a sigh. He sure looked nice tonight. More than nice. Attractive. Stirring up longings she didn't need to revive. She didn't need to get lost there.

Mrs. Kelly's abstinence devotional with the pottery wheel came to mind, along with the messy relationships of her past.

Star ripped her gaze away, but Paul stepped even closer, eliminating all distance between them.

His hair smelled so nice. Clean and woodsy. His arms, strong but gentle, encircled her, and she let herself snuggle in.

The music played on, some songs slow and mournful, some silly about fishmongers and mermaids. She and Paul kept the same spot, slow and steady, but her heart danced its own wild beat.

"I could stay like this forever."

"What?" Paul stepped back and smiled.

Nooo. Had she said that out loud? "Nothing."

Returning to his spot, he whispered, "Me, too, but I imagine they'll make us leave eventually."

Oh, he'd heard. But such a sweet answer. "Yeah, your mom would— Oh, my word. Have you seen Will? I completely forgot about him."

Star slipped from the warmth of Paul's embrace, worry

snaking around her chest as she frantically scanned the room for any sign of Will's profile.

"I don't see him." Paul checked his phone. "No texts."

Star dug her cell from her back pocket. "No service."

"Stay put. I'll go look in the men's room and ask around."

Groaning, Star whispered a prayer. "Sorry, God. We had one job, and we failed. Let Will be okay, please."

Maybe he'd stepped outside. Star craned her neck to see around the crowd but was unable to get a good view. In fact, she didn't spot anyone from their group. She should go take a quick look outside. No telling what an eighteen-year-old could be doing. She hated to think about the stuff she'd done at that age.

After filtering her way through dancing couples and patrons with pints, she pushed open the exit door and stepped onto the cobbled sidewalk. As she walked farther away, the brisk night air whipped around the old buildings, sending a chill through her. The street quieted past the pub.

If Will was doing something he shouldn't be, he might've tried to find cover. Star walked to the next corner and scanned a darker alleyway. Nothing that she could see. She stepped farther down and squinted. Nothing. She wasn't dying to wander around an alley in a foreign country.

Had they passed a Chinese restaurant or pizza parlor? Will was thin, but he sure put away the food. She took a few more steps.

"Alone, eh?" A male voice spoke from close behind her, the accent unfamiliar.

Spinning around, Star found a tall blonde man only inches away. Great. A drunk. Heartbeat ramping up, she dropped her gaze to search the ground for something—anything—to use for a weapon if she needed one.

"I'm looking for my friend." She sized up the guy. Late twenties, thin but muscular, Scandinavian looking.

A sickly smile lifted the guy's mouth. "Me too. Let's be good friends."

Ugh. She tried to step around him, but he blocked her path.

If only she'd kept her guard up. She knew better. "Look, buddy, I need to get back inside."

"Not yet." His eyes roved her. "You're American, right?"

A swift, well-placed kick would have to do. *God, I know Christians are supposed to turn the other cheek and all, but I need to get away from this guy. I could use some help.*

"It's none of your business. Move." She leveled her harshest stare on him, then tried to step past him. He grabbed her, shoved her against the wall. The pain exploded in her shoulder.

Every punch, every belt lash, every kick that her stepfather landed against her young body slammed full force in Star's mind, and her adrenaline roared to life. Despite her pain, she thrashed fists and knees at her attacker. She'd never go down without a fight.

Chapter 30

Where in the world was Star?

Anger steamed through each pore as Paul strode outside into the chilly night air. Colin should have told them he'd walked the rest of the group back to the hotel. Instead, the guide had come back and ordered a pint, not bothering to fill them in.

Which way would Star go to look for Will? Left toward the hotel or right, farther into town? If she'd walked toward the hotel, she might've seen Colin. Paul turned right, moving away from the music and chatter streaming from the pub.

Two blocks more, nothing. Only dark and quiet. Maybe he should turn around.

"No!" A woman's voice rang from down the street.

Star? Heartrate ramping, Paul sprinted toward the sound. Following scuffling and slapping noises, he rounded a corner into a dark alley.

A tall blonde man's body pinned Star against the wall.

Fury thundered through Paul. "Get away from her!"

The guy's head spun Paul's way. Paul grabbed for the weasel's shoulder, only to catch his shirt. The man cursed, released his hold on Star, and turned on Paul with a massive right hook.

Paul ducked and shoved the man. Hard. Sweat beaded on Paul's forehead while adrenalin roared through his veins. A snarl formed in his throat. "You disgusting excuse for a man!" Paul lunged toward him, but the guy spun and tore off down the alley. He'd chase the degenerate coward, but he didn't want to leave Star.

She turned her back and curled into herself.

Rushing to her, Paul wrapped his arm around her waist, careful of her shoulder.

Eyes wild, she swung blindly at him.

"Star. It's Paul. I've got you," he crooned, despite the blows landing on his chest. "You're safe now."

Her movements slowed, and her gaze found his, finally focusing.

"It's okay. I'm here." He stroked strands of hair from her face. "Did he hurt you?"

"I can't find Will." Her voice quivered.

"He's fine. Colin took him back to the hotel and didn't bother to tell us." Paul wanted to strangle him. And Will. And everyone else in the group.

"Is Star okay?" Colin ran toward them from the main road. "What happened?"

"You happened," Paul growled. "She was looking for Will."

"No." Star shook her head. "I should've waited for you to come outside."

"It's not your fault someone attacked you." Paul strained in the darkness to see whether she was bleeding or bruised.

"Here?" Colin's voice rose. "Dingle is a very safe town."

If Star weren't already traumatized, Paul would've tackled the guy. "Are you an idiot? No matter where a woman is—"

"It's not his fault." Star's hand covered his. "And I don't think that guy was Irish."

Colin came closer. "I'm so sorry. Do you need a doctor?"

"No." Star straightened.

"We can call the police to make a report." Colin pulled his

phone out.

"I really just want to go back to the hotel."

"I'll get you a cab then."

"You don't have to." She stepped away from the wall but stayed near Paul. "We can walk."

"It's the least I can do."

"Let him," Paul insisted. "You might change your mind once you start moving around. Sometimes shock numbs a body." He'd seen it in Africa, young children beaten and bloodied, walking like zombies into the orphanage.

"Okay." She finally agreed, and they headed together toward the main road, Paul keeping a loose hold around her waist.

"It'll be two minutes. He's not far." Colin tried to act chipper after making the call, but Paul still wanted to give him a piece of his mind. "Want me to come back with you? Or would you prefer—"

"We don't need you." The last bit of Paul's patience evaporated, but he bit his tongue to keep from spewing more.

He and Star didn't speak on the ride back, but Paul covered her hand with his own. Once he helped her out and they entered the brightly lit lobby, Paul stopped. "Let's make sure you're not hurt."

Gaze downcast, Star stilled.

Paul nudged her chin to examine her face. No marks or bruises that he could tell. He took her hands. Her knuckles were red. They'd likely bruise and swell. The girl was a fighter. And he hated to think of how she'd had to learn to be one from childhood. It wasn't fair.

Her sweater and jeans covered her body, leaving him no clue as to injuries there. "What about your shoulder? The rest of you?"

"I'm fine. Really." At last, her gaze met his, her eyes glassy and red. "Can we sit out back on the patio of the hotel for a while? I need to decompress before I see your mom. Get my head together."

"Sure. Can I get you some water…tea…anything?" Would the vicious attack reopen the wounds from her past—drive her to want a drink? Or use something else? If he were in her place, he'd probably like a few shots of tequila.

"No." Her voice was a whisper.

They walked through the lobby and out the French doors to the patio. Alone in the cool night air, they sat on a bench, staring out at the bay. Moonlight illuminated the waves that gently crested against the shore. A million pricks of light dotted the sky and shone over the faint outline of green hills.

But only one Star captured his attention.

Though one may be overpowered, two can defend themselves. A cord of three strands is not quickly broken.

Another verse. But not quite as annoying as the ones before. Again, Paul reached for Star's hand and covered it with his own. "You deserve better—you deserve someone to watch over you, to treasure you. Someone to make sure no one ever hurts you again."

She turned and gazed up at him, eyes shining. "No one can promise that. But having someone to go through the bad times with is—"

"I'd like to try." He cupped her cheek. "Maybe you and I could spend time together. Back home. Figure out where to go and what to do next. Together."

A tiny lift of her lips drew him closer.

"What do you think?" His voice came out husky.

Her smile tipped, and her eyes held his. "I might like that."

"You might?" Only inches away now, and the magnetic

pull of her mouth was more than he could fight. His lips brushed hers, softness and sweetness filling his senses.

She responded with intensity, roaming, exploring, and deepening the kiss. Warmth flooded him. And a fierce longing. A longing to hold and protect. To show her a different kind of life than the one she'd known. To show her how a good man could treat her.

Which probably started by showing her respect. Despite the fires raging within him and urging him on, he relinquished her lips.

Expelling a long breath, he rested his forehead against hers. "That was everything I'd hoped for and more."

The tinkle of laughter came from Star. "We've come a long way, haven't we, Perky?"

The wind swirled between them, ruffling her hair and heightening his already spiking senses. "You speak the unvarnished truth, Princess Shining Star. As usual."

He pressed another kiss to her forehead, lingering, savoring the soft feel of her skin, the intoxicating scent of her hair. This woman—beautiful in any light, shone a light all her own.

~~~

If only she'd spoken the truth.

Still enveloped in Paul's arms, Star touched her tingling lips, guilt trickling over her. She'd wanted to tell him that the Someone who would always walk through hard times with him or her, with anyone who invited Him, was Christ. She'd wanted to remind him of how they lived in a fallen world, a temporary world, but God's love lasted forever.

But Paul's offer to be with her back home, his closeness, his infernally beautiful hazel eyes, his kiss—everything about Paul Kelly in that moment had shut down the voice shouting in her head.

Because she'd wanted him to kiss her so badly.

"We should go in. You have to be exhausted." His voice was soft, gentle even. "And Mom might worry."

Or maybe they should worry about Mrs. Kelly, but his mother's date seemed like another subject she'd rather not bring up. "I'm ready." She forced herself to pull away from his warmth and stand.

He rose, closing the distance between them, and slipped his arms around her. "Decompressed enough now?" His lips again teased hers, soft and playful, unleashing a swarm of butterflies in her stomach.

"I don't think decompressed is the term I'd use to describe my feelings at this point."

"Oh, really? How would you describe them?" His breath tickled her forehead. Then he brushed light kisses on her temples, her cheeks, her neck. She wobbled a bit with the weight of desire sweeping through her.

"A time-to-say-good-night-before-I-do-something-stupid kind of feeling."

"Know it well. Sometimes fail." He laughed and released her.

"A poet and a pilot? I need time to get to know you better, Mr. Kelly."

"I've got all the time in the world, and you may not believe it, but I'm a patient man."

Shaking her head, Star tsked. "I'll believe that when I see it."

"Ah, another challenge for me to take up." He slipped her hand in his. "I'll escort you to your room now, princess."

"Thank you, kind sir."

Walking inside and down the maze of halls, Star savored

having Paul at her side. A defender. A friend. And now maybe something more.

They reached the door, and he gently held her close. "Are you sure you weren't hurt tonight?"

"I'm fine." Except, if her arm moved to a certain position, pain seared through her shoulder as if someone were ripping the limb from her body. But Paul didn't need to know that.

Because, in this moment, next to his firm chest, nothing had ever felt so right.

Chapter 31

Over a week of ancient castles, spectacular views of green Irish countryside, and dozens of sweet kisses later, Star stared at Paul's hand covering her bruised knuckles. She relished the feel of how nicely she fit, snuggled next to him, while they traveled the last few miles toward Dublin on the bus. She still couldn't get over how her emotions for this man had transformed.

Her mind circled back to the day in Mrs. Kelly's driveway when she'd told Paul he disgusted her. That was hardly the case now. She couldn't seem to get close enough to him. Couldn't seem to breathe in enough of his crisp linen scent. Couldn't stop staring at those hazel eyes. And after their sizzling good-night kisses, she couldn't stop reliving them most of the night.

"You look deep in thought," Paul said as the bus rumbled to a stop in front of the large brick hotel in Dublin.

She lifted her gaze to meet his. "I can't believe we only have a few days left in Ireland."

"Me neither." A grin played on his lips. "You know what they say about time flying."

Oh, those lips. "And I've been having fun."

"More than just fun, I hope." His expression turning serious, he lifted her hand to press a soft kiss against her palm, sending flutters through her whole body.

"More." The only word she could squeeze out as her breath caught. Just the sight of him undid her now. What a dramatic turn life had taken these past couple of weeks.

Colin stood near the driver and announced their next

meeting time in the hotel lobby would be just before dinner. The group began to exit.

Star stepped into the aisle, her sling constantly hindering easy progress, but Paul had asked her to keep wearing it. To be safe. And her shoulder still throbbed if she moved the wrong way.

The phone in Paul's shirt pocket rang. A silly button-down number covered in rainbows and bearded leprechauns they'd come across in a gift shop. She couldn't wait to put on the jewel she'd found to wear tonight. A cat riding a llama with a spaceship circling. Who thought of this stuff? And who wore it, other than people who'd lost their clothes on vacation and were in a contest to look ridiculous?

He stopped to check the number on his cell. "I'd better return this call. I'll catch up with you and Mom later." His smile flickered but quickly faded.

Star exited without Paul, immediately missing him and feeling a bit like she'd taken a punch to the gut. That old fear of abandonment raised its ugly head.

Maybe the call was about his job. Despite the great time they were having, his lack of employment surely still nagged him. Her own situation in that department would slap her in the face as soon as she returned home, especially if her shoulder was still messed up and the gym wouldn't hire her.

Mrs. Kelly waited on the sidewalk with her suitcase. "Hey, sweetie. I was hoping you and I could unpack, then maybe have a cup of tea before dinner." She flicked a glance Paul's way. "Just the two of us."

"Of course." Star smiled at her friend. "Is everything okay?" Will's grandfather—Bradford—had taken over as Mrs. Kelly's touring companion since that crazy night in Dingle. The arrangement had worked out well for her and Paul's new…thing. Whatever it was. But right now, Bradford had gone on ahead. Had something come between them? Already? Would she and Paul fall apart that quickly?

"Perfect. Let's go inside." Mrs. Kelly reached to roll the bag. "I'll get a porter to bring up our luggage."

Efficient. She must really want to talk.

Jazzy music played inside the fashionable lobby. Sleek metal chairs with bright purple accents gave the large open room a modern feel. The wall of windows were all closed, so this place must run their air conditioning. First time since they'd arrived. Not that they'd needed it—though the locals had claimed the seventy-degree temperatures to be a fierce heatwave. At least they'd had a few days with no rain.

A bellman took the luggage to the room while they checked in. No sign of Paul, so they found an elevator that took them to their floor.

Inside the spacious, modern room, Star plopped down on the bed. "Is everything okay?"

Mrs. Kelly trudged over and sat beside Star. "I guess we can talk here. I didn't want you to feel awkward."

"The longer we wait, the more convinced I am that something's wrong."

"Nothing's wrong, exactly." Mrs. Kelly directed a sad smile Star's way. "You and Paul seem…close now."

Mrs. Kelly didn't approve. A boulder sank in Star's gut.

She should have known. Tears burned in the back of her eyes. She wasn't worthy. "I'm sorry. I know I'm not the kind of girl you'd pick for your son."

"Oh, darling, don't you dare think that." Mrs. Kelly patted Star's knee. "The truth is, my Paul isn't the kind of man I'd choose for you. Anymore, at least. He used to be, but since he lost his faith…"

"Oh." Star studied her sweet friend. "He's still a good man, just not…"

She closed her mouth and allowed the Voice she'd been squelching to be heard. "He's not a believer."

Mrs. Kelly gave a slow nod. "Do you remember my lesson with the pottery wheel?"

"Of course." Another thought she'd been shoving away.

"Remember what I said about the pressure?" Her brows lifted over kind eyes.

If only she could forget. "Pressures come from inside, and pressures push from outside. The walls build. The piece that isn't centered from the beginning collapses. Makes a mess."

"You're a good student, Star." Mrs. Kelly cleared her throat. "Could that lesson apply to your situation with Paul?"

Her insides in knots, she blinked away tears. "I guess it might. Yes."

"I don't have all the answers about what you should or shouldn't do. I'm only concerned for you. But hear this." Mrs. Kelly's gnarled hand covered Star's. "There is no one I'd rather have for a daughter-in-law than Star Youngblood. If Paul Kelly ever gets himself right with the Lord."

~~~

"You're kidding?" Paul pressed the phone harder against his ear to drown out the sound of cars whizzing by. "The new guy's already had it with Kenneth, huh?"

"Yep." Charlie scoffed. "I told the boss I didn't think you'd come back, but I'd try."

Paul let his chin drop. Just when he'd decided to move on and find a new life, the old one slunk back around. Visions of the spoiled CEO throwing a tirade echoed through Paul's mind—the rudeness, the cursing, the refusing to allow scheduled time off, the constant changes in flight plans. Sure, the money was more than most corporate piloting jobs, but was the difference in salary worth the torment? Even if he could quit on his own terms next year, the thought of going back sickened him worse than the idea of riding a boat around a harbor again.

Plus, Mom needed him.

And there was Star.

The thought of her blazed through his midsection. But more than that, her sweet vulnerability, wrapped in her tough façade curled around his heart and held tight. She needed him too. And he wanted to be with her.

"Sorry, Charlie." Paul's answer was firm. "I'd rather work on a janitorial crew in the Sahara Desert than fly that man's plane."

"I thought you'd say something like that now that you've tasted sweet freedom from tyranny." Charlie groaned. "I guess I'll let you in on another great gig I heard about in Atlanta. In case you need an income or something silly like that."

"Really? You weren't going to tell me unless I said no?" Paul leaned against the rough bricks of the hotel's exterior.

"Every now and then, I have to think of myself. Working with you is the only thing that's made the job here bearable."

At least that was a compliment. "Fair enough. Tell me about this job in Atlanta."

Ten minutes later, Paul read an email on his phone while seated at a table inside the hotel lobby. Voices from the bar cheered. Probably a rugby tournament or soccer game on TV. The link to the job Charlie had sent took Paul to a listing with a well-known commercial flight company. Charlie had also given the name of a friend who worked there and was involved with the hiring. Sweet deal.

Atlanta hadn't been the plan, but if Mom had her surgery

soon and recovered well, this job could be the answer. A big city would have plenty of retirement facilities, and if she didn't want to move there, Atlanta was only five hours from Hilton Head or St. Simons, depending on traffic. If they got Mom settled someplace safe in either of those towns, he could commute on his off days. Some pilots flew four days, then had three days off. It could work. At least until he finished saving enough money to open a flight school.

A text chimed as he pocketed his phone.

What now? He pulled it back out of his pocket.

Francesca.

Paul massaged his forehead before reading the text.

Ciao, love. I heard you are in Dublin. So am I, for a fashion show. Where are you staying?

Good grief. He couldn't deal with Francesca right now. He had no reason to ever see her again. The whole relationship, if one could call it that, had been an irresponsible blunder. His life had taken enough unexpected turns—more like twists and spirals and corkscrews. No way did he want to throw another woman in the mix. Besides, he'd basically invited Star into a relationship.

Another chime.

Paul?

Apparently, Francesca wasn't giving up. Who even told her about his trip? It had to have been Charlie.

Paul typed out a text.

Sorry. I'm with my mother.

An immediate response. *I'd love to meet her.*

No. No. No. Life kept throwing him curveballs, and they were clocking him in the face. *Not a good time. We have a busy schedule. Have a great trip.*

Maybe that would put an end to the conversation. He'd

turn off the phone, just in case.

At the front desk, he checked in and picked up his key. This hotel rated highly, and he looked forward to a long hot shower and maybe a catnap before dinner.

"Sir," the cashier called as Paul turned away.

"Yes?"

"I apologize, but I forgot you had a delivery."

"Really?" Please let it be his wallet.

"Your baggage and another envelope." The man laid the duffle bag and a white express envelope on the counter.

Could it be both? Paul grabbed the letter first. It felt stiff. Good. He opened it to find several other envelopes inside. New credit cards. Thank you.

Up in his room, he showered, humming to himself. He couldn't wait to put on his own normal clothes and surprise Star at dinner.

~~~

This shirt looked hilarious on her. Star couldn't help but laugh as she checked herself in the mirror. Not only was the design totally weird, but the fabric swallowed her and hung loosely around the neck on one side, making the cat riding the llama in the middle appear a little drunk and the spaceship in the sky askew. No way would she lose the ugly shirt contest wearing this number.

"Well. Aren't you...something I can't find words to describe?" Mrs. Kelly chuckled. "You've made losing a suitcase into something fun for Paul. I'm so proud of your attitude. And for making this trip the dream of a lifetime for me." She pulled Star into a soft hug.

"I love you," Star whispered into her friend's shoulder, but immediately blushed. What was she thinking? Mrs. Kelly was her employer, not her mother. "Sorry. I—"

"I love you too, darling." She tightened the hug. "Don't you ever doubt it."

The words soothed some of the ragged edges of Star's heart. No matter what happened between her and Paul, Mrs. Kelly would always be special to her.

"Are you ready to go to dinner?" Mrs. Kelly released her.

"My hair's still a little damp, but it takes forever to dry." Star grabbed an elastic band. "I'll put it up." Like most days on this trip, a twisted bun would have to do.

"If you'd prefer, you can dry it and meet us in the lobby." Sniffing, Mrs. Kelly hobbled toward the door. "I'd hate for you to catch a cold too."

Star paused. Irish evenings could get rather chilly. "I don't want you to go down without me. We can text Paul."

Mrs. Kelly clucked her tongue. "Nonsense. There's an elevator ten feet down the hall that will take me to the lobby. I'm fine."

"Okay." She held the door while her friend limped through and watched until she reached the elevator and entered it.

Once Mrs. Kelly disappeared, Star took her time combing and drying and styling. She even applied eye shadow and mascara—not something she'd made time for most of this trip. Tonight would be one of the last here in Ireland, and she wanted to savor her time with Paul. When they returned home, life would crash into them with a vengeance. They'd both be back to the reality of looking for a job. Would they be able to withstand the world's pressures?

Thoughts of what Mrs. Kelly had said about Paul being an unbeliever made her heart pinch. The last thing she wanted to do was give him up. He'd been a believer, and maybe he still was deep down, only he'd been hurt by all he'd been through. He was a good man. He could come back to faith.

Couldn't he?

She checked her hair once more and opened the door to the hall. After one step, she stopped short, holding the door open. By the elevator, Paul stood talking to a woman. Not just a woman. A knockout. Tall. Perfect body and beautiful face. Long, dark, shiny hair.

Paul wore a starched, light blue button-down and khaki pants. Where did he find that outfit, and when?

The woman, dressed in tight leather pants and a red, low-cut blouse, stood close to him. Really close. She ran her hand up and down his sleeve. The touch was intimate.

Paul made no move to step away.

Star strained to hear as they spoke. She shouldn't, but she couldn't force herself to stop.

"That night in Rome was a mistake." Guilt layered Paul's gaze at the woman. "You should work things out with your husband."

Like a fist squeezing her throat, the words cut off Star's oxygen. Paul had slept with another man's wife. Nausea swept over her, Mrs. Kelly's warning rolling in Star's mind.

The woman dropped her hand and took a step back. "I believed Paul Kelly to be a good man, but you are not." She pointed her long finger accusingly at him. "You are like all other men, after only pleasure for yourself."

"It's not like that, Francesca. I never meant for that to happen." Paul's brows furrowed. "Now I've met someone I care about. And I know you still love Matteo."

Met someone. Star sucked in a breath. He was telling the hot mama with an accent no, because he'd met someone he cared about.

Her?

Two doors down, a man exited his room, the clatter

drawing Paul's attention her way. He spotted Star, and his mouth gaped for a second, then he waved at her. "Hey."

Mortified at being caught eavesdropping, Star flinched but waved back. She took one step into the hallway and let the door shut behind her. Oh, why did she have to be wearing this stupid, ugly shirt?

Francesca's gaze bounced between Paul and Star. Then up and down Star again. An awkward silence stretched between them for a moment.

This was ridiculous. Star strode down the hall toward the elevator. And toward Paul and Ms. Fancy-pants. She wouldn't keep Mrs. Kelly waiting any longer.

Chapter 32

Why couldn't he catch a break?

A startling pain ripped through Paul's chest as Star strode toward him. Francesca, who'd not been invited but had searched him out anyway, stood her ground. What if he lost Star because of his one night of stupidity in Italy?

Then again, he hadn't even met Star back then. Why should he feel bad? Star had obviously made mistakes. She'd had boyfriends, and apparently, a couple of really messed up ones, at that.

When Star reached the elevator, Paul pressed on a smile. "I thought you were downstairs with Mom already."

"Heading that way." Her words were clipped.

"This is my friend Francesca." Paul nodded toward the glaring woman beside him, hoping neither would freak out. What else could he do? He knew more about flying in zero visibility than he did about women, yet even he realized he had little chance of landing safely in this storm.

Star extended her hand and smiled at Francesca. "It's nice to meet you. Where are you from?" Her expression appeared genuine and kind.

Francesca responded with cool professionalism, her pretty face void of any emotion, though her eyes narrowed. "Near Florence." She paused, then added, "Italy."

"I bet it's beautiful." Star kept her smile in place. "This is my first time out of the United States."

"You should see Italy." Francesca flicked a strand of her

long dark hair from her shoulder and slid a harsh gaze Paul's way. "There are many beautiful places in the world, as Paul can attest. We both travel extensively."

The word *we* sliced into Paul. "Not together." He pointed his thumb toward Francesca. "She's a model. And I'm a pilot so…" What a bumbling mess. He should shut up.

Both women arched an eyebrow, then Star took another step toward the elevator and pressed the button. "Nice meeting you. Safe travels."

"And you." Francesca's lips drew taut, and her dark eyes searched Paul's face, unnerving him.

Sweat broke out on his upper lip. "We should go downstairs now." He cleared his tight throat and shrugged. "Mom will be wondering what happened to us." As he was. He couldn't fathom the next disaster he'd crash into.

The elevator opened with a chime, and they all shuffled in. The doors closed, and Paul kept his gaze locked on the lighted floor numbers. He'd noticed Star's amusing shirt, but obviously, now wasn't the right moment to mention it. She'd been so sweet to make losing his suitcase fun. He should have kept up the game instead of changing into his regular clothes tonight. Especially since she probably felt awkward right now.

Time moved snail-slow from floor to floor, the uncomfortable silence twisting his insides. His face scalded as he imagined Francesca mentioning their night in Italy in front of his mother. As much as he'd discarded the rules he'd grown up with, the thought of disappointing his mother tore him up.

At last, the elevator opened, and Star rushed through the sliding doors into the lobby.

"Star, wait," Paul called after her.

Her feet halted, and she glanced over her shoulder, her lips pressed in a flat line.

Paul's gaze bounced between the two women.

"Ciao, Paul." Dejection distorted Francesca's picture-perfect features. She pivoted on her high heels and walked away, slapping Paul with guilt.

"Bye." The most he could think to say. He'd explained that he couldn't see her, but she hadn't listened. Hurting her had never been his intention, but that was exactly what he'd accomplished.

"You coming or what?" Star's voice spun him around. Shock and thankfulness lifted his feet. She hadn't gone on without him. She was still speaking to him. She'd shown such poise in an embarrassing situation.

"Definitely." He caught up to her side. "I'm sorry."

"For what?" She kept her gaze straight ahead as they walked toward the front of the lobby to meet the tour group.

"She texted that she was in Dublin, and I told her I was busy." That sounded lame even to him. "She and I were never in a relationship. We were really only friends...mostly." Also lame.

Her perceptive gaze slid his way and laid him bare. Even if she hadn't overheard his conversation with Francesca, Star still knew the score. The girl had street-smarts.

"Can we talk here a second?" He didn't want to have this discussion in hearing distance of the others.

Stopping, she turned to face him.

"I made a mistake with her." Paul lowered his voice and stepped closer. "We used to flirt when we ran into each other at the airport, but she was married. One night, she was upset. She and her husband had separated. We had wine—"

"Got it." She held up her palm, then let her eyes close. "No need to draw a picture."

Shame hung like ice weighing down the wings of a plane,

pulling it toward the ground. "I don't know what to say."

"All of us do things we regret." Star's eyes became glassy as she held his gaze.

For all have sinned and fall short of the glory of God—

"Please stop." Paul smacked his forehead with his palm.

"Stop what?" Confusion knotted Star's brows.

"Not you." Gingerly, Paul slid his hand to catch hers. "Ever since I started this trip, I've been getting these weird thoughts popping into my head, which is crazy but…" He sighed, not knowing how to finish.

"What kind of thoughts?" Star's piercing gaze sliced into him like a scalpel.

Paul's gaze roamed the lobby. Confessing his insanity hadn't been his intention, but lying to her didn't seem like a good idea either. Especially now. "Verses."

Her head cocked. "Like of a song or from the Bible?"

"Not a song." He couldn't stop an eye roll because he knew what was coming.

~~~

"Huh." Star had no words. Paul was hearing Bible verses in his mind. That had to be a good thing. It had to be God working on him.

Yet, he'd asked for them to stop. She searched his face for some clue as to what exactly was going on in his head.

God, what should I say?

Nothing profound came. Other than Mrs. Kelly's advice. It seemed God was pursuing Paul, but Paul kept rejecting Him. So far. Could that change, and, if so, what was her part to play?

Let go and let God. The slogan from her AA meetings floated through her mind. Maybe it was God's job to convict Paul, not hers, despite the fact she was dying to tell Paul to listen to those verses.

She chewed her lip a second. Keeping her mouth shut sure proved to be as hard as giving up bad habits.

"We should catch up with the others." She took a step back and turned away from him, though he still held her hand. She relished the sensation, and the way he seemed to want to protect her. And even with his supermodel friend, he'd obviously tried to be honest. Sort of. A lot of guys wouldn't have been.

They strode over to the waiting group. Mrs. Kelly chatted happily with Will and Mr. Palmer—aka Bradford.

"At last, things are grand, now that Perky Paul and Shining Star have arrived." Colin beamed Star's way. "We couldn't leave for our fancy dinner without our princess. And don't you look wild but adorable with your festive shirt."

Paul squeezed Star's fingers and slid a glance her way, his lips pinched. She couldn't help a snicker. He deserved a serving of jealousy after the supermodel appearance. And him wearing his normal clothes without warning her.

They stepped out into a cloudy, dark evening. A chill wind nipped at her, bringing a shiver. No sign of stars or moon as they traversed the few blocks to the restaurant. She should have brought an umbrella or raincoat. As if the sky heard her, lightning split the darkness. A thunderclap followed, bringing a collective gasp from pedestrians on the sidewalk.

"We're almost there, and I'll hire cars to drive us back afterward," Colin called over his shoulder. "No worries."

"I guess we used up our foul weather passes the last few days." Paul shook his head. "This storm is more par for the course in this part of the world, though. Rainy and cold."

"Then I wouldn't want to live here." Wind slapped Star's hair onto her cheeks. "Is London the same?"

"Pretty much. But I was hardly ever home." He lifted one

231

shoulder.

"Yeah, I heard you traveled." Star couldn't stop the sarcasm in her voice.

"Sorry." He groaned. "At least, I don't have to go back there now, other than to get the rest of my meager belongings. And more clothes." He glanced down at his fresh shirt and pants. "My suitcase arrived, by the way."

"I see that. Nice. Any idea where you'll locate next?" Where would he go? Back to his mother's? She tried to sound neutral rather than desperate to have him near.

"Actually, Charlie, my copilot, hooked me up with a job possibility in Atlanta." They reached the restaurant's green awning, and Paul turned to face Star, brows raised. The other members of their tour continued inside, but he motioned that they'd be along in a minute and let the door close. "I could keep St. Simons as a home base. Or Hilton Head." He mumbled that last part.

Fire scalded her cheeks, and a scoff flew out of her mouth. "You still think your mom needs to move?"

"Not right away, but eventually. The community I showed her is really nice. She liked it. Really."

"What's so much stinking better about that part of the coast?" She huffed, squelching the rest of the words boiling up inside her.

Paul let go of her hand and cupped her cheeks. "Nothing if you're not there."

And her heart melted like butter on a hot stove. Did he really mean it? He cared for her that much?

His lips neared hers, then brushed them lightly. He rested his forehead on hers. "A friend is retiring soon and wants to sell his flight school near Hilton Head. My dream was to buy it. Be my own boss." His eyes pleaded and shone in the low light spilling from the window.

"I guess if your mom wanted to move there…"

So Paul didn't think she was incapable of caring for his mother. He simply wanted his mother close to him. And telling Mrs. Kelly what to do wasn't her place. Part of her knew she was being selfish in wanting things to stay the same. Maybe even cowardly and clingy. Because she had no idea what her own future would hold if she didn't work for Paul's mother.

A moment later, he'd captured her lips. Sweet but strong. His fingers feathered through her hair, down her back. Too soon, he pulled away, leaving her breathless.

"We better go in now, before I decide I'm not hungry." His teasing gaze held her captive.

His kisses sparked a fire within her that both pleased and terrified her. She'd not felt this way. Ever. Not for Blake, certainly not for Vince or any of the other losers she'd dated. What if Paul never became a believer though?

She swallowed hard, then forced herself to breathe. "Yeah, you know I can't miss a meal."

Chuckling, he opened the door for her. "After you, princess."

Inside, small candles adorned tables with white cloths. In the low light, Star spotted their group at a long table in the back. Two chairs waited for them, though not together, but across from each other. Colin sat between the seats at the head of the table.

A low growl came from Paul. "That guy never gives up."

"He's just trying to be friends. We're the only people his age on the trip."

"Believe what you want."

Paul pulled out the chair for her and smiled, then took his seat.

"Thought we'd lost you to the storm." Colin pretended to be afraid.

A waitress holding two carafes approached Star. "Red or white wine for you?"

"Water is fine."

"Wine's included with tonight's meal." The waitress held the white bottle near Star's glass.

"*No*. But thanks."

"You could try a sip."

"I don't drink." Star jerked her hand over the crystal, accidentally tipping it over.

"Don't have a canary. I'll get your water." The waitress set the wine on the table and stood the glass back up.

"We'll both have *just* water." Paul gave the woman a stern look.

"Really?" That was a first on this trip. "You can have wine if you want."

"I don't need it." His hazel gaze held hers. "You're intoxicating enough."

Heat rushed to Star's cheeks. Whew. She was going to need a lot more water.

Once Snippy-Girl filled both flutes, she took off, probably to throw some dirt on their plates.

The meal began in small, fancy courses—a savory leek soup, a salad topped with fennel and radishes, then an appetizer drizzled with garlic butter. Every bite melted in her mouth.

"Knock, knock." Colin leaned close to Star's ear.

She glanced at Paul before answering. He and Morris had leaned close together and were deep in conversation about Africa and politics. "Who's there?"

"Irish." A grin lifted Colin's stubbled cheeks.

Star smirked back at him. "Irish who?"

"Irish you weren't going home soon." He raised his brows, and she couldn't help but laugh at the corny joke.

Sighing, her gaze drifted back to Paul. "Yeah. Me too."

"That lad should feel like a mouse in a cheese shop." His shoulders sagged with the odd statement.

"Who?" Star pivoted to face him, her elbow resting on the table.

"Paul." He gave her a look that said *duh*.

"And why is that?"

"Because you're mad about him, obviously." And Colin seemed none too pleased with that admission. Paul might be right about the guy.

"Did I hear my name?" Paul reached across the table and caressed Star's arm. Tingles zipped across her skin at his touch.

The rest of the night sped by, despite the many courses. Paul's lingering gazes captured her attention more than the gourmet food, stirring up forgotten longings deep within.

Colin stood and clanged a fork against his glass. "Tomorrow, we begin our day with a tour of St. Patrick's Cathedral and Christ's Church. After that, we'll visit Trinity College and the Chester Beatty Library. Be prepared to walk a good bit, or you may hire a car and meet us there. Let me know this evening if that's the option you choose."

Star let out a sigh. The trip was almost over. They'd all be back home soon. Would this vacation romance survive the cold reality of normal life?

~~~

An hour later, Star stood outside the hotel under wide eaves, held close in Paul's arms. Her pulse throbbed as he laced her neck with soft kisses. She drew in a shaky breath, the air between them crackling with electricity. Rain splattered the sidewalk, and thunder rumbled the clouds above. Every part of her savored his touch, felt alive under his hands, but her breathing stalled. She needed to put a stop to this before things became too heavy.

"We should call it a night," she finally managed. "We have an early day at St. Patrick's."

"Forget St. Patrick's." His mouth covered hers again, his arms pulling her closer, eliminating all the distance between them.

Star lost track of all space and time there in his arms until voices tracked down the street. She pulled away, her lips feeling swollen and tingly.

"Come back to my room," Paul whispered against her hair.

The implication popped her eyes open wide. Despite the desire stealing her breath, her spine stiffened. "Paul, no."

"I care about you. I want to be with you." His voice came out ragged.

Being physically intimate with Paul went against what she'd learned in Bible study. From Mrs. Kelly—his own mother.

The raw look on Francesca's face came to Star's mind. And she knew why. Intimacy outside of commitment—marriage—laid the soul bare, open to pain. This past year she'd been taught that God's design was the best way.

Thunder rumbled closer, rattling the windows. Star chewed her lip, deliberating what to say.

"Paul, I'm not claiming to have been perfect in the past, but I'm a new person now."

Sighing, Paul's forehead dropped to touch hers. His hands rubbed up and down her arms. "I'll wait as long as you need."

Her heart both expanded and broke. Did he get that she meant until marriage? Maybe they could talk about that back home. "So, see you at breakfast?" She nuzzled his nose with hers.

"Breakfast, but I'm not going to St. Patrick's or Christ's Church."

Star pulled back to study him. "Why not?"

His expression soured. "I have no desire to pay tribute to a phony belief system that's robbed millions of people for two thousand years."

"Paul, that's not what the church is or was ever intended to be, and you know it. Sure, there've been some bad people who claimed they were Christians, and there always will be, but the true church is the Body of Christ, the people who bow their knee and offer everything to a loving, risen Lord."

His hands dropped to his sides, a damp chill taking their place. "I don't find anything loving about the God who demolished my dreams and killed my father."

She pictured the spinning clay at the potter's wheel. *When two people believe different things, the weight will be off. It makes a mess.*

She and Paul were too different. If they continued on like this, one or the other of them would bend on what they believed.

And she refused to let it be her. As much as it tore her to pieces, she couldn't let this relationship go any farther.

Determination rose up within her. She'd come too far in the past year, and she wouldn't give up her faith or her heavenly Father.

"I can't do this." She backed two steps away from him.

"What?" His mouth gaped. Lightning flashed and reflected in his eyes.

"You and me." Tears burned behind her eyes.

"I don't understand." Disbelief creased Paul's forehead. "You love Mom, she loves you. I'm crazy about you. I've never felt this way about anyone." He reached out and caressed her cheek. "I...I'm falling in love with you. I'll take care of you. We'll take care of each other."

Star's tears dripped and cascaded to the ground, matching the storm raging around them. "We don't believe the same things. A plane won't fly with two pilots trying to go separate places."

"You mean the stuff I said about God? The church?" He scoffed. "You'd let your Christianity stand between us?"

"I'm falling in love with you, too, Paul. Like as-deep-and-wide-as-that-ocean-we-crossed in love with you. And I adore your mom. There's nothing more I'd want than to be part of your family." Her voice broke, and she took his hand. "But I can't. Because I think you still believe in God. You're just furious with Him that life didn't go the way you wanted it. Now you hate Him." She shook her head. "And that's why I can't do this. Because as much as I want to be with you, I love Jesus more."

"You're choosing God over me?" He spat the words at her and ripped his hand away.

What else could she say? "I'm praying for you to come back to Him."

"Don't waste your breath." He pivoted and shot off into the hotel, leaving her alone in the rain.

Chapter 33

A heaviness buried Star, deep and weighty like the crashing waves in the Atlantic. Alone at the hotel restaurant in the early morning, she sipped hot tea and then let her chin rest on her palm. No one else had made it to breakfast yet, but since she hadn't been able to sleep, she'd come on down.

The night had been a fitful one, thrashing beneath the hotel's crisp cotton sheets. And not because of Mrs. Kelly snoring like a swamp full of bullfrogs. The anger on Paul's face branded on her mind—the hurt. She'd tried to do the right thing, but now... she felt like she'd blown it. She'd only driven Paul farther from God.

"Good morning. Can we join you?" a woman asked.

Star looked up to find Morris and Linda. "Sure."

Linda took the seat next to Star, her head tilting to the side as she took in Star's features. "Everything okay?"

A loaded question. Star shrugged her good shoulder. "I'll be all right." Surely Linda and Morris didn't really want to know.

"Mind if I ask if this has something to do with Paul? Or am I being too nosy?" Linda gave her a kind gaze.

Maybe she did want to know.

Morris cleared his throat. "I forgot something upstairs. Be back in a minute."

Once he left the dining room, Linda patted Star's hand. "You can talk to me. For days, I've sensed that you needed me."

"Really?" Another surge of regret ran through her, and talking with someone might help.

"You and Paul seemed to have grown…really close on this trip." Linda poured tea into her cup from the kettle on the table.

"I told him last night that I couldn't be in a relationship with him anymore." Star swallowed at the enormous lump in her throat.

"What happened?" Linda's full attention rested on Star.

"He used to be a Christian, but some bad things happened, and he's walked away from God."

Linda nodded. "I'd gathered that much from his conversations with Morris about Africa. So sad."

"As much as I've grown to care for him—maybe even love him—I realized our differences on faith would become a huge problem." Star took a sip of her tea to try to soothe the throbbing urge to cry.

"That's a mature decision, but carrying it out had to be hard." After bending down to retrieve her purse, Linda rummaged until she found a business card and held it out. "Come to Jacksonville and stay with us when you get back. See what our ministry does. I meant what I said about the job. I know in my heart I'm supposed to offer the position to you."

Morris returned to the table, and Star took the card. "Thanks."

So Linda was serious then. She cared, and she meant it about the job.

Reunite Global. Star stared at the name. After the mess she'd made with Paul, even if Mrs. Kelly didn't move to a retirement community, there was no way being her aide could work now.

Others from the group shuffled in, looking sleepy. Star

smothered a yawn.

"This has been an amazing trip, but sleeping in my own bed is starting to sound nice." Morris directed a sweet gaze at Linda. The kind of gaze Star prayed to have from a husband someday. A husband who would be a partner in all ways.

Her heart pinched. Oh, how she wanted that partner to be Paul.

As if summoned, he entered the room with his mother. Mrs. Kelly's eyes were red and glassy, her lips downturned. What had Paul said to her?

Paul avoided looking Star's way and aimed for a table at a far corner. Hesitating, Mrs. Kelly waved at Star with an apologetic glance, then hobbled slowly across the room to catch up with her son.

Every fiber of Star's being hurt for Mrs. Kelly. Sadness roped around Star's stomach and cinched tight. There was no way she could eat now. She stood on shaky legs. "I'm not hungry."

Pity filled Linda's gaze. "I'll order you a pastry or something for later and tuck it in my purse."

Across the room, a clatter rang out, and then a gasp. "Mom!" Paul's voice cried.

Star pivoted in time to see Mrs. Kelly slump across the table. Cups tumbled. Paul tripped over his chair, but caught his mother in his arms and set her in her seat.

"Someone call for help!" Paul shouted, panic paling his face.

Star ran to his side. "Did she hit her head or anything? I can—"

His hazel eyes shot hateful missiles at her. "Get away from my mother! I told you this trip would kill her. You've done enough."

His words punched her in the gut, the blow swift and fierce.

A flashback of her stepfather tunneled her vision. That look of rage. The kicks, pushes, and fists knocking her down the hall of the trailer. She and Skye wore matching pink dresses, sweat pouring from the late summer heat beating down on the metal building with no AC.

That was the day she'd decided to fight back.

She blinked and looked back at Paul. No one would abuse her, verbal or otherwise, without getting scarred themselves. But she wouldn't shout back at Paul.

Because maybe he was right. All she'd done was cause him and Mrs. Kelly problems. She loved Mrs. Kelly, but there was nothing she could do for her anymore, but pray. Paul would never let her back into their lives.

The pain of the loss slashed into her. She'd always been on her own, not belonging, not mattering to anyone. Why did she think that would ever change? Turning on her heel, she ran out of the dining room, through the lobby, and up the stairs to her room. In five minutes, she had her bag packed and plowed outside to hail a cab. Tears blinded her as she threw her suitcase into the trunk.

At the airport, Star begged a ticketing agent to move her to an earlier flight. Maybe it was the tears, or the sling on her shoulder, or the desperation in her voice, but finally, the guy found a spot on a plane departing in four hours. He charged her a hundred dollar fee, but that would be worth the price to get away from this pain.

"Here you go, lass." Compassion filled the middle-aged man's voice. "I've a daughter about your age. Please, be careful."

She nodded. "I will." She'd guard her heart for sure.

Star sat in a lonely corner of the airport staring into space, trying to let her mind blank out. She'd prayed for Mrs. Kelly and Paul, which was all she could do, but the hamster-wheel of grief and worry kept reeling her back in, scrambling her thoughts, racing her pulse, and leaving her shaky palms clammy. In her life before Christ, she would've been racing for something to take the edge off.

And at the moment, the bar down the hall seemed to be calling her name. A drink or two would numb the pain. Enough alcohol could wash away the excruciating memory of Paul's face. The urge pulled hard.

Lord, help me. Please be with Mrs. Kelly and Paul. Let her be okay. I feel so helpless and awful. I need You.

Chapter 34

"I found you."

Star looked up at the words as, breathless, Linda planted herself in the chair beside her. "Finally."

"How did you get past security?" A lump rose in her throat. She couldn't believe her eyes. "Why would you?"

"To be with you. And, don't worry, Morris will text if there are updates on Mrs. Kelly." Linda took Star's hand and squeezed. "I prayed God would help me figure out where you were and what flight you'd been switched to so I could change my ticket to be with you. I happened to end up with a really nice agent who seemed to know exactly what I needed. Off the record, of course."

Rivers of tears flowed down Star's cheeks. "Why would you do that?" She hiccuped. "For me?"

"Come here." Linda held out her arms and folded Star to her chest. "This may sound crazy, but I've learned to obey what I feel God is telling me to do. And I think I'm supposed to sort of…adopt you. I want you to be a part of our family."

Through wet lashes, Star gazed up at the woman she'd known only two weeks. "I'm not a minor, you know?"

"But you don't have a family, do you?"

"My friends at Re-Claimed." Her chest shook as she spoke. "And I had Mrs. Kelly." She was being such a baby, but she couldn't seem to stop.

"Morris and I have grown children with families of their own. They're living busy lives in other cities, so we have room for you in our home and in our hearts." She gave Star a gentle hug. "For as long as you need us."

Warmth settled over Star's wounded soul, along with a sense of hope. Though her heart had been laid bare, God had provided comfort. Stranded and alone, she'd called out to her Father for help, and He'd answered.

"Linda, if you're serious, I might take you up on that." Star gazed up toward the ceiling. "God knows I could use a mother's advice."

A sweet laugh bubbled in Linda's chest. "And I might be guilty of doling out a lot of my opinions to my daughters and son. So join the club."

"I like the sound of that." Despite her sling, she lifted her arms to hug Linda, but her shoulder slipped out of place, stealing Star's breath. "Oh," she gasped at the sharp pain.

"Did I hurt you?" Linda let go of Star and sat back to look her over.

"I moved wrong." She spoke through gritted teeth.

"We're going to get that shoulder looked at as soon as we get home." Riffling through her purse, Linda retrieved her phone. "I know a great orthopedic doctor. I'll send an email and see how soon they can get you in."

"Wait. I don't have insurance." And there was no way she'd let Morris and Linda pay her medical bills.

"I heard Priscilla tell you she had trip insurance, and you hurt yourself on the trip. We'll figure it out, and once we hire you officially, our ministry has benefit options for fulltime employees."

A job with benefits and a family? *God, You sure are good. Please be good to Paul and Mrs. Kelly too.*

"You're thinking of Paul again, aren't you?"

Hunching over to hide more tears, Star bobbed her

quivering chin. "And Mrs. Kelly. What if she...?" Her voice broke.

"Don't think the worst." Gently, Linda rubbed circles on Star's back—the way she'd always imagined a normal mother would. "Morris went to the hospital with them. He'll text us." She huffed. "As for Paul—and I've told my daughters this many times—unless a male is wearing a diaper, you can't change him. That's God's job."

Star couldn't stop a blubbering laugh. "I'm going to enjoy getting motherly advice from you."

~~~

Mom had to be okay. This couldn't be the end. The white walls and the smell of antiseptic closed in on Paul, squeezing his chest, choking the oxygen from his lungs. "I hate hospitals." He whispered and slumped in the hard plastic chair, not really speaking to Morris beside him.

"Places of pain, but also places of healing." Morris rested a hand on Paul's shoulder.

"I wish they'd tell me something." Frustration and guilt boiled inside him. If only they'd never come on this trip. Mom would be safe and home. And he never would've had his heart shredded by another quote-unquote Christian. All night he'd fumed over how Star could just toss him out like one of those stupid ugly T-shirts they'd bought. For God.

Still, the wounded look on her face when he'd yelled at her split him in two. He shouldn't have taken out his panic over Mom on her.

Morris dropped his hand and folded his arms in front of his chest. "I know you may not want to hear this, but I'm praying."

"I figured," Paul mumbled and rubbed his pounding temples. "Not that it'll do any good."

"If you keep massaging that wound, it'll become more and more infected with bitterness." Morris's voice held compassion, but the words bit into Paul, ripping at the scars covering his heart.

"I served God. I prayed." He scoffed. "Your God didn't answer."

"His ways—"

"Aren't our ways." Paul held up his palm. "Got it." He wasn't trying to be rude to the guy, but he'd heard that verse from his mother when Dad had died. And he couldn't believe how she could be okay with that lame excuse.

Morris sat back in his chair and crossed his arms. "Paul, God isn't some Santa we write a letter to, telling Him what we want. Prayer is part of our relationship with our Creator. It's communicating and listening more than it's telling Him what we'd like Him to do."

Five feet away, the emergency room doors swung open, and a thin brunette in blue scrubs exited and aimed at Paul. His pulse skittering, he sat up as she approached, trying to determine if her expression gave anything away—good or bad.

"Mr. Kelly, you can come back to see your mother now." She directed him with a sweep of her hand.

Paul scrambled to his feet and followed.

"Want me to go with you?" Morris moved to the edge of his chair.

Did he? He swallowed in an attempt to wet his dry throat and then glanced at the nurse. "Is she...okay?"

"Awake and insisting she wants to leave." The nurse smiled.

Relief loosened Paul's tense muscles, and he pivoted toward Morris. "I'll go back alone if you don't mind."

After passing through two short halls, the nurse led Paul

into a small room. Mom sat on a small cot propped up with a few pillows, and a young doctor in blue scrubs stood at her side.

"Oh, Paul, I'm so sorry I worried you." Mom's tired face crumpled. "And poor Star. Is she here?"

He wasn't about to relay that bit of information yet. "What's wrong with you?"

His mother gazed up at the doctor. "The good news is, I just have an ear infection and vertigo."

The doctor smiled down at her. "The bad news is, she has a severe ear infection and a harsh case of vertigo."

"Vertigo?" Paul blew out a long breath.

The doctor turned his attention to Paul. "We ruled out heart issues and stroke. There was a large amount of fluid behind her right eardrum. We're treating her with an antibiotic, but until she's better, she'll feel as though she's tumbling through space. With her arthritic stability issues, she'll need to rent a wheelchair for the last part of your tour, due to the dizziness and balance disturbances that go along with the condition."

Mom let her eyes close. "I guess that cold I had caused it."

The doctor nodded. "Probably, but when you get home, you'll want to see an audiologist if the problem continues."

Not only that, the plane trip home would be a bear.

Once the doctor finished giving written instructions to Paul, he excused himself and left.

Mom squinted her eyes open and aimed a hard look his way. "You never answered about Star."

Oh, man, he was going to be in trouble.

Chapter 35

Oh, honey, how could you? That poor girl's been through enough in her short life.

In the four days since they'd left the Dublin hospital, Mom's words had continued to stab Paul's chest. The two sentences played over and over like a song stuck on repeat. They sank down deep, gashing open his heart, which had already been torn open by guilt and grief. Not only did he feel shame, he missed Star. Missed everything about her. The way she fiercely protected those she cared about. The silly game she'd conjured up when their suitcases had been lost—which he realized she'd done to pull him out of the funk he'd been in. How she'd let the awkward situation with Francesca pass so easily. Not many women would've.

And of course, he missed holding her in his arms. He missed the softness of her hair when he ran his fingers through it…and those smoldering kisses. He sucked in a deep breath and closed his eyes.

A dozen *if-onlys* paraded through his mind. If only he'd not let his desire press her into an uncomfortable situation that last night. If only he'd been willing to tour a couple of old churches and not make such a big stinking deal over it. If only he hadn't lashed out at her when he thought his mother was dying of a heart attack.

Paul left his perch at the window. Rain barreled down from the late afternoon London sky, the same as it had every day since they'd arrived. He eased into an armchair in the small living room of his flat where Mom snored quietly on the sofa. He'd taken her back to London to recover before trying to fly over the Atlantic with an ear infection and vertigo. While they were here, he'd pack his belongings and arrange to ship them to St. Simons. No sense delaying.

He'd scheduled an interview in Atlanta for the following week. If he received an offer, he'd ask the company to allow him to start work after Mom's heart surgery. She'd agreed to have the procedure as soon as possible. She'd been excited—as excited as a person could be over having open-heart surgery—knowing he'd move back to the States to care for her.

He looked at her now. Smile lines carved deep in her temples, and a whirlwind of emotions stirred inside him. She was such a good person, a good mother… What if he tanked when Mom needed him most? Dad would've been a better caregiver for this surgery. Paul hated the unfairness of a life that took people way too soon. And even worse, what if Mom didn't make it through surgery? He'd read up on the risks over the past three days—infection, heart attack, stroke. Even the risk of anesthesia.

Mom's snores stopped with a gasp. Her lashes fluttered as she woke.

"Hey, hon." A little wobbly, she pushed herself up to sit. "How about we try out my sea legs and go to dinner?"

"Are you sure? It's pouring out." He pictured her falling and breaking a hip on a slippery restaurant floor.

"I feel better, and you can't keep me caged up here forever." Glancing down at her wrinkled top and slacks, she chuckled. "By the time I get ready, the rain may stop."

"I'll make a reservation somewhere nice, then." He stood and retrieved his phone from the coffee table. "Maybe we can do a driving tour of the sights, too, and measure how you handle the motion."

"Great idea." She smiled at him, then sobered. "Did you apologize yet?" She still wasn't letting him off the hook.

He'd meant to tell Star he was sorry—typed out at least twenty different texts, only to delete them. Punched in her number to call but chickened out. What kind of man was he that he couldn't admit he'd been a jerk?

He smothered a groan. He knew what he was. A prideful man who was in love with a woman who wouldn't have him. A man with a broken heart.

He made a decision. "I'll do it while you're getting ready."

~ ~ ~

"That's a real nice lady you got to adopt you." Davis grinned and nudged Star's good shoulder after he'd loaded the last of her few belongings into Linda's car. "Think she needs another son? I'm available."

Star couldn't help but laugh. "Find your own family that takes in grownups."

"Selfish." His teasing gaze swept over her, then he sobered. "I'll miss you."

A cool morning breeze rushed between them, stirring golden leaves of massive oaks that lined the sidewalks of St. Simons outside of Re-Claimed. "I'll miss your goofy self too." She sighed and sagged against the car's hood. Linda would be out of the house soon—once Gabby finished talking her ear off—and they'd be on the road to Jacksonville. She'd said goodbye to all her friends, and now she'd start a new life. The thought both excited and terrified her. "I'll miss everyone."

"But, you're happy about moving and the new job and all, right?" He studied her.

"Oh, yeah. It's an answer to prayer for sure." She bobbed her head. "I'm pumped." Her voice sounded fake in her own ears, though.

"Uh, something tells me you're down, too—about more than moving and your messed-up shoulder." He took a step closer and crossed his arms. "You know when you asked me about what was between you and me at the hospital, I—"

"Please, please forget that moment. Wipe it forever from your mind." She rubbed her forehead to try and hide some of the heat creeping to her face. "I was worried sick about Mrs. Kelly and frustrated about...you know...her son." She still was. Tears burned behind her eyes, and she sniffed.

"You miss her." Davis toed a piece of gravel. "And what about that son of hers? Paul. You don't seem to be able to speak his name."

Looking at the tree limbs and then the scurrying, fallen leaves on the sidewalk—pretty much looking everywhere other than at Davis, Star scrambled to find an answer. Davis was too perceptive for his own good. For her own good.

"You and him? Really?" Davis gasped. "Now, I gotta know."

"What?" Star scoffed. "I didn't say anything."

"You think I was hiding behind the door when they passed out brains or something?" He crossed his arms over his muscular chest. "What happened?"

Letting her chin fall, Star growled. Talking about Paul hadn't been the plan, but she might as well. Davis was like a dog with a bone if he thought something might rock someone's sobriety. "Long story short, we got close on the trip. Then I realized our differences in faith"—she rolled her eyes— "or rather his lack of, would be a huge issue down the road. I broke it off. He got angry."

"He didn't hurt you, did he? Because I'll rip him—"

"No. No. Nothing like that. Nothing physical." Only her

heart. She pinched her lips to keep from bawling again. Like she'd done in the shower and the quiet hours of the night when she'd had time alone to grieve.

Gently, he tipped her chin with the edge of his index finger. "You deserve a good man. No, you deserve the best man. Like Captain-America-Christian-Hot-Guy man."

A laugh bubbled up despite the tears coating her eyes. "I've got Jesus. He's the best."

He pulled her into a loose hug. "I'll be praying for you, and I can come visit when you have surgery if you want."

"Only if you don't try to steal my new parents."

Davis was a good friend. And that was all. She realized the emotion now for what it was, friendship. She'd not had many guy friends in the past. Maybe none.

Her phone dinged in her jacket pocket, and Davis stepped back. She pulled it out and stared at the name on the text. Her heart stuttered.

"You're looking at that thing like it's an anaconda or something. What's wrong?" Davis craned his neck to try to see the screen.

"It's him." She forced herself to speak his name. "Paul. I hope nothing's happened to Mrs. Kelly."

Chapter 36

"Good night in the morning, read the thing," Davis huffed.

"I'd rather poke myself in the eye with a sharp stick." Star grimaced at the thought of reading Paul's text. Nothing but pain could come of it.

"Just pull the rotten tooth and get it over with."

"Fine." Cheeks heated and heart racing, Star spun around, away from Davis's prying eyes. She was being silly. Her and Paul's relationship hadn't even lasted that long. Leftover chili had a lengthier shelf life.

I'm sorry for everything that happened the last night and morning you were in Ireland. I was a jerk and an idiot.

An ache spread across Star's chest, and with it, the hollowness of missing both Paul and Mrs. Kelly. Now that she was moving to Jacksonville, she'd likely never see either of them again.

But their separation was for the best. Still, how hard had those words been for Paul to write?

Or maybe his mother pressured him into apologizing. She'd never really know if his remorse was legitimate.

"I'm still here." Davis tapped her elbow. "And I'm still nosey. What did the man have to say for himself? He better not be harassing you. I'll put the hurt on him."

Star turned back to face Davis and shot him a quizzical stare. "Really? What about love your enemies and all that?"

"Okay, I'll pray God slaps some sense into him. Like knocks him silly hard."

She gave him a sad smile.

Praying for something—anything—to get through to Paul had consumed hours of her own thoughts. She held up the phone. "He apologized."

"Huh." Davis looked up to the sky. "Maybe God is slapping away at ole Paul. You gonna answer him?"

"None of your beeswax." Because she had no idea what she'd say. Her answer required prayer. She wasn't going to shoot off the first words that came to mind.

"We're coming," Gabby called. At last, she and Linda exited the Re-Claimed women's house and strode down the sidewalk. Gabby still talked nonstop the entire way, while Linda nodded and smiled.

"Well, sister. This is bye, I guess. For now." Davis gave her another side hug. "I'll miss you, kid."

"I'll miss you too." She smirked at him as he stepped away. "Mostly."

"I know you will." Grinning, he puffed out his chest. "I mean, I'm a Davis original."

Shaking her head, she laughed. "God broke the mold. And maybe for good reason."

"Truer words have never been spoken." Gabby approached and wrapped Star in her long arms. "You're always welcome back here. We love you."

Tears gathered in the corners of Star's eyes. "Love you too," she managed to squeak out.

Davis leaned close to them and winked. "Remember, you'll feel better when it quits hurting."

Gabby rolled her eyes. "Take him with you. Pleeease."

"I already told him no." Star slipped from Gabby's warm embrace and walked around to the front passenger side of Linda's Camry. She waved, then slid into the seat, and Linda did the same.

"Ready for an adventure?" Linda smiled at her as she started the engine.

"Ready." She struggled to fasten her seatbelt over her sling and breathed a sigh. Davis—in his own crazy way—was right. She would feel better when it quit hurting. She just prayed that time would come soon.

~~~

I forgive you, and I'm praying for you and your mom.

Paul sat in the chilly surgery waiting area of the Jacksonville hospital. Ironically, the best medical center for this heart surgery ended up being in the town where Star had moved.

He read the text for at least the hundredth time over the past two weeks. How easily Star offered grace.

He'd texted Francesca and apologized, explaining he'd never meant to hurt her. The reply she'd sent hadn't been as generous. Not that he deserved anything from either woman.

He massaged the back of his neck. Already a tension headache threatened, and the nurse had just taken Mom back. A long, awful day and night awaited. The doctor had warned Paul that between prepping Mom, the operating room, and then the recovery room, she'd be away at least four to six hours. Then she'd be in the ICU.

Waves of anxiety smacked him as he imagined Mom having such a large incision down her chest. He cringed at the thought of the procedure itself, splitting her open, messing with her heart. Nausea swept through him. She had to make it. If she didn't...

Please—

No. He wasn't begging anyone.

No answers had come to his prayers in the past. A wasted effort.

Shaking off the thought, he refused to go any farther down that road. He reached for the book of company policies and the manual he'd brought from the flight company in Atlanta. He could prepare for his new career—his new life in Georgia.

"Is that seat taken?" a man asked.

Paul looked up to find Morris, dressed in jeans and a long-sleeve T-shirt. The same shirt as when they'd first met in Ireland. It read *Reunite Global.*

"What are you doing here?" He'd known the guy all of two weeks in Ireland. Morris had to be here for some reason besides Mom.

"We came to sit with you." Morris plopped next to Paul, so close their shoulders touched.

"We?" Paul's forehead drew together. Had Star come with him? A rush of hope tore through him.

"Bradford and I." Morris thumbed toward the entrance. "He had to make a detour into the men's room."

His throat thickened. Of course, Star wouldn't come. He'd kicked her out of their lives.

But Mom and Bradford? He still couldn't get used to the idea of his mother dating. "Thanks. Linda didn't mind you taking off?" Yes, he was fishing for information about Star. He could kick himself, but he couldn't stop.

"Star's surgery is today too. At Mayo. We have staff handling the ministry. All will be fine." He clapped Paul's arm. "And Linda will take good care of Star, in case you're worried."

A pang of guilt pierced his heart. "Her shoulder was that bad?"

Morris nodded. "MRI showed tendons shredded to pieces in there."

"I should've been the one to protect Mom that day on the cliffs."

257

"Paul, there was years of old damage to her shoulder. Not your fault in any way." Morris's throat made a low growl. "That monster of a stepfather."

And the knife of guilt sank deeper. He never should have yelled at Star.

"Hey, stranger." Bradford cruised in, the gray-haired man smiling with kind blue eyes. He moved with the speed of someone twenty years his junior.

Paul stood and shook his hand. Tight grip too. "Thank you for coming." He'd learned his lesson on being rude. And the thought of sitting alone for hours overwhelmed him, so company might be nice.

"Priscilla is a special lady. I've been praying for her nonstop." He clasped Paul's shoulder and squeezed.

Thickness coated Paul's throat. He didn't want to be comforted by prayers. He wouldn't give the possibility of supernatural help purchase in his heart.

"What's Will up to?" he asked to change the subject.

"He's joined the air force."

"You're kidding?" That came as a shock.

"Your talk of piloting inspired him. You don't know how much I appreciate it. Will needed some kind of direction." Bradford leveled a serious gaze at Paul. "And I'm free to be here for the long haul."

Paul blinked hard. He couldn't go there right now.

"Linda just texted. They've begun Star's surgery." Morris held up his phone, as if they could read the message. "Let's say a word of prayer."

Paul's stomach sank faster than a boulder rolled from a cliff. Maybe he would rather be alone.

Chapter 37

"How's it going so far?"

Paul looked up from his perch in the hospital waiting room to find Mom's neighbor, Cooper Knight, approaching with a plastic food container in hand. Why had he driven the hour from St. Simons?

"I've been sent to deliver this healthy cookie concoction from my wife. She's in town for Star's surgery this morning, but I'm only here for a quick visit. She says to tell you Phoenix the possum is being taken care of." Cooper opened the lid of the bowl and held it toward Paul. One side of his mouth lifted. "I'm the possum keeper now."

"Thanks. For both. It was nice of you to come down here." Paul took a cookie-thing and examined the brown lump. Something poked out of the bran surface—maybe carrot and raisin chunks. Not super appetizing, but a nice gesture. He took a bite. Not as bad as it looked. Fruity and moist, a hint of cinnamon.

Behind Cooper, the mouthy guy from the Bible study appeared wearing a bright orange T-shirt and holding two large cups from Starbucks. "Sorry I got lost. Ran into someone I knew." His gaze landed on Paul. "Hey, dude."

Not him. Paul tried to school his features. "Hey." He forced the single word. He wasn't in the mood for a sermon today.

Or ever.

"I come bearing a caffeine offering." The guy—wasn't his name Davis?— shot him a goofy grin.

Paul took the cup with a nod of thanks, soaking in the aroma of chicory. The coffee looked far more appealing than the cookies had, although he'd have preferred the brew had come from someone else. He pointed with his head to the men beside him. "This is Morris and Bradford, friends we made in Ireland who came to…be a support."

"That's kind of you." Cooper shot them a smile.

"Well, I'll be a monkey's uncle." The men stood, and Davis shook their hands. "You came all the way from Europe? I thought we came a long way from St. Simons."

Morris laughed. "We were on the tour with the Kellys and Star. We're actually from the Jacksonville area."

"Ooooh, one of you is Star's new dad, I bet."

New dad? What did that mean? He'd heard that Star worked for Morris and Linda's ministry.

"That would be me." Morris nodded. "She's just out of surgery. All went well."

The good report loosened some of the knots in Paul's shoulders. If only Mom's operation could be over. It'd been hours.

"Praise the Lord." Davis breathed an exaggerated sigh. "That girl deserves something good." He cut his gaze toward Paul. "She deserves the best."

Heat like burning coals waylaid Paul, steaming up from his chest and searing his cheeks. A snarky reply clamored to be spit out, but Paul bit his tongue. Obviously, Star had confided in the guy. Why, he couldn't fathom.

"Sorry I can't stay longer, but I'll come back if you need anything." Cooper punched the cookie container toward Davis, then looked at Paul. "I have to get back to the gallery, but we wanted you to know you were on our hearts. Your mother's a special lady. And I'm leaving this guy with the cookies to keep you company."

Davis pushed back at the plastic bowl. "You keep those balls of nothing. I'll order pizza or something more manly for us."

No, please, don't stay. For the love of all.

"You don't need to." Paul set his cookie on the coffee lid and stood. "I've got people with me." He thumbed toward Morris and Bradford, then shrugged. Maybe that sounded rude, and he was trying his best to do better since Ireland. "I mean, I don't want to keep Davis from work or anything. Thanks for coming, though. I know it was out of the way for you."

"This is my work." Davis stayed rooted in place on the white tile. "And I drove down separately."

"What work?" Exasperation laced Paul's voice, despite his best efforts.

"I'm going into ministry, so people are my work."

Paul's jaw clamped tight. Why did this keep happening to him? Christians surrounded him everywhere he went. He couldn't seem to slow the onslaught. He sank back into his chair, Morris and Bradford following his lead. At least they were quiet.

Cooper placed the cookie container in Morris's hands and made his way out.

Unfortunately, Davis remained. Still standing, he patted his stomach. "I'm so hungry my belly is rubbing against my backbone. What kind of pizza can I get y'all? I saw a place not far from here."

Paul stifled a groan. At least that might keep the guy busy for a few minutes, and maybe his mouth full too. "Any kind of meat."

"That's what I'm talking about." The guy pumped his fist.

The phone in Paul's pocket rang, jolting him straight in the chair. He set the coffee on the floor and scrambled to get his cell. "Hello."

"Mr. Kelly, this is your mother's nurse. The doctor would like to meet with you in a few minutes. I wanted to make sure you're still in the waiting area."

"Yes." A furious pounding began in his chest, and his breathing stalled. "Is something wrong?"

"The surgeon will go over everything with you."

A few minutes later, Dr. Johnson strode through the door in blue scrubs, his expression grim. He removed his cap and ran his fingers through his thin hair. "Paul, come with me to a meeting room so we can talk."

Swallowing hard at the boulder lodged in his throat, he stood.

"Want us to come?" Morris rose to stand beside him.

Paul let his gaze roam over the three men who'd been waiting with him. As much as he didn't want company, he also didn't want to be alone. "Okay."

He followed Dr. Johnson until the man stopped, opened a door to a small meeting room, and held it for them.

Once they entered, the doctor motioned toward some chairs. "Want to sit?"

"Just tell me what's wrong." Paul fisted one hand and squeezed it with the other.

"Your mother's surgery went well until we were closing." Dr. Johnson pressed his lips together before continuing. "Then her blood pressure and vitals bottomed. She'd thrown a clot. We administered IV anticoagulants for the clots, which is delicate during this type of surgery because of possible blood loss. In her case, she had a brain bleed—a small one, though."

Paul squeezed his eyes shut as if he could lock out the flood of unwanted words crashing over him. "Is she...?"

"She's alive but unresponsive and on a ventilator in ICU."

"Unresponsive, like in a coma?" He couldn't stop the crack in his voice.

"Yes."

A familiar agony plowed through Paul—agony excavated from those long, grueling hours spent begging for his father's life.

All for nothing.

"Paul, don't give up." Dr. Johnson exchanged the professional tone for a hushed, compassionate one. Still, the words seemed to be coming from across a long chasm, their meaning plummeting before reaching Paul.

A hand rested on Paul's shoulder and squeezed. "God can still work miracles." Morris's voice came from behind.

Covering his forehead and eyes with his palm, Paul cursed. He knew better than to expect a miracle.

Chapter 38

"Oh, Lord, please save her." The pain in Star's shoulder faded as grief carved into her heart. Fear, like brutal hands, clutched her throat, taking her breath prisoner. If Paul lost his mother, the blow would devastate him. The anguish could destroy what little love he had left in his heart. And the thought of losing her dear friend pressed heavy as a cresting wave in high tide.

"She's still alive, so there's hope." Linda knelt on the rug beside the recliner Star had camped in since arriving home from the hospital. The woman had been so good to Star, serving homemade soup, tending to her every need. "God created life from dust, He can make Priscilla well."

"I know." Star sniffled. "And as much as I want her to live, I know if He doesn't heal her, Mrs. Kelly will wake in His arms. It's just that Paul…" Her voice broke. "I'm afraid this'll be the last straw. He's so angry with God. His heart will close to Him. And maybe close to everyone else forever." She let her eyes slide shut.

"Paul is an M-A-N. They don't do well with emotional pain. They don't do well with life spinning out of control, but Morris will be there for him." She made a sad laugh. "Women don't do well with this stuff either, honestly."

"How are you and Morris so good together? So happy?"

Linda slid up to sit on the couch. "Our marriage wasn't always so great. Don't let anyone fool you into thinking their lives have always been sunshine and roses. We almost split up years ago."

Star's mouth fell open. She swept her good arm around the living room of the beautiful four-bedroom ranch she'd been blessed to call home. "You're kidding? Why? Y'all seem so perfect."

"Typical story. When we were young, we both worked at different jobs, Morris with really long hours. We had one child in daycare, and Morris often traveled overseas for the ministry. Managing the household fell to me while he was gone, and when he came home, he just wanted to *relax*." She pinched her lips together. "As in, I had to do everything."

"That would tick me off." Star felt her brows furrow. "I can't believe Morris would ever act like that."

A sad smile lifted Linda's cheeks. "I was bitter and angry, believe me." Blinking at tears, she looked down at her hands and twisted the wedding ring on her finger. "I was so angry, I got involved with a coworker." Her gaze rose to meet Star's. "He gave me the attention I was so desperate for, and I'm ashamed to say I broke my vows."

"You?" Star couldn't stop a gasp.

Linda gave a slow nod.

"How did you turn things around?"

"When I told Morris I wanted a divorce, he begged me to go into counseling." Linda's gaze rose to meet Star's. "We had our son, so I agreed to try for his sake, but I honestly had no intention of staying in the marriage."

"Oh, my goodness."

"After a year of the ministry giving us support while Morris stayed in country, things started to improve. I quit my job where the other man worked. Morris helped around the house, worked on being a father and a husband." A real smile lit up Linda's face. "Slowly, but surely, God resurrected our dead marriage. And I believe God can resurrect Paul's dead faith.

And save Priscilla, if it's in His will."

Star let her head fall back against the plush leather chair. "I just wish I could do something."

"You can. But this battle will be on our knees. Well, you stay in that chair until you're better, young lady." Linda shot her a teasing, motherly look. "Let's pray now."

"Okay." Star bowed her head, and they lifted Paul and his mother before the throne of the Creator of the universe.

~~~

Bradford insisted on paying the bill for lunch at the noisy bistro near the hospital and then excused himself to rest at home for a while. The news from the doctor that there wasn't much else to do for Mom seemed to have robbed the older man's strength.

The clanging of silverware and the clatter of voices grated on Paul's nerves. Even the spicy aroma of the chili left on his plate irritated him. Three days of this torturous waiting. Bitterness grabbed at Paul's heart, seizing him like a spider's web he couldn't escape.

Standing, Davis rubbed his stomach after devouring the last of his food. "Thank God for chicken. Or anything fried, really."

Paul rolled his eyes. What an idiot. Thanking God for chickens. And didn't the guy know fried food ruined people's arteries?

Like Mom's. Though the doctor said the inflammation from arthritis had damaged hers too. So unfair.

Paul followed the men out of the restaurant and onto the damp sidewalk through a misty haze to head back to the hospital, where they waited like zombies. For nothing to happen. Nothing to change.

Cool air blasted through the doorways as they entered the

hospital.

Davis thumbed toward the chapel down the hall. "I'll be back in a bit." Other than the God comments he'd made, like at lunch, the guy hadn't involved Paul in the praying. He'd actually been considerate, bringing food and coffee. Mostly speaking only when spoken to. Davis hadn't been the irritant Paul had expected. Intense but steady, the short, muscular guy had stayed night and day at Paul's side. A fixed presence.

Why would Davis do that? Sympathy? Or for God? Likely a Jesus complex. A checkmark on a do-gooder box. For some reason, the thought raised Paul's blood pressure. He didn't need people, much less Davis, feeling sorry for him. Anger rose up inside, strangling him.

"I'll go with you," Morris added. "We'll be back. Text me if anything…"

"Changes?" Paul spat the word. "It won't. You're wasting your breath down there."

Morris placed a gentle touch on Paul's back and gave him a sympathetic look. "Come talk with us."

He didn't want to. There was no reason to. Still, Paul found himself nodding and following them down the beige halls, for no other reason than the fact that he had nothing else to do.

And he'd love to give them a piece of his mind.

Morris's phone rang, and he pulled it from his pocket to check the number. "Sorry, I need to take this real quick."

Davis and Paul took a few more steps to give Morris his space.

"I know you want to come, but you need to listen to Linda and the doctor," Morris spoke quietly, calmly. "You can't get out this soon." Morris ended the call after a few more words of encouragement.

Sadness pinched Paul's heart. Star obviously loved his

mother. Loved her enough to want to come here after her own painful surgery just days ago.

Selfishly, he wished she could. He'd love to catch sight of her, if even for a moment. His chest squeezed. That was him. Selfish.

They reached the small chapel and entered. Paul glanced around, took in the altar table, the cross, and stained-glass panels at the front of the room. It had been a while.

At least no one else is here.

A shadowy darkness fell across his heart as he sat on a blue cushioned chair on the back row. Maybe he *would* give them a piece of his mind.

Morris and Davis stood back a few feet, confusion clouding their features. They surely wondered why he'd agreed to come.

"Sit." Paul flicked his hand toward the empty seats. "Go ahead. Tell me what you really think of me. Get it all out. Why am I wrong about everything?" Emotion heightened, raised his voice. "Explain how God is doing a good thing by killing my mother. Why did He kill my father? Why, when I tried to serve Him in Africa, did He pull the rug out from under me? Explain what I've done to deserve the torture He's laid on me."

Thick silence punctuated by tension ricocheted between them.

"Really?" A frown twisted Davis's face as he sat. "You really want to know?"

"Yeah," Paul spoke between clenched teeth. "Let's clear the air and be done with it."

Davis shrugged. "Okay. I'll start with the fact that you seem like a bit of a self-contained train wreck in how you handled things with Star."

"True. Is that all you got?" Paul shot him a hard look.

"For now." In another surprise move, Davis clamped his mouth shut.

"And you?" Paul yanked his gaze toward Morris.

Morris leaned his elbows on his knees and clasped his hands in front of him. "I know losing your father hurt. I was close with my dad, too, and the pain of saying goodbye tore a gash in my heart. But you studied the Scriptures in seminary, so you know we live in a fallen world." Morris swept one hand around. "All of this is temporary, only a breath in God's timeline."

Paul had heard it before. Ad nauseum. "And my mission work?"

"I don't know why you chose that mission in Africa or if you prayed about it first. I can only speak from my personal experience. My own good intentions took my focus off God's plan. Doing things my way almost destroyed my marriage, so I grappled and prayed— finally listened—then I went where He was leading. And I found that if God is prying something away from you, it's because He loves you. Open your hand."

Memories inundated Paul. The pleasure on his father's face when Paul had announced he was going into mission work. Nothing had meant more than making Dad proud. The prestigious opportunity to work with the renowned missionary had sounded impressive, so he'd jumped on it. He'd been twenty-four, energetic, ready to save the world.

He knew better now. He couldn't save the world. He couldn't even save the people he cared about most.

Had he prayed about whether he should go to Africa? He didn't remember spending much time thinking anything other than that he'd wanted to go. He wanted to do good work and make Dad proud.

His head pounded, vision blurred by tears. His body numb

to his surroundings.

His mother was dying.

This can't be all there is.

His phone rang, pulling him from his chaotic thoughts and stabbing him with shards of fear. "Hello."

"Paul, can you come up to your mother's bedside?" Dr. Johnson's voice sounded bleak.

"Yeah." Paul cut the connection. This was it. They were going to tell him his mother was gone.

Chapter 39

"Her vitals are falling." Standing at Mom's bedside in the ICU, the doctor placed a hand on Paul's shoulder. "I'll be honest. There's nothing else we can do for her. Nothing short of a miracle will change the course she's on."

The course toward death. Paul squeezed his eyes shut to block out this weak and frail version of his mother.

He wanted the real version of her back. The vibrant one whose smile overflowed with life. The one who'd taken him to the beach to make sandcastles whenever he'd asked. The one who took in every lost or abandoned creature they came into contact with and nurtured it back to health. The one who'd shown him unconditional love, despite every stupid thing he'd done—past and present. Everything he'd done in Europe had been to have the freedom to come home and take care of her.

He'd failed her.

"I've heard playing music or reading to patients in a coma could help." Morris stood a few steps back with Davis. "Does she have a favorite song?"

Paul opened his eyes and directed a questioning gaze at Dr. Johnson.

The doctor nodded. "There are some cases reported where music or reading helped, but like I said, her body is failing."

This can't be the end.

Paul swiped his hand through his hair. He had to do something—try anything. Mom used to love to hear a good choir. And she'd loved to sing hymns around the house. No matter what he believed, he'd go the extra mile to try to save her. "It Is Well."

"What?" Confusion knit Dr. Johnson's brows.

Paul turned to Morris. "Her favorite song is '*It Is Well with My Soul.*'" He pivoted back toward the doctor. "Can we sing to her in here?"

"As long as you don't get too loud. I'll let the nurses know you have permission." His lips turned downward. "I'm so sorry this happened, Paul. Your mom is a really good woman."

Tearful, Paul turned to Morris. "Do you know the words? It's been a few years."

"I do." He strode to Paul's side, and they both moved close to the bed.

Paul took his mother's arthritis-twisted hand and cleared his thick throat. "'When peace like a river attendeth my way,'" he sang, squashing the sobs clamoring to escape.

Morris sang along, his soft tenor clear and on tune. Davis rounded the bed to stand on the other side, then he knelt and mouthed words that Paul assumed were prayers.

The significance of the song's history wasn't lost on Paul. He knew the author had penned the verses after losing his children in a shipwreck. Still, the man wrote a hymn telling God it was well with his soul. How could someone have that kind of faith in the face of loss?

They finished the song, and the sounds of beeping machines and the whooshes of ventilators took over.

"I can find more hymns on my phone," Morris offered. "Or find a hymnal, maybe in the chapel."

"Okay." If this helped Mom, if she could still hear him and know that he was there, even if it didn't save her, the sound would make her happy. He'd keep singing until…

He couldn't go there.

He'd keep singing. *"Blessed Assurance."*

They sang hymn after hymn, breaking now and then for coffee or a snack from the vending machine. Davis continued to quietly pray, saying he hadn't been raised in church, so he didn't know the older songs and didn't want to ruin them.

Something about Davis clicked in Paul's heart. No longer did the man rub him the wrong way. Maybe the guy *was* meant for ministry.

Paul scoffed to himself. Probably Davis ministered far better than he'd ever done.

But he'd tried. An ache spread across Paul's chest. He'd done his best to love those children in the orphanage the way he'd seen Mom care for strays. Giving them space at first, letting them come to him for affection when they were ready. Gently nurturing them. In fact, he'd lost his heart to more than a few of those little guys. That had been the reason it'd hurt so much to get sent home. He'd felt like he was deserting them, and those kids had been deserted enough in their young lives. Leaving them had ripped him apart.

Then Dad…

Hours passed, and Paul's voice had become hoarse. Morris's eyes drooped. Bradford had joined them. But nothing had changed. Paul turned to the men. "Why don't y'all get some sleep? Come back in the morning."

Morris shook his head. "We can stay."

"I'll be okay." His gaze fell to Mom's lifeless form. "Some alone time with her would be nice."

The men exchanged glances, then agreed.

"Here's my pocket Bible if you want to read to her." Hesitant, Davis held out the small NIV version. "If she has a favorite book or verse."

Paul stared at the book, lungs collapsing at the thought of

reading from its pages. It had been a long time since he'd touched, much less opened, a Bible.

For Mom. He'd do it for Mom.

Lifting his hand, he took the book. "She likes the gospel of John."

The men nodded and left.

In the lonely whispers of machines and nurses' shoes, Paul pulled up a chair and opened the well-worn pages. He stared at the familiar, ancient words and took a sip of water before beginning. "In the beginning was the Word, and the Word was with God, and the Word was God..."

He read on and on until he finished the entire gospel, then sat back in his chair and swiped the back of his hand across his wet cheeks.

One verse stood out in his mind.

A servant is not greater than his master. If they persecuted me, they will persecute you also.

The words he'd read had done nothing for Mom. She still hadn't moved. But something deep inside Paul cracked open and spilled to the surface.

Star's words that last night in Ireland came back.

...I think you still believe in God. You're just furious with Him that life didn't go the way you wanted it. Now you hate Him.

Maybe she'd been right. She was smart like that.

And Morris had questioned the motives for his African mission work, and now questions niggled in Paul's mind as well. Had he gone primarily to make his father proud? And to make himself feel good?

Instead of going to glorify God? Instead of going where God wanted him to go?

As an only child, he'd often realized, intellectually, that he'd been a bit spoiled...had thought the world revolved around him. Not intentionally, but true.

The way he'd treated Francesca. A married woman.

Shame slid over Paul like slimy mud, bringing bile up his throat. He'd never had any intentions of being in a relationship with her. He'd just allowed his desires to rule, no matter who he hurt.

He was no better than the cheating missionary he'd reported in Africa, and the thought disgusted him.

Realization and truth landed on him like a crashing jet. He, Paul Kelly, was selfish. Self-centered. Self-absorbed.

A hypocrite.

A sinner.

All the rude things he'd said about Christianity had caused his mother stress and disappointment. He'd surely added to her heart disease.

Then the terrible way he'd treated Star. Pressuring her to come to his hotel room.

Oh, God, I'm the worst excuse for a human. I should be there in that bed, dying. I deserve death.

A bitter laugh rose up.

Why was he talking to God now? Why would God ever want to hear anything from him after the fool he'd made of himself? He didn't deserve for God to hear him.

Paul let his head fall into his hands and quietly wept.

Humble yourself before the Lord, and He will lift you up.

The verse floated clearly through Paul's mind, sending chills and waves of holy fear over him. The first verse sent his way since he'd asked—or rather demanded—that they stop. Why had he been so obnoxiously bold?

Quivering with horror, Paul fell to his knees beside his mother's bed.

"If You're there, God...if You're listening. I'm the worst

kind of sinner. I don't deserve anything. I've scoffed at You and Your Word. I don't deserve a miracle. I've been prideful. Angry. I was the one who wasn't listening to You."

He sniffled and swiped at the tears streaming down his face. "But Mom, she's good. She's taken good care of Your creatures." Star's face came to mind. "Your people. And now she's got a second chance at love. Take anything—take everything—I have. Send me anywhere you can use me. Take my life. I'll gladly die in her place." He sobbed and reached out to caress his mother's hand. "I'm so sorry, Mom. I'm sorry, God. Please forgive me. And if it's Your will, take me instead."

He breathed a long shaky breath. "But even if you take her, I trust You, Lord. It is well with my soul."

Peace washed over him like none he'd ever felt. He stood, pulled a chair next to the bed, then rested his head against the railing.

Chapter 40

Face still pressed against the railing of Mom's hospital bed, Paul's eyes slid open at the sensation of a hand touching his hair. Strange for a nurse, but maybe she felt sorry for him or thought he'd gotten sick.

How long had he been asleep?

He glanced over his shoulder but saw no one nearby.

Who…? His heart stammered, and he shot straight up in his chair. "Mom?"

Hazel eyes met his, weary and blinking, but definitely awake.

"Oh, praise God." He stood and pressed a kiss on her forehead. "I need to get the nurse." His voice projected way too loudly for the ICU.

"Right here." A fortyish redhead made a rapid path into the room, her blue eyes glistening. She held a finger before his mother, slowly moving it from side to side. "Don't try to speak, but can you track my movements with your eyes?"

Mom blinked and then followed with her gaze. All the while, Paul's pulse pounded in his chest. Could this be a dream, or had Mom really pulled through? He reached across his body to pinch his opposite arm. Pain followed. Real enough.

"Excellent." The nurse continued checking Mom's vitals and testing her reflexes. When she finished, she directed a smile at Paul. "I'll get in touch with Dr. Johnson, but it looks like your prayers were answered." She gazed back at his mother. "You have a good son. He's barely left your side and prayed hard for you all last night."

Mom's eyes shifted to Paul, and a single tear rolled down her cheek.

With emotion clogging his throat, Paul could only manage a nod, but he couldn't stop grinning. *She's alive.*

Two hours later, the doctor made a special trip in, checked Mom from head to toe, and said he couldn't believe how well she was doing. He even had the team extubate her. Now her breath came with only the aid of oxygen tubes attached at her nose.

Over and over, Paul praised God both in his head and out loud to every medical professional who stopped by.

"And what have we here?" Morris spoke quietly as he and Bradford entered.

Bradford gasped and made his way to Mom's side. "Priscilla. Thank God you're back."

Paul grinned and pointed upward. "He worked a miracle for us."

"It seems that way." Bradford pushed Mom's hair off her face. "And I think He worked one in your son's heart too."

She mouthed the word "Thankful."

Morris snagged Paul's arm. "Davis stopped in the cafeteria to pick up some breakfast. Want to go catch him?"

"Sounds good." He could use a few moments to decompress. "I'll be back, Mom. Bradford." He nodded to them and then followed Morris into the quiet hall.

Morris texted Davis to let him know they were on the way, then they walked without speaking until they neared the dining area. As the intoxicating aroma of bacon circled around them, his neglected appetite kicked in.

Davis waved from a table filled with food—eggs, biscuits, bacon, and fruit. He smiled and lifted a large cup of coffee.

"Got your name on it."

"Thank you." Paul pulled out a chair beside him, sat, and took a deep swig. "Nectar of kings. I needed this."

Morris took the seat across. "Paul's got good news. Tell us what happened."

"She woke up. She's doing well."

"For real?" Davis's mouth fell open. "Not that I didn't believe the Big Guy could do it, but…"

Paul nodded. "I understand. Things looked really bleak."

"Bleak?" Davis's brows lifted almost to his hairline. "I'd say black as asphalt."

A laugh shook Paul's shoulders. Man, it felt good. Relief swarmed him, flooding his weary bones, but in a good way. "After y'all left, I read the Gospel of John. Over and over, the people who were supposed to be religious leaders harassed Jesus. They tried to trip Him up—as if that were possible—and even accused Him of being demon-possessed." Paul took another sip of his coffee. "Something hit me over the head when I was reading. While I served in missions abroad, I'd encountered only a sliver of the troubles He went through, and I'd folded."

"He packs a powerful whack." Davis bobbed his chin.

"He does." Paul smiled, tears forming in his eyes. "I wanted to please my father by doing missions. I wanted others to know I was doing righteous things. I went into missions for all the wrong reasons. My good works glorified me instead of being an effort to glorify God. I was an approval addict."

"Hmmm." Davis's forehead crinkled. "There's probably a twelve-step program for that somewhere."

"Then I need to join." Paul grabbed a slice of bacon, took a bite, and savored the salty meat before continuing. "Convicted, I asked God to forgive me, and—if He was willing—to heal Mom. But I accepted His will either way. And honestly, I fully expected His answer would be no, and that Mom would join my dad in heaven."

Morris leveled a serious look Paul's way. "So you understand that God is still answering prayers even when life doesn't go the way we want it to? Even if your mother hadn't made it?"

"A servant is not greater than his master." Paul quoted the scripture.

A smile lifted Morris's lips. "Now we're talking."

Chapter 41

Seven months later

"I love being back in Malawi." After pecking Morris on the cheek, Linda smoothed her shoulder-length brown hair and shot a huge grin Star's way. "The ladies will be so excited to meet you."

Would they? Nerves knotted Star's stomach as she stared out the plane's window. What did she have to offer to the people of Malawi? She felt so inadequate. She had no idea what being a missionary meant, but Linda had convinced her to come and see the ministry for herself this week—said being there in person would help her understand better what they did and why.

Star loved her job with Reunite Global—with Morris and Linda. Everyone in the office treated her well, and she'd never worked with employers who'd started the week off with Monday staff prayer meetings like they did. Already, she'd been blessed, plus Linda had encouraged her to take the GED. After a few months of study, she'd passed. Not the best score in the world, but now she could continue her education if she wanted.

They unbuckled and prepared to deplane onto the tarmac. The journey to Africa had taken much longer than traveling to Ireland. A smile played on Star's lips, remembering all the annoyances Paul had endured on her first crazy flight. And a few times, she might've imagined him sitting beside her, holding her hand, when they'd encountered turbulence on the way to Johannesburg, South Africa.

A warm breeze greeted them, along with bright sunshine. A flat green landscape stretched beyond the airport grounds. Around them, passengers spoke in a variety of languages and accents as Star followed Morris and Linda toward the terminal bus. God had provided her with an unexpected family in Morris and Linda, and she'd always be grateful. Still, she missed Mrs. Kelly.

And Paul.

After sliding into a seat, she turned on her phone and punched in a quick text to him.

Made it.

The phone chimed back immediately, despite the time difference. Had he been waiting up?

You got this. Praying for all of you.

Thanks! Turning phone off now, but give your Mom my love.

Will do. We love you too.

A wave of warmth swirled within her, lighting up shadowy places deprived of hope. She and Paul had exchanged texts and emails for months, ever since he'd regained his faith, but they'd still not seen each other in person. Her heart told her to allow the time and space to prayerfully figure out God's will and direction. For both of them.

But maybe someday…

After exiting the bus, they plodded inside the airport. In Lumbadzi, the system lagged a decade or so behind the other terminals they'd flown through, but the building pulsed with voices and activity. Crowded together in lines, the passengers went through the slow process of filling out entry paperwork and then paid fees to serious officers dressed in blue uniforms.

Once they cleared the airport and picked up a car for the twenty-mile trip, she settled in the backseat behind Morris and

Linda, then soaked up the passing landscape. Canopies of green trees dotted the rusty dirt. Simple houses and thatched huts stood scattered along the plain that stretched toward stark gray mountains, which seemed to spring from nowhere. Sparse, low-hanging puffy clouds shone white against a brilliant blue sky.

Soon, they entered the dirt drive leading into the ministry compound. Women and children ran their way, waving, and their dark, beautiful faces, smiling. Behind them, the house parents, the Brelands, followed. Star returned their greetings, excitement surging through her. With God's help, she'd try to serve them. For Him.

Her worry had never been over the food or accommodations or even the travel, but more a fear of what would she have to offer to these people. Barely educated herself, a bad family background, only a few months of training in their customs—how was she supposed to be of any service to them?

When they parked, Morris and Linda slid out, slamming their doors behind them. She couldn't just sit here. Taking a cleansing breath and whispering another prayer, she stepped out of the car and stretched her stiff legs.

"Welcome. I'm Lindsay Breland." The short, muscular woman made her way to Star. With a slight bow and curtsey, traditional in this culture, she offered her hand.

"Nice to meet you in person rather than just through work emails." The thirty-something woman's freckled face split into a warm smile.

"You too." Star returned the gestures and shook her hand. A few cords of anxiety loosened. "How can I help?"

Lindsay chuckled. "Wow, I never hear that question so quickly from first-timers. Usually, the jet lag has them running for a cot to rest a bit."

More than a dozen children neared, studying Star, shy smiles and large brown eyes sweetly hopeful. Almost as many women followed them, a graciousness flowing from their faces. Star could almost feel their open hearts inviting her in. She could do this. With God.

"There's no way I could sleep now. I'm ready to get started."

~~~

Early morning sunlight spilled through the windows onto Paul's Bible. Sipping his second cup of coffee, he read as he waited for his copilot in the small commercial terminal on the north side of Atlanta. They had a long flight ahead today to the West Coast.

The door leading in from the runway opened, and a passenger from a plane that recently landed entered. A passenger Paul had met on another flight.

When the guy spotted Paul, fear carved a notch in the muscular pro football player's forehead. "Captain Kelly, I didn't do squat, so don't be quoting Scripture to me again."

"I've never quoted scripture to you, Isaiah." Paul couldn't stop a smirk. The star running back had a tough Competitor in pursuit of his heart. And Paul knew that feeling.

Six months ago, on one of the first flights Paul had taken with his new company, Isaiah had brought a woman on the plane with him—not his wife. As soon as Paul laid eyes on Isaiah, the guy had freaked out and sent her home in a cab. Oddly—or maybe not—they kept running into each other, even though Isaiah always asked to be assigned to a different pilot since that trip.

Isaiah shook a finger. "I know you're a Christian, and every time I see you, some verse my old granny taught me starts shouting in my mind and won't let me go."

"That's not me." Paul shook his head. "Someone else is chasing you." He leveled a hard gaze on the man. "Maybe you should let Him catch you."

Scoffing, Isaiah's brows pinched.

"What's He saying today?" Paul asked.

"You are my witnesses," declared the Lord, 'and my servant whom I have chosen..." He threw up his hands. "I mean, what is that?"

"Really?" Paul's breath caught in his chest. The same verse had been playing on repeat in his own heart all week. Ever since Morris had called with the job offer. Again. Paul had promised to pray about the position, and he had. Almost constantly.

"Yeah. Really." Isaiah grunted, headed toward the exit, and pressed the door open. Then, he paused, allowing the late spring humidity to rush into the air-conditioned building. "I guess I'll try to figure out what it means."

"You might as well. It's foolish to keep kicking against the goads."

Isaiah whipped around. "Do you know my granny or something? She's said that for the past ten years."

"What happened ten years ago?"

The guy's eyes narrowed. "You do know her, don't you? She told you."

"Never met her, but she sounds like a smart lady. You should listen to her."

Mumbling and shaking his head, Isaiah left the terminal, hopefully, to zip away in his luxury sports car to his home in North Atlanta. Luckily, his wife hadn't left him yet, despite a few scandalous tabloid photos last year.

The verse came back to Paul's mind. *You are my witnesses...* What did that mean for him, personally, to be a witness? Why was it plural?

Did it mean in this job as a commercial pilot or the mission position Morris had offered? Paul ran his fingers over his Bible. His copilot still hadn't arrived yet, and Paul had the plane prepared for takeoff, so he had a few more minutes to read and pray. And he'd learned his lesson about charging ahead in his own will. Though he'd completed the application and jumped through all the mission board's hoops to be a part of Morris's ministry, Paul would go only where God led him, not follow his own will.

He had a new Boss now. A perfect One.

He knew it didn't matter how much good he did or how many missions he went on. If he hadn't bowed his knee and surrendered all to Jesus, he'd missed the jet. Or the J-train, as Davis called it when they met in St. Simons to talk over coffee.

Not that it would change his decision, but he couldn't help wondering what Star would think about him working for Reunite Global.

Man, he missed her. They'd shared texts the past several months, about Mom and her fantastic recovery, about Star's shoulder rehab and her new job, about the first trip she'd made to Malawi and how much she loved serving there. And he'd loved hearing from her...was happy for her.

He was happy for Mom too. She'd decided to move into a retirement community in Jacksonville Beach, close to the Mayo Clinic and, of course, close to Bradford. Mom didn't need him much now.

Seemed like everyone he cared about most lived near Jacksonville.

He turned his attention to the Bible and whispered a prayer. "I am your servant, Lord. Lead me. Give me direction."

Thirty minutes later, his copilot arrived. Not long after,

three members of a pro soccer team they'd be flying to LA boarded, along with three women they'd added to the flight plan at the last minute. The rowdy men stank of stale beer and continued their midmorning partying while in flight.

About halfway to their destination, the flight attendant entered the cockpit in tears. "I can't take this anymore. They won't keep their hands off me. One guy threw up all over the place, and I can't control…" Her voice broke.

Adrenaline pulsed through him. This woman was a consummate professional—experienced in handling pawing, wealthy men accustomed to getting their way. In fact, he and his crew were well-versed in how to deal with the bad treatment, so this group must be off the charts. Paul and his copilot exchanged frustrated glances. "You take over, and I'll handle those clowns." Paul unbuckled and walked through the cockpit into the cabin.

The foul mess these guys had made would run upward of fifty thousand dollars if they had to replace the couch or carpet. He put two fingers between his lips and whistled. "Hey! Turn off the music."

The guys stopped their cavorting. One of the women lowered the volume. A guy wearing a stained blue polo staggered toward him. "Aren't you supposed to be flying the plane?"

"Let me get something settled. This"—Paul's voice boomed as he swept his arm around—"is not acceptable. What would your mothers think of how you are treating my flight attendant? Would you want your sisters to be treated this way?"

The men exchanged glances.

"You will treat my crew with respect," Paul continued, "or I will put this plane down at the next airstrip, even if it's in the middle of the desert, and leave your behinds there." He nailed each man with a hard gaze.

"And if you are allowed to stay on board, you will clean up this mess and pay whatever it costs to clean what you can't. Do I make myself clear?"

Solemn expressions covered their faces. One answered with a slur, "Yes, sir, Captain, sir." The others started picking up cups and bottles. The three women helped.

He stood and watched to ensure they did what he'd asked.

The flight attendant leaned close to his ear. "Thank you. I'm done after this month. I've seen most of the world, and I can think of better things to do than babysitting rich people. I think you can too."

Her words sank deep into him. He'd flown movers and shakers, adulterers, prostitutes, drunks, rich and famous actors, rock stars. He'd flown kind-hearted people, and way too many unhappy people with more money than they knew what to do with. But this didn't feel like the ministry he was called to. His story was meant to be told somewhere else.

And he was pretty sure he knew where.

Chapter 42

Ready to fly again. And with time to spare.

Star lifted her luggage and carried the bags from her bedroom to the front door of Morris and Linda's home. Her home. *Thank you, Lord.*

Soaking in the joy of her blessings, she leaned against the doorframe. God had not only provided her with a wonderful family, but her shoulder felt better than ever. She hadn't realized how damaged the tendons around the joint had been.

The three of them should be leaving soon for the long trek back to Malawi. She'd fallen in love with the sweet people on her trip two months ago, and she couldn't wait to design pottery with the single ladies in their ministry. Paul's prayers and encouragement bolstered her confidence too.

Relieved of the pressure of physical intimacy, she'd come to know a whole different side of Paul. They discussed ministry and their travels and even the most trivial details of their everyday lives. The truth was, she loved him more than ever.

This new Paul loved the Lord. He texted photos of sunsets and mountains with Bible verses. He told fascinating stories about the wealthy people he'd flown and a few opportunities he'd found to share his faith. That last night in Ireland, she'd never imagined God would pull off this transformation.

She rummaged through her purse to find her phone. More often than she'd like to admit, she obsessed over the photos Linda and Mrs. Kelly had snapped of her and Paul against the Irish landscape. She opened her favorite, the one on the top of the Bunratty Castle, the wind whipping her hair, the look on Paul's face as he smiled down at her. His eyes. Those beautiful pools of greens and golden brown had drawn her in, even then.

Would their paths ever cross again? She hoped and prayed they would, but she accepted whatever God had in store for her. And for him. She'd grown up in a dysfunctional home and entered into messed up relationships in the past. This time, she wanted to do things God's way. Already, He'd given her the seeds for ministry to women who'd endured even more difficult lives than her own.

Women suffered much in Malawi. Besides AIDS and other disease issues, men could divorce their wives easily. If the women had no family to take them in, they gave up their children because they had no way to earn enough money to feed them. Some families wouldn't take the women back, as they didn't have funds to care for them either. Though some men might marry divorced women, they often wouldn't accept the kids. So, again, the women gave their children to the orphanage in order to survive.

Reunite Global worked to put children back with their mothers by educating the women, teaching them business skills, or training them in crafts so they could earn a living wage. Star's heart had soared when she'd worked with the women to create fabric purses on the last trip. And that was when she'd come up with the idea of teaching them to create a line of pottery to sell at the market. Maybe even ship to the US.

Morris and Linda embraced the idea and had several wheels donated and delivered, along with tons of clay for their upcoming trip. Her friend Rivers created a unique design for the new line, and soon they'd have their own brand. Of course, she'd teach the women the abstinence lesson Mrs. Kelly had taught her. Joy didn't begin to describe the thrum of Star's pulse when she prayed for this ministry to flourish.

A text chimed from the phone still in her hand. Linda. They must be running late.

We sent a car to pick you up. Should be there any minute. We're running behind, but we have our luggage with us and will meet you at the airport.

Hmm. Star hadn't noticed them loading up before their meeting this morning, but she'd been busy packing herself.

Star opened the door and pulled her luggage outside, then locked up. She searched her purse until she felt her sunglasses to shield her eyes from the warm Florida sun. After placing them on her face, she unwound her hair from her ponytail and ran her fingers through the damp strands. Maybe she should have had it cut shorter for the trip, but she'd barely had time to gather the long skirts she'd wear each day and the other supplies she'd need while doing administrative work for Linda. Add to that the need to go through the mission board's training before she left on this trip. The intense program included a psychological study that required a ten-page questionnaire of her life history. Somehow she'd been deemed sane enough to work in ministry. A miracle in itself.

A blue sedan pulled from the street into the drive and stopped. The car door opened, and a man dressed in khaki pants, a light blue T-shirt, and a baseball cap exited. He hadn't looked at her, but something familiar tapped against her heart. Who…?

The man ripped off his hat and pivoted her way.

"Paul?" Star's pulse throbbed in her ears, and heat crept across her cheeks as she lost the ability to breathe.

"Hey." He spoke as if his being there were perfectly normal. His brown hair had grown to touch his collar, and he could use a shave. Still, he was handsome as ever. Then a smile lit up those hazel eyes, and an easy, relaxed expression loosened his forehead. She'd never seen this look on him. And she loved it.

"What are you doing here?" She managed to squeak out and lifted her sunglasses, propping them on her head.

He walked closer, and the rest of the world seemed to fade away. "I'm traveling with y'all to learn the ropes of Reunite Global. Morris and Linda plan to start another ministry next year in rural Kenya."

"What? You? How?" None of this made sense.

One of his brows quirked. "I quit my job. Mom's moving to a retirement village here to be near Bradford."

Could she blow this any worse? "I normally handle all of Linda's correspondence in Jacksonville, and I never saw your paperwork."

"Morris processed my application. I hope you don't mind. Linda seemed to think…" His smile faded, and his gaze dropped to the pavement. "We should've told you. I'm sorry. I'd hoped…"

"You hoped what?" She managed to breathe, though Paul's proximity alone rekindled a powerful longing in her heart. But the desire for him had transformed into something untainted by worldly lust as she'd come to know him on a deeper level. A spiritual level. She'd prayed for him for months. But she still loved God first and best.

And she needed to see that Paul felt the same way.

"I've been praying since I took the job in Atlanta. I've met with your nutty-but-spiritual friend Davis on my days off, talked to Morris on the phone, tried to listen to the Lord's leading. The other day I felt that confirmation in my soul."

All good news, but she had to know more. She had to be

sure. "How?"

"A verse." Paul's eyes lifted and held hers.

"What verse?" Her breathing stalled again.

"'You are my witnesses,' declared the Lord, 'and my servant whom I have chosen...'"

The same verse that had been pressing on Star's heart all month.

Arms thrown out wide, a laugh bubbled from deep inside her. "Get over here, Perky."

He closed the gap between them in one long step and pulled her against him. She relished his strong arms around her, soaked in the crisp linen scent of him, closed her eyes, and leaned against his firm chest to hear the heartbeat of a man who'd been transformed by God. A man she could love and trust with her heart. And not end up in a mess.

"I've missed you, Princess Star." He breathed the words against her hair.

She raised her gaze to meet his. In their depths, she found a different kind of love shining down at her. No longer did his gaze hold the anger over his past or the desire that had almost swept her away, but a tenderness that sent her heart soaring.

"Would it be okay if I kissed you, just once, before we head to the airport?" He tipped her chin. "In Malawi, PDA is inappropriate, so..."

Another laugh splashed up from deep inside, like a spray of cool water on a hot Florida day. "Make it a good one then, Perky."

Mischief danced in his gaze. He brushed her lips with his, slowly at first, then with a passion and a warmth, so lovely. The emotion spread between them with a promise of something pure, but surely an exciting adventure together.

When finally he relinquished her lips, he pressed his

forehead against hers and sighed. "What do you think about possibly being a copilot with me in Kenya? Down the road, of course, with a little more time together under our belts."

Joy exploded in her soul at the implication. She'd love nothing more than to serve the Lord at his side. If that was God's will. "We'd better start praying about that move, and make sure God is in the control tower."

He pressed one more kiss against her cheek. "Amen."

Epilogue

"I was hoping for more of a destination wedding for my first time officiating. Like a lions-and-tigers-and-bears-oh-my destination wedding." Davis waved one arm around Linda and Morris's green front yard. With the other hand, he pulled at the stiff white collar buttoned around his muscular neck, a bit too tight for the eighty-degree temperature.

"The flight to Africa would be too hard on Mom, and there's not much in the way of bears in Kenya anyway." Sliding a snarky glance toward his friend, Paul straightened his tie for the seventh time. Man, his nerves hadn't bundled this tight in over a year.

Spring came early in Jacksonville. Birds chattered in blooming dogwoods, and butterflies bounced along the daffodils blossoming in the sculptured flower beds. Not that he could concentrate on any of the decorations Linda had set up for the wedding, or on their friends Cooper and Rivers, or on any of the other twenty people sitting in white folding chairs in front of them.

Long shadows spread across the lawn, and the music changed from a slow instrumental melody to a haunting tune that floated on the air with strains of fiddle and flute, a traditional Irish style. Nice touch. God had used the trip to Ireland to change all their lives, after all. *Thank you, Lord.*

Morris and Linda's front door opened, and Paul's pulse spiked. Bradford led Mom down the two steps into the yard, then to the seat reserved on the front row of the small gathering. She directed a bright smile at Paul, still looking giddy as a twenty-year-old bride herself since she and Bradford had married two months prior.

The Irish melody transformed into a lyrical version of the wedding march, and the door opened again. Morris stepped out and then turned back, offering his arm to the woman in the long white dress behind him.

Star stepped forward, and a flood of emotion deeper than he'd ever felt consumed the oxygen in Paul's lungs. She strolled down the short aisle of grass, her gaze locked on his.

He'd never seen anything or anyone so beautiful, inside and out.

Finally, she reached his side. Morris kissed her cheek, then took his seat beside Linda.

Winking, Star grinned his way and whispered, "I love you, Perky."

Warmth and joy radiated through him. God hadn't answered all Paul's prayers the way he'd expected. He didn't know why some prayers were answered with miracles, and others weren't. He still missed his father—wished Dad could be here. He still hurt for the orphans he'd been forced to leave in Kenya years ago.

But he trusted that God loved him, loved Star, loved his mother, and all the people of Kenya. God would do what was best for each of them. Paul would open his hand and give every single one of the people he loved to the Lord to care for in His infinite wisdom.

Davis cleared his throat. Loudly. "I'm up here, you gooey-eyed people." Snickers circulated through the guests.

With a teasing raise of her arched brow, Star pinned Davis with a sassy look. "Don't make me dock your pay, preacher boy."

"Yikes." Davis straightened, pretending to be afraid. "I've heard about you Bridezillas."

"You'll see one if you don't get this show on the road. We're ready to get on with our adventure. Honeymoon first, of course." Her fiery gaze swung back to Paul, setting him ablaze. "Right?"

Tough but fragile, beautiful and strong, Paul couldn't wait to go anywhere God led him with this shining Star at his side. "What she said."

"Smart man." Davis chuckled. "Let's do this. Dearly beloved…"

The End

Don't miss the next book by Janet W. Ferguson.

Would you like to be the first to know about new books by Janet W. Ferguson? Sign up for my newsletter at https://www.janetfergusonauthor.com/

Have you read other Coastal Hearts stories by Janet W. Ferguson?

Magnolia Storms, Falling for Grace, The Art of Rivers

Have you read the Southern Hearts Series by Janet W. Ferguson?

Leaving Oxford, Going Up South, Tackling the Fields, and Blown Together

Did you enjoy this book? I hope so!
Would you take a quick minute to leave a review online?
It doesn't have to be long. Just a sentence or two telling what you liked about the book.

I love to hear from readers! You can connect with me on Facebook, Twitter, Pinterest, the contact page on my website, or subscribe to my newsletter "Under the Southern Sun" for exclusive book news and giveaways.

https://www.facebook.com/Janet.Ferguson.author
http://www.janetfergusonauthor.com/under-the-southern-sun
https://www.pinterest.com/janetwferguson/
https://twitter.com/JanetwFerguson

About the Author

Faith, Humor, Romance
Southern Style

Janet W. Ferguson is a Grace Award winner and a Christy Award finalist. She grew up in Mississippi and received a degree in Banking and Finance from the University of Mississippi. She has served as a children's minister and a church youth volunteer. An avid reader, she worked as a librarian at a large public high school. She writes humorous inspirational fiction for people with real lives and real problems. Janet and her husband have two grown children, one really smart dog, and a few cats that allow them to share the space.

Made in the USA
Middletown, DE
20 March 2020